POPULAR PUBLICATIONS · FACSIMILE EDITIONS

Terror Tales #3
(November 1934)

Starting in 1934, editor (and publisher) Harry Steeger unveiled *Terror Tales*: perhaps the flagship magazine in Popular Publications' so-called "Weird Menace" lineup of titles. Running for almost 50 issues, *Terror Tales* showcased some of the best suspense, mystery and terror stories to see print in the pulps. This facsimile of the November 1934 issue contains stories by Arthur Leo Zagat, G.T. Fleming-Roberts, Wyatt Blassingame, Nat Schachner, and Laurence Donovan, among others.

Authors:

Arthur Leo Zagat, G.T. Fleming-Roberts, Wyatt Blassingame, John Flanders, Nat Schachner, Laurence Donovan, George Edson

Illustrators:

John Newton Howitt, Amos Sewell

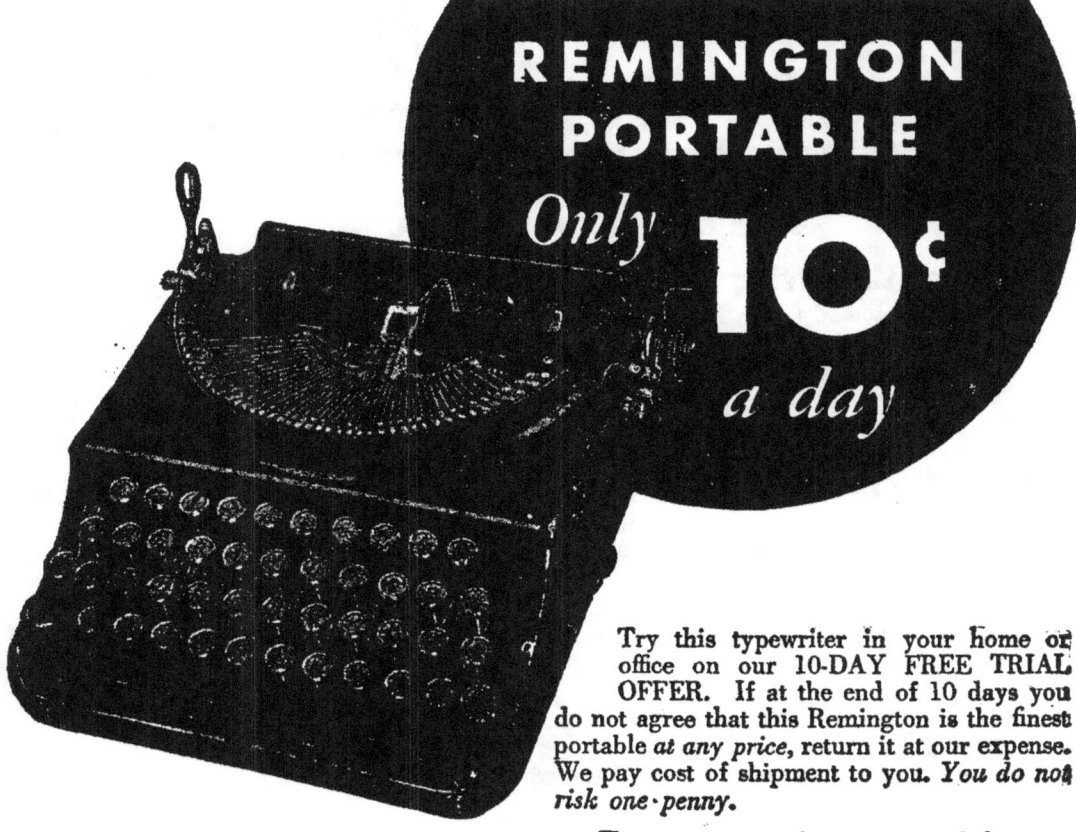
1

TERROR TALES

Volume One   November, 1934   Number Three

Cover Painting by John Howitt

Story Illustrations by Amos Sewell

Published every month by Popular Publications, Inc., 2256 Grove Street, Chicago, Illinois. Editorial and executive offices,
205 East Forty-second Street, New York City. Harry Steeger, President and Secretary, Harold S. Goldsmith, Vice President
and Treasurer. Entry as second-class matter pending at the post office at Chicago, Ill., under the Act of March 3, 1879.
Title registration pending at U. S. Patent Office. Copyright, 1934, by Popular Publications, Inc. Single copy price 15c.
Yearly subscriptions in U. S. A. $1.50. For advertising rates address Sam J. Perry, 205 E. 42nd St., New York, N. Y.
When submitting manuscripts kindly enclose stamped self-addressed envelope for their return if found unavailable. The
publishers cannot accept responsibility for return of unsolicited manuscripts, although care will be exercised in handling them.

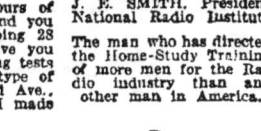

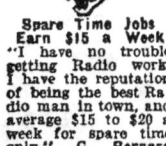

4

Prepare Quickly at Home in Spare Time

FOR A
Good Pay Job
IN THE
Fast-Growing
AVIATION
INDUSTRY

WALTER HINTON: trail blazer, pioneer, explorer, author, instructor, AVIATOR. The first man to pilot a plane across the Atlantic, the famous NC-4, and the first to fly from North to South America. The man who was a crack flying instructor for the Navy during the War; who today is training far-sighted men for Aviation. Hinton is ready to train you at home in your spare time. Get his book.

My famous course trains you right in your own home—gets you ready for one of the good ground jobs—or cuts many weeks and many dollars from flight instructions. Send for my big free book today.

Don't sit back and envy the men who are in the midst of the romance, adventure and fascination of Aviation. YOU DON'T HAVE TO. For right in your own home, in your spare time, I'll give you the training you need to get started in this growing, well-paid industry. Get my free book. It tells *all* the facts.

Many Make $40, $60, $75 a Week

Through the amazingly simple method I have worked out, I can train you at home to fill many well-paid jobs in Aviation. Naturally, before you can fly, you have to take additional instruction in a plane. Even on that instruction I save you time and money. But when you graduate from my course you have the necessary foundation to fill any one of the many interesting, well-paid ground jobs. Many of my graduates quickly get into jobs paying $40, $60 to $75 a week. Others, with the additional low cost flying instruction I arrange for, become pilots at $300 a month or better.

Aviation Is Growing Fast

Get into Aviation now—when you are still getting in on the ground floor of a new industry—when you have a chance to forge ahead without having to displace lots of older men. Aviation is a young man's industry, where young men earn real money. The President of the biggest air line in the World is only 35 years old. Most famous

---

Here are just a few of the many well-paid jobs in the fast growing Aviation Industry:

On the Ground

Airport Superintendent
Instrument Specialist
Electrician
Shop Foreman
Hangar Crew Chief
Traffic Manager
Purchasing Agent
Aerial Mail Clerk
Motor Expert
Radio Operator
Airplane Mechanic
Field Work

In the Air

Air Express Agent
Air Mail Pilot
Aerial Photography
Airport Manager
Test Pilot
Aerial Passenger Agent
Private Piloting
Weather Observer
Flight Instructor
Commercial Pilot
Field Manager
Transport Pilot

---

pilots are in their early thirties, or even younger. It is a young man's industry, which means that there are plenty of opportunities to forge ahead. But just because it is run by young men, don't get the idea that Aviation is a small business. Millions are being spent yearly to develop and improve airways and planes. Thousands of men earn good livings from the business. And many, many thousands will enter it in the future. It is a great and growing industry, this Aviation, an industry that still brings romance, excitement, thrills—even while it is bringing big opportunities and good pay.

I Have Helped Secure Jobs for Many of My Graduates

Due to my widespread connections with aviators, plane manufacturers, airport managers, etc., I am in an especially favorable position to locate jobs for trained men. My Aviation friends know that Hinton-trained men are well qualified to fill any job for which I recommend them.

Send For My Free Book Now

Now is the time to act. Don't sit content with a humdrum job with no future. Act now—to get yourself into Aviation—the industry that is slated to grow into a giant business in the next few years. Get into Aviation. Study at home in your spare time for a well-paid job with a real future. Mail the coupon for my free book today.

Walter Hinton, Pres.
Aviation Institute
Washington, D. C.

These Men Made Good With My Training

$75 a Week as Instructor

Robt. N. Dobbins, a Hinton graduate, writes: "I cannot thank you enough for the assistance you gave me in getting my present position. Last week they promoted me to Chief Instructor, at a big salary increase."

Now District Traffic Agent

"When I finished your course I became connected with T. A. T. and am happy to state that promotion has come very rapidly. I shall always be grateful for your interest and cooperation."—C. E. McCollum, District Traffic Agent, T. A. T.—Maddux Air Lines.

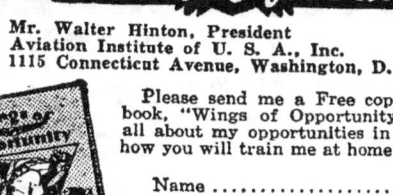
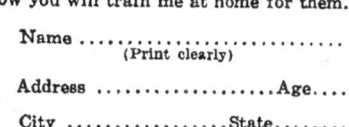

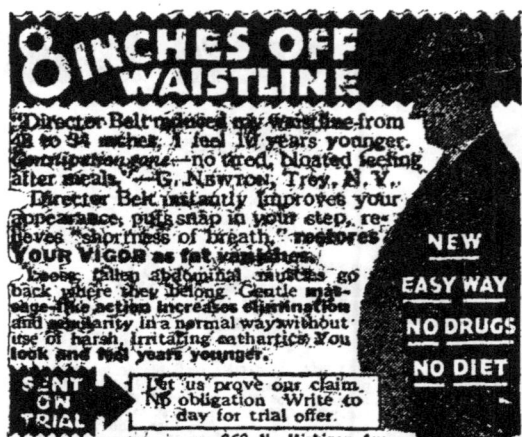

"SELDOM SEE AN I. C. S. GRADUATE OUT OF A JOB"

"IN ALL THE YEARS I have known of the International Correspondence Schools, I have seldom seen one of your graduates jobless."

A business executive made this statement in a recent letter commenting on the I. C. S. graduates and students in his employ and expressing regrets that it was necessary to reduce his personnel.

"However," he added, "all I. C. S. graduates and students will be retained, for I fully realize their value in my business."

• •

The reason so many I. C. S. men have jobs is because they are *trained men!* A recent investigation into the working conditions of 1000 I. C. S. students revealed only ten unemployed. You, too, can be an I. C. S. man.

Mark the coupon and mail it today! It has been the most important act in the lives of thousands of men.

Thirst Of The Living Dead

By
Arthur Leo Zagat
(Author of "House of Living Death")

Strange, horrible tales were told of the lake that the Iroquois had called the Eye of Evil . . . but none so strange and horrible as happened that hideous night when Ralph Dean fought, a pain-wracked madman, for his body and his soul— fought the angry gods of an ancient race long dead, and the thirsting Things, dead yet alive, that crept through the howling storm in search of warm red human blood!

T HE Iroquois called the lake Eye-of-Evil. They were long vanished and their harsh word was unpronounceable and therefore forgotten by the few leathery-faced mountaineers who had succeeded them in the region. But Lake Wanda's unsavory reputation still clung to it. And indeed, seen from the summit of Mount Toran, whose forest-cloaked thousand feet soared gloomily above it to the west, the sharp-ended oval with its single, round central island did startlingly resemble a great eye. All day, deep-sunk in its socket of encircling hills, that eye was darkly-shadowed, brooding and somehow ominous; but just before dusk it turned a lurid red, glaring balefully at a baleful sky. Then night would rush down Toran's slope, would engulf the lake like black lids closing—and, to believe the old tales, nightmare horror would stalk its shores.

Whether or not those whispered legends were true—of stealthy murder, agonized suicide and drowned men who would not stay in their watery grave—Ralph Dean did not know and did not care. Solitary

Complete Mystery-Terror Novel

except for his dog, Scout, in the living-room of the ancient house on Oldun Island, pupil of the Eye-of-Evil, he stared into the flames of the fire that was its sole illumination, and read in it only the tale of his anguished loneliness. He was but dimly aware that the smoked rafters of the huge, dim room shivered under the blows of a howling tempest, that the night outside was cataclysmic with sky-rending lightning and earth-shaking thunder, that the lake was lashed to fury by shrieking wind and torrential rain and the tall trees on the island itself bent almost double by the gale. Another such storm, exploding without warning from a starry sky, had a week ago darkened his life with a desolation so black and abysmal that he thought himself dulled forever to any emotion other than grief.

If he had known what grim terror this new storm was to pluck from the wild night and cast up on his threshold, he might have pulled open the great oaken door bisecting the long, oak-paneled wall behind him and plunged out into chaos— to throw himself into the bottomless depths that had taken his oldest friend, Anton Walder, and Ralph's laughing-eyed, flaxen-haired wife, Myrtle. Even the thought of two-year-old Billy, forgetful already of his mother and sweetly asleep in his crib upstairs, would have lost the power to hold him back. . . .

Now Scout whimpered in his sleep, and Dean's bronzed, big-knuckled hands clenched on his knees. He was reliving that evening, hearing again the words that had condemned Myrtle to death: "You go with them dear; you enjoy night paddling so. I'll stay with Billy. Don't worry, I shan't be lonely. I'll think of you and Anton and Sonia out on the water. . . ."

The wind thudded at the door as if some soft hand were pounding for admittance, moaned through the trees. The dog woke with a start, heaved to its feet. It stood stiff-legged, its hair bristling to a thick ruff around its neck, its livid eyes fastened on the shadows of the arched embrasure wherein the portal hung. Tiny whimperings came from the back of its throat, whimperings of ancestral fear.

Dean's sharp, grief-lined profile turned slowly to the animal, and he watched its antics somberly. Just so had Scout acted when, after a night of frenzied, fruitless searching, the two had found the overturned canoe floating in a cove on the other side of the island, and Sonia Walder's body under it. The clothes had been pounded from her by battering rocks, her head mashed to a pulp. One foot had twisted under a thwart of the frail boat and anchored her there as if the lake were sending to Ralph a mocking token of the others' fate.

"Down, Scout. Down, old boy. There's no one there. Come here, old fellow. You miss her too, don't you?"

CURIOUSLY, the Airedale paid no attention to his master's voice. What did he see, there in the dark, what phantasm to which human eyes are blind? Ralph pulled a shaking hand across his own forehead. He had been seeing things too, ever since Lake Wanda had swallowed Myrtle and refused to give her up. The flick of pale garments in forest aisles, a shadowy form moving among the trees just beyond the range of his burning vision. He had heard things, too, wandering aimlessly in the woods; the familiar timbre of Myrtle's voice, her words not quite distinguishable; Anton's guttural rumble. Once there had been a scream, on a moonless night, and he had rushed pell-mell from the house, sure that Myrtle had called for help. He had found no one, of course. . . .

And now he fancied someone was at the door, was begging wordlessly for admittance, for refuge from the tempest. It was against all reason; there was no living thing on the island save the three within the house and the dog, impossible for anyone to have come across the waters through the storm. It was the wind, only the wind. Dean licked dry lips and told himself again that it was only the wind.

Was his loss driving him mad? The natives—Ira Toombs and old Eri Halden—

certainly had thought him so when he had insisted on remaining with Billy on the ill-omened island. He wanted to be there, Ralph had said as they ferried what was left of Sonia to the mainland, when Myrtle's body was washed ashore.

They had looked at each other queerly, and then old Eri had drawled: "Ye'll stay here forever then. Ol' Wanda don't ever give up her daid, leastways not their corpses. Mebbe thet's why—"

A warning hiss from Toombs had cut him short, and Ralph, only half-hearing, had foreborne to question what the end of the sentence was to be. But later, an obscure fear had peered from Charity Halden's old eyes when he had offered what to her must have been a small fortune to assume the care of Billy and the slight duties of the household. Nor had her excuse, that the frequent storms isolated Oldun Island so that it was impossible to reach the mainland, been sufficient to account for her obdurate refusal—a refusal only abandoned when the curly-headed child had smiled endearingly up at her and snuggled his warm, confiding palm into her work-worn hand.

Charity Halden was upstairs now, asleep in the nursery. . . . Scout's lips pulled back from his black gums and he growled. The wind dropped in a sudden lull—but the fumbling at the door continued. There was a rasp to it, as of feeble nails scratching at the wood, low down. And that—that certainly was a moan, faint, only just audible. . . .

Ralph shook with a sudden chill. The moan came again, burbled, trailed off to silence. The renewed howling of the wind was like the wailing of a lost soul.

There couldn't be anyone there, anyone —human. But suppose there were; suppose . . . Dean dared not word the thought that came to him. He fought against unreasoning fear, fought himself out of his fireside chair and to the door. The metal of the doorknob was hot to his icy fingers. They closed around it, slowly; turned it, every thirty-second of an inch of movement a new victory over protesting nerves and rigid sinews.

Abruptly the bolt left its socket and something hurled the door inward, knocking Ralph aside, to his knees. The wind raged around the big room, the rain drove in, a solid wall of water. There *was* something on the threshold; a sodden, shapeless heap. It was a human form, the form of a woman, face down in muddy water that swirled, a foaming flood, across the threshold.

Dean got hands on her soggy garments, dragged her in, heaved erect and launched a battle against the storm to shut it out. It fought him back, shrieking with the voice of a thousand fiends, determined to hold the territory it had gained. Before the door clicked closed Ralph's back-muscles were stabbed with fire, his legs quivering with exhaustion. But he dropped at once to the woman's side, his knees squelching in the soaked rug.

What she wore had lost all identity, so drenched it was, but it covered her completely. And yet—there was something familiar about the hidden lines of the figure beneath it, something . . . Dean's lips were bloodless, his eyes black flame in a ghastly face. His arm slid under the cold, wet form, turned it over gently, tenderly. His other arm pillowed the lax head. The shawl fell away from the woman's face. . . .

THE whimper that broke the tumult-encircled hush of the big room came from his throat. Oh God! Oh merciless God! The bloated, clammy-white, blue-lipped face into which he stared was Myrtle's face. *Myrtle's!* Changed, horribly distorted, but he could not mistake it. His wife was back. His wife . . . Lake Wanda, the Eye-of-Evil, had thrown her corpse up, in wanton mockery, on his very doorstep. "Here she is," the storm howled at him. "You waited for her and we give her back to you. This is the face that will haunt your dreams forever now, this horror—instead of the beloved vision that otherwise would have been yours to cherish."

But what of the fumbling at the door, the scratching, the moan—the moan that had not been the voice of the wind? . . .

Fearfully, not daring yet to hope against the black despair flooding him, Ralph's hand found an opening in the sodden fabric cloaking the limp form, crept within. His hand felt flesh—gelid, clammy flesh that tingled his fingers with the cold feel of death. Bloated flesh that dented to the pressure of his hand—and a vague, dim flutter, a hint of movement where the beating heart should be! A pulse, vague yet perceptible. She lived. Miracle of miracles, *she was alive!*

Then Ralph, too, came alive. He lifted the flaccid figure, surging to his feet with her in his arms as a new, unfamiliar strength surged within him. In seconds he was across the room, had laid her tenderly on the bearskin rug before the roaring fire, had forced a drop or two of brandy between her lips, and was chafing her arms, her dear hands.

"Myrtle," he babbled. "Myrtle dear. . . . Wake up. Wake up." He mumbled broken, pathetic phrases from out their lexicon of love. Again he felt for her heart. It beat a little more strongly now, but the wax-white lids still hid her eyes, and her flesh was still cold, cold as death itself.

Warmth! She needed warmth, blankets. "Charity," he called. "Charity! Bring blankets down. All we've got!"

Ralph did not think then, did not dare to think, of how Myrtle came to be alive, of where she had been in the week since she was supposed to have drowned, of

how she had gotten home at last. He did not think, even, of where Anton might be, of whether he too might not have been saved from the lake. He was absorbed, wholly absorbed, in bringing Myrtle back to consciousness, in fanning the flickering spark of life that was still in her, the spark that threatened momentarily to go out.

Where was that woman? "Charity!" he roared again. "Charity!"

There was no answering thump of bare feet on the floor above; no querulous, age-thinned voice. Nothing but silence reached him, and the tumult of the storm. She slept too soundly; he must get the blankets himself.

He slid carefully out from under Myrtle, surged to his feet and was running up the broad steps that lifted from the other end of the room. The hall was dark, upstairs, except for a line of dim light under the nursery door. He jerked that open as he passed, yelling "Charity," glanced within. And he stopped abruptly.

The cot where the woman should be was empty! A night-light floated in a glass of oil, and by its vague luminance he could see the white covers thrown back, the mark of her form on the undersheet and the dent of her head on the pillow. And he could see something else on the pillow. There was a fleck of red on that pillow-case . . . another, a third . . . tiny drops of blood still freshly scarlet!

Steel fingers of fear pronged his heart as he whirled within. The baby! But Billy was in his crib, blond locks curling about his white forehead, smiling in sleep disturbed by neither storm nor shouting.

Billy was asleep, but on the floor there were other droplets of blood. Ralph's eyes followed them to the window. Good Lord, the pulled-down shade, the sill, were wet. Wet by rain! And Dean himself had closed that window when he had come up to hear his son's prayer and kiss him good-night, twenty minutes before a drop of rain had fallen!

The fact that only a few drops showed, on pillow and floor, was somehow more fearsome than if the room had been a shambles. There had been no struggle here, no fight. But a vein had opened, somewhere on old Charity's scrawny body, and she had gone—out of the window, out into the storm!

The floor rocked to that storm's buffeting, the dark exploded into blue light; Ralph was deafened by blasting thunder. A cataract pounded down upon the house, streamed across the pane. She couldn't have gone out into that of her own free will!

Dread was a tangible presence in the room, dread of something that threatened the child. He couldn't leave Billy alone here, alone with the tempest and—whatever it was that had left those crimson drops. But Myrtle was below—restored to him from the dead—needing him. Dean's neck corded and a visible pulse pounded in his temples.

A furry body brushed against his legs. Ralph gasped—jumped back. The Airedale looked up at him, whimpering. Dean gasped again—but with relief. "Scout," he snapped. "Scout! Stay here. On guard, Scout. On guard!"

The dog whimpered again. But he stalked across to the crib, whirled, stood stiff-legged, shaggy lips curled back from white fangs. Nothing human, nothing animal, would get past that faithful sentry to harm the boy. "Guard him, good Scout," Dean said, and knew he was free to get the blankets and minister to the other, below. But as he blundered down the dark hall his brow wrinkled. The dog was afraid—somehow he knew it—was terrified of something in the house that the man could not sense. . . .

CHAPTER TWO

Hungry Fangs

DEAN knelt by Myrtle's side. He had gotten her sodden clothing off, had wrapped her in layer upon layer of thick, warm wool. Heat from the fire up-beat on her. Her nostrils vibrated, slightly, with faint breathing. But the gray shadow of death still lay across her cruelly distorted countenance, her brow was still clammy white, her lips still blue. What could he do? What more could he do?

Anxiety, helpless futility, tore at him. And the storm rattled at the windows, howled about the house, seemed to be demanding her back from him. He could hear the roar of the wind-lashed lake, its angry roar. . . . *"Ol' Wanda don't never give up her daid. . . ."*

"Myrtle," Ralph groaned. "Myrtle darling. . . ."

His pulse pounded. Her eyelids were trembling—were lifting—were open! She was looking up at him . . . No! She was looking up, but not at him, not at anything! Her eyes, her blue eyes that once had glowed so with love for him, for little Billy, stared unseeingly up at the ceiling. He looked deep into them; they were blue caverns of emptiness, soulless and dead. But under his fingers the pulse in her flaccid wrist beat, beat more and more strongly, and the blankets that covered her rose and fell with her breathing.

Dread—the living dread that had filled the nursery above—seemed to have seeped down into the shadows that waited behind him to quench the firelight, seemed to quiver there and reach out for him with pallid hands. . . .

A scream threaded through the racket of the storm, a thin scream from outside, a woman's scream! It came again—quavering with infinite terror, yet retaining, oddly, the querulous edge of Charity's aged voice. "Help!"

He could not ignore it. Could not, though every fiber of his being clamored to stay here with Myrtle, to bring life back to her dead eyes, to her recovered body. Charity was out there in the storm, was crying to him for help, and he must go. Somehow Dean got to his feet, got to the door, lunged through, battled to get it closed again.

The storm took him, buffeted him. Impenetrable blackness swallowed him, blackness alive with tumult, solid with wind and water that battered him, dazed him with its fury. It was as if the lake had lifted from its bed, had engulfed trees, house, the island itself in a mad effort to destroy them, to have done with them once and for all. And he, he was a pigmy, an unconsidered mote in the grip of cosmic forces. . . .

Blue flame burst the sky, jetted down Mount Toran's precipice, flicked Lake Wanda's foaming surface into being and was gone. But Dean did not hear the world-crashing peal of thunder at all. For he had seen—among the trees silhouetted against the white sheet of the storm-whipped lake—two black, struggling forms. He lunged toward the blackness where they had been. He caromed off an unseen tree-trunk, fought underbrush clogging his plunging legs, distinguished a threshing just ahead that was not the threshing of the tempest. His fists clenched. . . .

Then he sensed someone beside him. He whirled toward it—too late. Something crashed against the side of his head, white flame exploded within his skull! He spun dizzily, staggered, sank to his knees.

Vertigo swirled about him, but through it he heard a mocking laugh and the sound of a heavy body moving away through the underbrush, a sound that merged with the crash of the storm and was gone. His head cleared; he was on his knees in the swimming underbrush. Ahead of him the

house he had quitted was a dark bulk, a looming bulk against whose darkness fire-lit oblongs flickered. A single pale rectangle above was the shade-covered nursery window.

Dean's skull throbbed with dull pain, wind-driven leaves whipped across his face, stung sharply. It was difficult to breathe the water-filled air. Yet he could not move; the blow from his unseen assailant seemed to have paralyzed him. He remained kneeling, leaning forward on stiffened arms, hands pressing down into mold, watching the house, waiting for the return of strength enough to lift himself, to get back there to Myrtle and Billy. . . .

And abruptly then he knew that the snatching of Charity from her bed, the scream that had lured him out here and the blow that had been launched at him from the dark were all part of some obscure threat that moved against his curly-haired, sleeping son in the room behind that nursery window!

A formless shadow jogged the edge of the pallid oblong, moved across it and was gone! Terror exploded within Ralph, heaved him to his feet, hurled him toward the house. He reached the door, got his hand on its knob, turned and pushed.

It did not move. It was locked, locked from within! Someone—inside—had shot the bolt that never, since the two couples had rented the house, had been touched. . . . And that someone was upstairs now —in Billy's room!

DEAN pounded the unyielding panels, screamed anathema. The wind howled taunting answer, battered him against the door; the rain lashed him with its fury. He twisted away, pulled himself along the rough stone of the structure's side to a window, pounded his fists through the glass.

Thunder-roll quenched the crash of the

glass, rain-pour washed blood from the jagged cuts on his hands and arms. Ralph heaved himself up to the sill, heaved himself through. The fire roared as the storm gained entrance through the breach he had made, the fire roared and the tempest wailed. But otherwise there was silence, dreadful silence, within the room.

Silence, and emptiness. A frenzied glance showed Dean only a pile of moist, thrown-back blankets where he had left his wife. Nothing more! God! Had the lake taken her back, had she returned to its storm-lashed depths? He pulled a hand across his aching head. It was an insane thought, but everything was insane, mad as the storm itself. Billy! What was happening to Billy?

Ralph started toward the stairs, stopped. He stared at the pitiful little heap that lay at the foot of their broad curve—the contorted, broken-backed form of Scout, the dog he had left on guard. The dog's lips still snarled back, his fangs were still bared in futile defense of his little master; but lips and teeth were scarlet with blood that dripped to a little pool on the floor. Scout was limp and lifeless!

Dean rocked back on his heels. A red mist swam before his eyes, blinding him. Then it had cleared and he was leaping across the floor in great strides, was pounding up those ominous stairs, a sob rasping his tightened throat. He thudded to the top. The hallway was dark, but a bar of light showed the nursery door to be open. And a soft murmur came from that room, the limpid sound of someone talking.

Afterward Ralph Dean could not explain what halted him, what sent him stealing silently, noiselessly down the hall. An instant before he had been hurtling to his son like a thunderbolt of vengeance; now he crept, fighting an inexplicable revulsion, fighting a horrible fear. Not fear for himself, but fear of what he should find in that room, marrow-chilling fear of what that eerie, liquid babble portended.

He got at last to the nursery door. His groping hand closed on the jamb, his lips tightened; and his head thrust slowly past the screening wall. His glance flicked past Charity's still empty cot with its blood-drops, past the little table where the night light flickered, found the crib. And pent breath brushed past his dry lips.

Billy was still asleep. But bending over his little bed, face close to his chubby one and lips pressed just under a shell-pink ear, was the white, nude form of— Myrtle. A warm flood of relief, of thanksgiving, welled up in Dean. Billy was all right, and Myrtle. She had regained her senses while he was out in the storm, had hastened up here to the crib-side of their son, to give him the mother's kiss he had so long been denied!

Both his loved ones were together here, safe. Let the storm howl now, the lake foam along its shore. He had them back. . . .

And then Dean froze with horror. From the spot where his mother's lips were tight against the tiny fellow's flesh, from under those very lips, a filament of blood seeped out. It crawled leisurely down his little neck, reached the white coverlet and stained it a vivid, screaming red!

A STEEL band constricted Ralph's forehead, a soundless shriek tore at his throat. That was not Myrtle, that was not his wife, that did this evil thing. It was something the lake had sent to him in mockery of his grief; something vile, infinitely vile that it had vomited up from its dark depths.

"Ol, Wanda don't never give up her 'daid," Eri Halden had said. No. But she spewed out other things, unmentionable things, in the guise of the dead she held. . . .

The awful realization shook him; a shout trembled on his lips. He choked it back. If the sharp teeth hidden by those bloated, blue lips clenched and tore once, only once, nothing could save his son!

Billy's heavy-headed croquet mallet leaned just inside the door. Ralph's hand flashed to it, gripped its handle. He was stealing noiselessly, furtively across the floor, taut with fear that—she—might hear him. He was just behind her now. The mallet arched up. One blow it would take to crush the skull of the thing that sucked Billy's blood, to send it back to the unholy death from whence the lake had spewed it. His biceps corded to deal that blow.

But it did not fall! Her maize-colored hair, dry now, coiled in soft tendrils along her neck just where his fingers had delighted to stroke it. The very cant of her head was like, too like, the Myrtle for whom his love had been an ardent, consuming flame. Whatever she had become he could not strike. . . .

"Myrtle," he whispered, in agony. "Myrtle. You'll wake him."

The woman stirred, straightened and turned. Faint color now tinged her cheeks, that had been so terribly white, and her eyes were dreamy, absorbed, but no longer wholly dead. Ralph shuddered as he thought of the reason, but his cold lips said steadily, "Come, Myrtle, come away. You'll see him in the morning."

She followed him as he backed from the room, her once slim legs moving automatically, as if she were walking in her sleep. There was something infinitely horrible in the slow, noiseless way she glided toward the door—something unhuman. Ralph shuddered again. His skin crawled with revulsion as she reached him and he took her icy hand, but he led her away and she came with him, strangely complacent.

"Come down to the fire again," he said. "You need its heat."

And thus they went down the staircase, past the shattered corpse of the dog that had been faithful to death. They reached the fireplace. At a word from Dean she sank docilely down on the blankets, let him make a cocoon for her, slip a cushion under her head. She sighed, seemed to relax almost at once in sleep.

The wind beat in at the broken window, swirled about the room. Moving dully, his brain clogged by horror, Ralph picked up a small rug, stumbled toward the gaping aperture with some idea of stuffing it against the gale. But as he reached it, the slap of the cold rain across his face woke thought. He remembered Charity, remembered that she had been struggling with someone and that he himself had been attacked, had been brought to his knees by a crashing blow.

What was going on, what had the storm brought to Oldun Island? He was certain there had been no one on the island before it broke. He and Scout had gone all over it just after supper. No boat he knew to be on the lake could have reached it after that. And yet—Myrtle had gotten here somehow, and at least one person else. Icy prickles ran up and down his spine. Had neither of the two needed a boat?

He peered out into the tumultuous dark. Lightning split the sky, and he froze. Someone had moved among the trees, just then, had ducked back out of sight, not quite quickly enough. He had glimpsed a swarthy face, staring eyes. Someone was watching the house, out there in that uproar.

"Who's there?" Dean called sharply. "Who's there?"

Howling crescendo of wind through the vibrant branches of storm-torn trees, snare-drum rattle of rain on leaves and ground and bass roll of thunder, orchestrated the terrific symphony of the tempest; but through it, through the echoing diapason of the gale, a weird ululation rose to shrillness. Dean's scalp tightened as he heard it, and primal terror gripped him. It was like the lamentation of a bodiless phantom in eternal torment, like the wail of an outcast soul riding the black wings of the storm in endless, despairing search for peace forever denied it.

The eerie sound died away. The wind dropped to a sudden lull as if Boreas himself bated his breath in awe at the utter desolation of that cry. Then, out in the darkness, a fiddle-string twanged, and something thudded into the sill alongside the utterly shaken man.

A red finger of light reached out from the fire behind him, reached past the black shadow of Ralph Dean's head, and fumbled at the incredible thing that had catapulted from out of the furious night. It quivered still like a thing alive, a straight shaft of hickory, the feathered tuft at its end a gray blur.

Ralph stared at it, the blood in his veins an icy stream, stared at it and whimpered as Scout had whimpered, afraid of things that were not, that could not be. An arrow, an Indian arrow! Great God in heaven, had the world gone entirely mad? . . .

CRASH! Dean whirled to the smash of splintered glass behind him. A black, radiating star showed in a window at the other side of the room. The wind whistled through it, and still bounding across the floor was a round object, white, red-flecked. Even as he turned it thudded to rest at his feet and Ralph saw that it was a fist-sized stone, saw that something was twisted around it, a bit of white fabric, blood-stained.

Dean gasped. That white stuff, scarcely wet, was fuzzy, warm-looking. It was like the flannel of which Charity's high-necked, ankle-long nightgowns were made. He bent to the thing, picked it up. The flannel was tied to the stone by a raveling of its own material, and the red on it was strangely like a letter, like the letter S.

Ralph picked at the knot, loosened it. The rag straightened in his shaking hands. Those *were* letters on it, letters scrawled in blood. An S, a K, a space, then a C and an O. SK—CO! He stared at the gory message. His brow wrinkled, his mouth was a straight, grim gash across his pallid face. What could those cabalistic ciphers mean?

Then suddenly it came to him. On the other side of the island, gouged into its shore, was a tiny bay—the very place where he had made the gruesome find of the shattered canoe and Sonia's battered corpse. When Halden and Toombs had arrived in response to his frantic signals and he had started to describe the spot to them, one of them had interrupted him.

"Yeah," he had said. "We know. That's Skull Cove, where some 'un found an Injun skeleton oncet. That wuz th' last loon crazy enough to live in this house. Th' lake took him too, twenty years ago. . . ."

SK—CO. Skull Cove! Undoubtedly that was what the letters meant. Somehow, by what means he could not fathom, Charity had contrived to get this message to him. Inscribed in blood on a bit torn from the only garment she wore, it was a cry for help, a piteous cry for help. . . .

His eyes lifted from the thing, strayed to the bundled form before the fire, came back across the room and sought the shadowy staircase that led to the room where Billy slept. How could he answer the woman's call for help, how could he go out into the storm and leave the child alone with—the thing his mother had become?

No! Ralph's fingers closed on the rag in his hand, twisted it, flung it from him.

No! He would not go. He could not. Charity would have to take her chance alone. Billy came first, helpless little Billy with the blond curls tight around his white brow. Charity's life was nearly run; a year or two more would make no difference. . . .

But he had made her come here, against her fears, against her premonition of danger now all too well fulfilled. She had come for Billy's sake, to mother the motherless child, and Billy had already learned to love her. One faithful friend of the child's lay there, at the foot of those stairs, stiffened now in death that had come to him in the child's defense. The harassed father could not deliberately abandon another to what awful fate he could only guess at, and guessing, shudder. He must go to her. *He must.* . . .

Fishing paraphernalia lay on a table, disused since tragedy had come to Oldun Island. A reel of strong line . . . Ralph's hands flew as he lashed Myrtle's sleeping form with it, lashed her so thoroughly that she could by no remotest possibility free herself. A rod—the butt section was heavy, lead-weighted. It was better than no weapon at all. And then, not stopping to think—not daring to think—Dean plunged out into the storm once more.

Head bent, arm thrown up across his face in a pitiable attempt to protect his head from the clubbing blows of the almost solid wind; deafened by the continuous pealing of thunder, by the crash of uprooted forest giants and the piercing shriek of the gale; half-drowned, he ploughed through the tempest-riven woods inch by painful inch. Every step was a torment, every yard a battle won against impossible odds. But he went on, slowly on. . . .

He was not alone in the storm! Nothing he saw, nothing he heard, made him aware of it, but he knew it; knew it by the drying of his throat, by the chill that struck into the marrow of his bones, by the unreasoning terror that was an icy lump at the pit of his stomach. Something—an unseen shadow in the Stygian murk—was following him, was keeping pace with him, was waiting the moment to spring.

A creeper caught his feet; he stumbled, scrambled to keep from falling. One arm swept out aimlessly, *touched wetness, wet skin, sinewy muscles rippling beneath it.* He twisted to it, saw something loom, black against black. Fingers gripped his outflung wrist, jerked downward.

And on the instant he was fighting for his life, fighting with a slippery, naked antagonist he could not see; a powerful being whose blows were bone shattering, whose taut muscles were armor against the pounding of his own fists, the blows of his club. A *something* that snarled bestially, that growled and pressed in and gave no quarter. . . .

CHAPTER THREE

Skull Cove

FROM the instant that battle in the dark began Dean knew that he stood no chance. His unseen antagonist was gigantic, unbelievably powerful, merciless. Agony seared the wrist that had been grasped in the first onslaught; it felt as though broken, and the hand was paralyzed. Half Ralph's blows with his improvised club were wasted, thudded harmlessly against tree-trunks, bushes, anything but the invisible assailant. Yet he fought on, plunged in again and again to meet the other's attack, his pile-driving jabs, the irresistible impact of his cruel blows. Dean's fist glanced off a bristling jaw, another blow rebounded from a steel-hard abdomen. Then suddenly a sinewy leg was between his own, was jerked back, Ralph crashed down, the sweaty body of the other pounding down atop him.

Dean was pinned helpless in the mud. Hard knees ground into his chest, steely fingers were at his throat, were clamping slowly closed. He couldn't breathe. He pounded at columnar arms, pounded more weakly. . . . His lungs were bursting, and blackness shot with light welled up in his brain. His neck was crushed between those squeezing fingers. Blood was salty in his mouth, his own blood. . . .

The wriggly light-worms inside his head merged into one, into a spinning, mad pin-wheel of coruscating fire that was jagged and lightning-blue. Two faces were limned against the glare of that mad pin-wheel: one, copper-hued, wild-eyed, drooling; the other—the gaunt, black-bearded, gimlet-eyed face of Anton, of his drowned friend, grinning horribly. Then the mountain fell upon him! . . .

Moments later Ralph weltered up through blackness to consciousness, to pain that seared his throat, to the roar of the storm and the buffeting of rain and wind. He was on his back in mud and water; tempest-torn blackness lay on him like a pall. He was alive—strangely, he was alive!

What then had become of the invisible assailant who had had him down? Why had he relented, why had he not killed him? There had been no doubt at all of the lethal ferocity of his attack, no doubt that he had meant to choke from him all semblance of life. But something had stopped him. Maybe Anton had beaten him off. Maybe—Hold on! Anton was dead, drowned. That wasn't really Anton he had seen, nor was the other an Indian. Those faces had been only delirious visions of his tortured brain.

Ralph was not yet fully conscious; he was dazed, mind-numbed by pain and terror. Had he been in full possession of his senses it is doubtful that he would

have had the courage to stagger to his feet, to reel again through the unabated ferocity of the elements toward the inlet that was so grimly named Skull Cove. But he did that very thing, driven still by the purpose with which he had set forth, like a mechanical toy that had once been wound and was not yet run down.

It is doubtful too, that he would have reached the Cove had it not been very near. As it was, he was more dead than alive when he dragged himself out of the thicket into the shelving space that bordered the little bay. He sprawled on the gravelly beach, lay there for long moments, let the wind play with him; let the foam, driven in from the turbulent lake, sting his throbbing temples.

A croaking sound, a sound only half-human, pulled his head up, jerked open his eyes.

The crescent-shaped front of the woods was like the van of a black-horsed Arab squadron, charging the lake pell-mell, threshing spear-points thrust out ahead. In front, their madly careering leader, a lone oak tossed wild arms. And limned against its creaking trunk, a blanched emblazonment on a black shield, was a pallid, straining figure—the white figure of a naked woman, of Charity Halden!

SOME power outside himself lifted Ralph to his feet, sent him plunging to her against the moving wall of the wind. A glimmer of more distant lightning aided his sight, showed him that she was lashed to the streaming bole, showed him her gaunt face, her bulging, tortured eyes, her straggly gray hair streaming about that anguished face and lashing its sunken cheeks.

He got to her. She saw him—and her thin lips moved. Somehow her hoarse croak was clearly audible above the shriek of the gale:

"The living-drowned. . . ." The guttural words burbled through water that filled her throat. "From the lake. . . ." Her countenance was a ghastly mask of terror. "They—" And suddenly her eyes were closed, she was hanging limply on the ropes that bound her scrawny body to the tree.

How, working with frantic, bleeding fingers, he loosened those water-soaked knots, how he got the old woman free and onto his shoulder, how he made his way back through the storm, Ralph Dean could never remember. But he accomplished the superhuman task, and the next scene that he remembered in the phantasmagoria of that terrible night was when he eased the flaccid burden against the jamb of the house door and fumbled with rigid, clumsy fingers at its bronze knob.

The portal opened and Dean staggered through. The woman slipped from his shoulders; he was dazed, blinded. Fighting to get the door closed again he was conscious only that he was once more in shelter, that the thick stone walls of the ancient house were about him, making an island of warmth and quiet in a world where all else was turmoil.

He quivered with dull pain, with exhaustion. The storm shut out, he leaned against the stout panel that vibrated under its baffled blows. Then his overtaxed legs buckled, and he started to slide downward. Forehead and palms against the wood, he held himself upright while his brain cleared and he remembered all there was yet to do. He forced himself around.

Black shadows, red-edged, danced in the great room. Charity's crumpled body lay in a watery pool at his feet. He must tend her, get her warmed, get her to the fire. It was so far, so far to the fireplace.

Dogged, flogging his water-weak limbs to the task, he bent, got the bony body in his arms, lifted. His bleared eyes drifted across the room, to measure the distance he would have to carry her.

The fire still flamed bravely. Myrtle. . . . Good Lord! She wasn't there! The blankets were there—suddenly clear visioned, he saw their crumpled mass—and the fishing line! But she couldn't have. . . . The line was cut, cut by a keen knife. Myrtle couldn't have done that. . . .

Billy! Like the jagged lightning still splitting the clouds without, terror for the child jabbed lividly through the billowing darkness of his brain. *Billy!* The old woman still in his arms, Ralph whirled, was plunging across the room and up the stairs. *Billy!* He didn't feel Charity's weight, he didn't know she was there! But the stairs were high as Mount Toran's steep, the light from the half-open nursery door glimmered at the further end of infinity. . . .

He reached it at last.

A great sob retched from the tight anguish of the father's chest. How could the child lie sleeping there, so peacefully, in the midst of so much terror? One small hand was curled, like a half-open blossom, on the coverlet; a tiny smile touched the cupid's bow of the child's lips. Ralph gained control of himself by a gigantic effort, and slid noiselessly into the room.

Charity's cot came across his vision, and she was suddenly an unsupportable weight in his arms. He put her down on the bed. Her cadaverous head dented the pillow just where minute, browning flecks still stained it. Dean jerked the sheet up to cover her nakedness, and turned to the crib of his son.

He thought he tiptoed silently toward it; but the child sighed and his lids fluttered. Just as Dean bent over the crib-side they opened. Limpid eyes, mistily blue, looked up at him drowsily, and the lad's smile deepened.

"Daddy," he murmured. "Daddy. Unc' Anton 'th back. Ith Mummy comin' back too?"

RALPH'S scalp tightened; grisly fingers clutched his throat. His hand tightened on the rail till his knuckles showed white. But he contrived to keep his reply in the hushed soporific tone a parent uses to a prematurely awakened babe. "You've been dreaming, big fella. Uncle Anton's too far away to come back."

"But I did tho thee him," Billy insisted. "He talked to me and he kithed me, here." Petal-like fingers came up to the spot, under his ear, that by compromising sanitary precautions and tender affection had been designated his "kissing place." Ralph was shaken anew by a swift vision of blue and bloated lips pressed to the satin skin, of sharp teeth mumbling the life-pulse there. Teeth of the living-drowned! "And then the Injun came an' he went away."

Pent breath whistled from between Ralph's icy lips, gusty with relief. The child *had* been dreaming, of course; that last statement proved it! "All right, bunchums," he murmured. "All right. Go to sleep and we'll talk about it in the morning. Go to sleep or there won't be any pancakes and maple syrup for breakfast."

The threat had its customary effect. "I did tho thee Unc' Anton," Billy muttered as his eyes closed again. "I did tho. . . ." His tiny treble trailed off into a long sigh. His father reached down to pull the rumpled cotton blanket more snugly about the child.

And a green leaf slid out of a fold and fluttered to the floor! Only a leaf. . . . but it was still wet with the rain against which the nursery window had been shut for hours. . . .

Terror, quivering dread, black premonition of an unknown, impossible menace, were once more tangible, living presences in the dim room. . . .

Ralph sat bolt upright on a backless stool in the center of the nursery floor. He had done what he could for the old woman. She lay on her cot now, still unconscious, whether asleep or in coma he was not physician enough to know. Billy was quietly asleep in the dim luminance of the night light. But there would be no sleep for him—he must keep awake, taut, on guard against the unnamable evil that prowled the storm-torn night.

He must keep awake—his lacerated fingers tightened around the croquet mallet that was his only weapon—though every exhausted cell in his throbbing body pleaded for sleep, for rest. For rest. . . . Tired lids drooped over aching eyes. He jerked them open, straightening. Rest. . . . The storm must be waning; now its noise was dull, muffled. . . . Tomorrow. . . .

The very blackness that engulfed him was palpitant with evil. Things that he could not see crawled through it, loathsome things from the watery depths where for centuries they had slithered through the slimed sockets of human skulls. Their clammy touch was horrible on his skin. He tried to brush them off, but he was rigid in the unholy paralysis of the nightmare. The Stygian murk swirled into an eye, a world-encompassing eye of evil, the cyclopean eye of Lake Wanda as he had seen it once from the cloud-piercing peak of the mountain. Nausea retched his stomach, vertigo was a giddy whirl in his swooning brain. The eye was drawing him down to it; down, down. . . . The boiling surface was just beneath him, a gigantic arm stabbed out of it, clutching for him. . . . Titanic fingers, flesh-stripped and bony, were closing. . . . And Ralph jerked awake.

He was awake, but the eye was still there, mirroring death in a face that was the gruesome white of decay. *Myrtle's face was thrust against his own, her clammy touch was on his neck and her blue lips snarled back from cruel teeth!*

THE nightmare paralysis held for an instant—then Ralph had struck at her, had leaped backward with the crash of the stool, was lunging to her again to grab her and wring her neck and make an end of terror.

His fingers clutched her arm. She jerked it from his hold. She whirled, was out of the doorway. Dean thudded against the slammed door. As he fumbled for the knob that momentarily evaded his frenzied hand he heard the swift pad of feet moving away to the right. He got the door open, leaped out. White flicked into a room to the right, their room. He threw himself down the passage, flung that door open.

The storm-glow was sufficient to show him every cranny of the familiar room. There was the double bed that had been so cold for a week, there the rough-pine wardrobe, its curtain shoved open and only clothing within. There was the smaller fireplace Myrtle had so loved and the up-ended box that she had frilled with a cretonne skirt for a dresser. Everything was open, wide open to his staring gaze. But nothing moved within. The white form, Myrtle's form, that instantaneously but surely he had seen, flick through the door of that chamber was not within it! The room was empty.

Then indeed, the harassed man went berserk. He plunged, frothing, into the bedroom. In minutes he had torn it apart. Clothing was strewn about the floor, a welter of flying feathers from the ripped mattress filled the air. He had raked, with clawing hands, the very ashes all over the cold hearth. The furious, illogical search had revealed no trace of that which he sought. He straightened, growling as Scout might have growled, and dived out again into the hall.

A strange, mad figure, wild-eyed and disheveled, he catapulted from room to room of the sprawling structure, tumbled down the stairs and spread desolation below. The thing in woman's form that he had welcomed as his loved one returned from the dead, had vanished, vanished utterly from the house! He raised shaking arms above his head; blasphemy formed on his white and twitching lips—but was not uttered.

The ceiling above him had thudded to the impact of a footfall! The dull sound came again. Faint as it was, it crashed within Dean's reeling brain like the Hammer of Thor on the Anvil of Doom. For an instant, as terror fought with reason for possession of that beleaguered mind, he froze. Then he had twisted again to the stairs, was racing up, heart in mouth, was hurtling through the nursery door.

His foot skidded just within the threshold, skidded on slipperiness, and he sprawled, headlong. The crash stunned him for an instant, then he was aware that he lay in a puddle of warm and viscous liquid, that it was blood, a pool of blood drenching the floor!

He rolled over, heaved erect. Charity's bed swam across his dizzy vision. It was a shambles dripping with gore! One thin hand gripped the encarmined sheet. Ralph's bulging eyes followed the scrawny arm, came to the shoulder, the throat —where the throat should be!

A gaping hole was there, beneath the sharp chin, a gaping hole that had been ripped through aged flesh, through muscle and cartilage and sinew, so that its edges, where the spurting blood left them visible, were jagged and horribly torn. Teeth had done this: long, sharp, cruel teeth. Nothing else could have made just such a wound. . . .

The man's teeth chattered, he mouthed words that made no sound. His hand groped for the door-jamb, gripped it so that he would not fall. An ague shook him as a terrier shakes a rat; his heart pounded as though it would burst its bony cage. Billy's crib was behind him, just behind him. He could see it by turning his head inches, inches only. But he dared not look. He dared not. . . .

He must! He willed his head to move; the muscles of his neck corded, his chin moved slowly through the necessary arc. The foot of the tiny bed came into view, the tousled blanket, the pillow! The pillow where only the depression of a small head was, the pillow from which that head was gone!

Dean spun around and a great cry burst the confines of his constricted throat. The crib was empty! *Billy was gone!*

CHAPTER FOUR

Print of a Naked Foot

THE fury of the storm had redoubled. The bowl of Wanda's valley was filled with the coruscating blaze of its unintermitted lightning, spilled over with the fulmination of its thunders. It battered at the house on Oldun Island as if determined once for all to sweep all sign of human habitation to oblivion. It howled maledictions down the brick chimneys, thudded ponderous fists against its rock-like walls, set the entire fabric quivering with the fury of its onslaught. Beams creaked and groaned as the gigantic battering ram belabored the centuries-old structure. At any moment, it appeared, the ancient jointures would be riven apart and the mansion collapse in ruin.

In the nursery-room on the second floor, the din of the gale, the sense of imminent destruction was overpowering. But Ralph Dean neither heard the turmoil nor felt the awesome majesty of the raging storm. Minutes had passed, long minutes, and he was still in the very pose that his body had assumed at the moment he had seen that untenanted crib. He stared at it with unseeing eyes, statuesque—petrified by a catalepsy of despair, motionless as the bedaubed corpse on its gory cot behind him.

The tiny night light guttered in its glass of oil and the blood dripped from the man's soaked garments and his clawed hands, dripped back to the welling pool whence it had come. The slow, regular spat was like the monotonous tick of some gruesome clock, marking the black, eternal seconds in a sealed sepulcher. . . .

At last the man stirred. Somewhere in the depths of his consciousness a tiny spark of courage had still burned, and now it flared a little more brightly so that its flame was reflected in the glaze of his hopeless eyes. Those eyes drifted from the little, empty bed, drifted to the floor of the room, to a gay-colored grass rug that lay in the middle of the floor. One of its figures was overlaid by a red blur.—Dean bent forward, scrutinizing it more closely.

The little hairs at the back of his neck rose, and his throat tightened to a growl. The stain at which he stared was a footmark, the print of a *naked* foot! He could distinguish the heel, the curiously splayed toes. It was a big foot, too big to be a woman's, too big to be Myrtle's. Not Myrtle's! Strange how the discovery lightened, infinitesimally, the blackness of the pall that enfolded him. . . .

There was another blood-smeared footprint on the bare floor beyond the rug— a third, fainter, at the window. Dean thudded across to it. The sill was wetter than before; the window must have been opened again; and there was a pink tinge to the film of water. He took hold of the sash, flung it up.

The gale howled triumphantly as it swept in and scurried about the nursery; but it might have been a gentle breeze for all the affect it had on Ralph. He thrust head and shoulders through the opening, his hot eyes searching. All of the storm that reached his consciousness was the flickering luminance of its electrical display, and that was because it gave him light by which to see.

Yes, the rough, jutting stone of the house wall offered ample hand and foothold to a climber, an ornamental ledge just beneath the window a firm resting place while prowling hands lifted the unbarred sash. This was certainly the way the killer, the kidnaper had come! Billy was in the hands of someone human— someone he could track down, could kill. . . .

Something glinted on the ledge. Dean reached down, touched metal. He pulled the thing up. . . .

And quivering terror of the supernatural swept over him again!

THIS that dangled from his icy fingers, this chain of threadlike silver links, its twin was about his own wrist. He and Anton had exchanged them as gifts on the day he had wedded Myrtle, and the two men had sworn never to part with them. They were symbols of their friendship, symbols that Ralph's victory, in the game of love and courtship the two had played for the girl, had not broken the chain of affection that had linked them for years.

Ralph remembered Sonia's passing some laughing jest about the chains just as the trio had shoved off for that fatal canoe trip; was certain, therefore, that Anton's had been on his wrist when he had drowned. And now. . . . Dean had found that chain where only the killer could have lost it, only the one who had stolen Billy from his bed!

"These chains will bring us together again, no matter how far we may be separated," Walder had said, his black eyes glittering, as they had fastened them about each others' wrists. An American would have been shame-faced about the sentiment, but the Russian had been unabashed. And he had been right, the chains had brought them together again—though separated by death! But not as Anton had meant—not as he had meant!

Ralph threw back his head, suddenly, and laughed. The shrillness of that mad laugh merged with the storm's wailing, with the husky roar of the foaming lake that had taken his beloved ones and sent him back in their stead ghouls that prowled the storm and were athirst for blood. Lake Wanda might have been evil for centuries, but never in the long aeons it had glared malevolently at the sky had it contrived so perfect a consummation of its evil!

Ralph laughed till his throat ached and foam flecked his lips. Somehow his laugh was in exact accord with the blood-spattered room, with the mangled corpse, with the insane maelstrom of the gale that laughed too, or chuckled in mindless glee at the destruction that it had wrought.

Then, quite suddenly, Dean's wild cachinnation choked to silence. The doorknob had rattled, behind him. He half-turned to it, half-turned and crouched, saliva dribbling from his mouth, reddened hands opening and closing, as if their gory fingers ached to be at someone's throat. He crouched, and his eyes, lurid with grief and terror and madness, were fixed on the slowly opening door.

The shadow of the portal hid from Ralph that which was moving it. But there was a paleness there, a tall glimmer, the ominous swaying of white fabric— of, it seemed to him, a death shroud. His lips retracted till his teeth were bared in a hideous snarl. He crouched lower, quivering with tenseness.

The black oblong widened, bit by stealthy bit. His sharpened ears heard the faint hiss of furtive breathing; his nostrils flared to a vague odor—the musty, earthy aroma of the grave, that threaded through the thick smell of drying blood. His own blood was an icy stream in his veins, and his scalp a tight cap that squeezed his brains.

Slow as the descent of a glacier, inevitable as Doom, the aperture widened. Now Dean could make out the swaying of the sepulchral drapery that clothed the entering figure, the pallid oval of its face. The door came wholly open, light sifted past its edge, and he was staring at Myrtle!

He saw that the white garment she had donned hung limply, drenched, that her lips were no longer blue, that they were a smear of scarlet across the death-pallor of her countenance. Even as his muscles tautened horror shook him. Oh God! Oh Almighty God! *Was she coming from an unholy feast at which she and Anton, had sucked the life-fluid from the body of her own son?*

HIS coiled limbs exploded; he leaped. And a sudden blanket of black swept over him from behind—thick, fuzzy cloth that blinded him, that tangled his legs and flailing arms, that drew tight about him so that he could no longer move, could scarcely breathe. He felt rope wind around the bundle he had become, felt its coils constrict till they cut into him, excruciatingly, even through the mass of the enfolding cloth. A muffled scream came to him. He thudded to the floor, heard muffled pounding as of running feet, bare feet.

He heaved, threw himself about in a desperate effort to free himself, knowing only too well that his writhings were in vain. Hands fumbled at him again; he was lifted, was jounced about on what might have been a shoulder. Water soaked through his blanket wrapping. He was dropped through an unknown distance,

banged into softness that squelched and might have been mud. Something thudded again, and once more he was lifted, once more he was being jounced on a powerful shoulder, was being carried—to hell itself for all he knew. . . .

God, oh God! Were they not yet satisfied? Would they not rest content till no living thing was left on Oldun Island? Myrtle and Sonia and Anton had died, days ago. Now Charity was dead, and Billy. He was the last of the group that had come here so joyously for a happy vacation in the isolation their close friendship craved. And he was a prisoner, a helpless, blinded prisoner in the power of Wanda's evil spawn.

Ralph Dean prayed then, prayed for the first time in long years, and he prayed that his death might be swift, that he should not live to feel the teeth of his friend pierce his skin, that he should not know when the lips he had so often kissed sucked the blood from his frozen veins. That which animated them was not, could not be, Anton's soul or Myrtle's, but the bodies were theirs, and he had loved the bodies too.

After a time the bumping, rough progress ceased, and he was thrown down, brutally, on some hard, rough surface. The clamor of the storm, was dulled, fainter, almost as if he were within some enclosed place. But that could not be, for there was no other building on the island. The storm must have lessened then. . . .

Strange. That sounded like the pad of bare feet going away. They were leaving him—his captors—wherever it was they had taken him. Perhaps they were filled, would come back later to drink from his veins. But Charity's blood had spilled, mostly, on the floor and Billy's body was so little, so tiny. They couldn't have drunk enough.

But wait—he had read somewhere, he remembered, that vampires must return to their graves at dawn, that only the night was free for them to prowl. That must be it. The sun was rising, Myrtle and Anton were going back to the lake, were even now sinking beneath its surface. But they would return with the night. He would be here for them, here for their grisly feast.

Would he? He had twelve hours—twelve hours to live. Seven hundred and twenty minutes. Forty-three thousand, two hundred seconds. Thinking of the numbers, calculating them, was giving him a hold on reason, was somehow quieting the swirl of utter madness in his brain. He had forty-three thousand, two hundred seconds, then, in which to defeat them. It was a long time and they couldn't stop him because they would be at the bottom of the lake.

He'd better start now. Some of those precious seconds had gone already, maybe there were only forty-three thousand one hundred and forty-nine left. Forty-eight, it had taken a full second just to think that number. But it was something real, and nothing else was. Nothing that had happened since he had found Myrtle lying outside the door. He was dreaming it all. He had fallen asleep in his chair before the fire and was dreaming all this. Scout was asleep too, on his favorite rug, and Charity was upstairs, asleep. Billy, too. Billy was in his crib. Billy. . . .

Ralph Dean sobbed, felt tears wet his face. He was weak, his vitality drained to the last drop. This was the first pause in the terrific surge of events, the first time he had had a moment to think. Desperate as his situation was, fear for himself was obliterated by the sense of dreadful loss that oppressed him. His grief for Anton, for Myrtle had been redoubled, increased a thousand-fold, by knowledge of what they had become. And his son . . . insanity would have returned, never to depart, if he had not in that mo-

ment closed his mind to speculation as to the child's fate. He must get free first. Get free. And then. . . .

He was enveloped in the clumsy folds of a blanket, roped tightly so that he could move neither arms nor legs. But he could move his whole body, and the surface on which he lay was rough. He could feel a sharp point digging into his aching back. His lashings wound about him spirally. He gritted his teeth and started to writhe, to chafe those ropes against the rough ground. Sooner or later, if he were not interrupted, the fibers must fray, must be worn through and part.

IT SEEMED hours that he had been rubbing back and forth, back and forth, till his muscles shrieked for relief and his head swam with the terrible monotony of the movement. At first he had paused every few moments to strain, to test the bonds, but at length the scraping had become mechanical. For a long time he had not stopped, had not thought of stopping. Had not thought at all, except to concentrate on keeping up that writhing motion. Back and forth, back and forth, scraping, scraping, scraping. . . .

And suddenly, he could move no longer. Overtaxed nature had revolted at last. His muscles stiffened, refused to obey the frantic messages of his brain. Ralph lay gasping, his sinews knotted, terrific cramps racking his exhausted body, his heart pounding a dirge of despair. Pain was a fiery net that meshed his frame, pain was a burning vortex that seared the void within his skull. He was done, he could do no more. He must lie here, bagged like a hen doomed to the slaughter-house, waiting for death, for worse than death.

What was that snuffling sound, that rasp as of claws on stone? They came nearer—faint but ominous. Dean forgot that he was bound, tried to jerk erect—

did jerk up to a sitting posture. That sudden jerk had parted the ropes—they *had* frayed through!

The realization brought back momentary strength. He surged to his feet, fought to cast the clamping folds from him. The blanket clung to him, he was tangled in it, could not get free—and something yowled, close by. The muffled sound was pregnant with threat, with feral menace!

Ralph struck out frenziedly. The sodden wool ripped, gave way. He threw it from him, whirled to the enraged scream of some animal close by in the blackness. Though cold air slapped his cheeks, pulled into his lungs, tar-barrel murk blinded him. But there, there in front of him, not five yards away, twin orbs of green light, level and low, glowed in the sightless dark.

Even as he caught sight of them they moved. That feline scream came again. They leaped at him. A shaggy body struck him, sharp claws ripped down his side, fangs sank into his arm, thrown up instinctively, and he thudded to the rocky ground under the tremendous impact.

The animal pounded down atop him. Its claws flailed, seared across his chest. Fetid breath stank in his nostrils, and the beast's avid snarls were loud in his ears. Dean clutched fur in his desperate hands, felt lithe muscles ripple beneath the pelt, felt a hot, slavering muzzle nose along his bared chest and knew that long fangs would be at his throat in seconds, would sink in, would tear. . . .

His right hand slipped, touched something that felt like a wooden stick, grasped it. . . . The animal winced, yowled. The stick was imbedded in its pelt; where it entered the fur was matted, stiff.

Dean's fist closed about the stick, thrust with it—deep. The stick went in. . . .

The beast's shriek was a scream of mortal pain. It was limp, suddenly, a flaccid weight over him, pinning him down. A warm liquid gushed over Dean's right hand, a viscous warm liquid that he knew was blood. But the beast that had attacked him did not move.

CHAPTER FIVE

Food for the Thirsting

RALPH lay under the animal's warm dead bulk for a moment, himself incapable of movement. Then a modicum of strength came back to him. He heaved, slid out from under the corpse of the beast. As his hand came away from the stick by which he had saved himself, his fingers brushed something that felt like feathers. Feathers at the end of a stick! They struck a chord of memory in him, something seen long ago, overlaid and forgotten by soul-shattering events that intervened. He recalled the fire's red finger touching a gray blur of feathers at the end of a shaft quivering in a window-sill. An Indian arrow. And this, this must be its twin!

Incredible! But incredible or not, the arrow had saved his life. Imbedded in the animal's flesh, painful but not deep enough to do any real damage, accident or fate had led his hand to it and he had thrust it in to reach a vital spot. Dean felt along the beast's flank, trying to find that arrow again. The thing felt like a cat, a gigantic cat. . . . Then Sonia had been right when she had sworn that she had seen a wildcat in the woods! . . . He found the arrow, tugged at it. It would make a weapon, some kind of weapon, for what lay ahead.

But who had winged that weapon into the cat's flank? Holding the lone arrow, Ralph rocked to the impact of the ugly question. Long years had gone by since the last Iroquois had folded his tepee and departed from the region—leaving the dead ashes of his fire and the bones of his dead. *The bones of the dead!* Lake Wanda had taken her toll of the redskins that had roamed her shores—were they, too, uneasy in her evil bosom? Did they, too, return to Oldun Island under cover of night's somber pall and wander, the living-drowned, seeking their unholy drink? *Were Myrtle and Anton only two of a gruesome band of dead-alive?*

Ralph's bleeding lips twisted in a wry, humorless smile. Twelve hours before he would have thought himself insane had such a thought come to him. Now it was his only refuge from conviction that he was mad. How otherwise explain the abduction and the killing of Charity, the kidnaping of Billy, his own presence here? The others had sated the thirst of the unholy band, but they would return to drink from his living veins. . . .

Not if he knew it!

His fingers clenched on the arrow, his arm swept out. The sharp flint reached the skin over his jugular, pricked it. Ralph held the stroke an instant, savoring the cosmic joke he was playing on his abductors. They would return to find him a corpse, to find the red fluid they had come to imbibe spilled, clotted and useless, on the rocky floor against which he had frayed their ropes. His biceps tensed for the slash. . . .

"Daddy," a tiny voice sobbed. "I want my daddy."

It was faint, faraway, somehow hollow, but it was Billy's voice, unmistakably Billy's voice! Just so had he often sounded when, repentant after punishment for some small misdeed or bemused by some childish nightmare, he had cried for Ralph from out of the night silences. "I'm thcared. Daddy, why don't you come?"

A great wave of exultation surged up within Ralph. He was alive, Billy was still alive! He was near, somewhere in this fetid darkness, and alive! The man peered into the sightless obscurity, trying to see some sign of the child's whereabouts, trying to localize the source of the vague crying, while his pulses beat a tattoo of jubilation in his wrists and temples. They hadn't killed him, they hadn't drunk his blood! "Daddeee!"

"Coming, son." Ralph held his tone low, hoping it would reach the child, hoping those others would not hear it. "Coming." It was hard, terribly hard to be sure of where that tiny wailing cry came from, but it seemed to be from his right. He would have to chance it.

The footing was stone, rough stone but dry; it pitched upward slightly in the direction in which he moved. "Hold on Billy, daddy will be there in a little while." Something crunched under Ralph's feet and somehow the sound was not quite that of a dried twig. Billy's soft weeping was perceptibly nearer. Dean's shoulder brushed against something solid. It was a vertical facing of rock, harsh to his hand but strangely clean.

This must be a cave, somewhere on the island, screened to the casual glance by the omnipresent thick underbrush of the woods; a cave or underground passage through Oldun's rocky foundation. The wildcat had used it as a lair, had returned to it to lick its wound and been enraged at finding its den preempted.

Ralph's toe stubbed against something. He started to fall, reached a hand down to break his fall. It struck something round, something that rolled with an eerie, rattling sound. He was on his knees, scrabbling for the thing that had rolled away. Here it was. He pulled it to him, trying to determine what it was.

It was dry, rusty. . . . His fingers found an orifice, another. . . . There was no doubt about it; this thing he had found was a dried and fleshless skull—a human skull!

THE grisly token of someone long dead shook in Ralph's hand. He tried to laugh off the chill prickling along his spine. No need to be afraid of this head— these teeth would never nip skin again.

Billy's sobbing was hushed for the moment, but another sound had replaced it, the distant lapping of water against a stony shore, the voice of the lake! This was a passage then, and it led to the lake. Was it through this tunnel that living-drowned returned to the world they could not leave? Was that why he and Billy had been carried here?

And then, suddenly, a freezing thought seared him with a fear that transcended all his previous terror, all the agony that had gone before. *He whose veins a vampire empties becomes himself one of their kind!* Was Billy, was his little, laughing son, one of *Those?* One of the dead that could not die?

Ralph's revolting soul cried out in an agony of denial, but the fearful thought would not down. There had been blood on Myrtle's lips—whose blood but that of her son? Ralph crouched, his icy lips pulled back from his chattering teeth. He must find Billy at once, and if the awful thing were so he must drive this arrow into the child's wee breast, through its tiny heart. So, and only so, could Billy be saved, only so could he be rescued from eternal anguish.

Dean surged to his feet, stumbled on again, driven now by an agony of haste that shuddered lest it find its goal. The man's sobs mingled with the renewed sobs of the little one, still ahead; the thud of his feet was a condemned man's march to the gallows. *If he had driven a pointed stake through Myrtle's heart when first he had found her on his doorstep this other, this greater sacrifice would not now be demanded of him!*

The passage curved, leveling out, and there was a red glow ahead, a bar of lurid light in the blackness. Fear that he had found the place where Billy was squeezed Ralph's throat, and he broke into a run.

The light-bar neared, but did not widen. Dean saw his hands and the arrow he clutched, red in the reflection of that uncanny light; saw rock, red-tinged; saw that the scarlet radiance came from a narrow chink in a rocky wall across the passage, a chink too narrow for him to pass!

He skidded to a halt, grabbing the rim of the crevice. He bent over, peered through the aperture. Light from within, red, flickering light, blinded his eyes accustomed for so long to darkness. He could see nothing save that lurid glare. But he heard the voice of his son—there, right there! "Pleathe Dod, thend me my daddy quick."

The prayer in that lisping baby voice cut him to the quick with poignant pity. "Billy!" he choked, "Daddy's here. Daddy's come!"

"Wheah?" As the piping glad little cry cut short the pathetic sobbing, Ralph's eyes accommodated themselves at last. He saw a cave, a stony bubble in the earth, saw a tiny blaze of twigs, saw a pallet of interlaced boughs, leaves uppermost on the cave's gray floor. And he saw Billy!

The child, his nightgown smeared and spattered with dried mud, stood in the center of that other cave. His face was streaked with dirt and tears, his tiny feet were caked with black loam, his hands were still folded in an attitude of prayer. "Wheah *are* you, big daddy?" His eyes were reddened by weeping, were bewildered and frightened; but they darted about eagerly. The light sparkled in their blue, eager depths, and his still quivering lips were warmly red as ever. Oh God! Oh thank God!

"I want you daddy, I'm thcared."

RALPH made his voice steady, calm and confident. "I'm right here, Billy-boy, right here where there's a hole in the wall. Come over here to me; I can't get in to you." Perhaps the crack was wide enough for the child to squeeze through. . . .

The tiny tad seemed bewildered, unable to locate him. "Billy," Dean said more sharply. "Come here! Over here!" How direct a child to whom right and left were cabalistic terms, a dazed and frightened tot? "Can't you understand, I want you to come over here where I'm talking from." The now frantic father fumbled at the crack in the rock. If he could get his arm through, Billy would see it. "Please Billy. I'm here."

The stony surface rasped the already lacerated skin of his arm, tore the raw flesh. "*Billy!*" The child had turned, suddenly, turned to the sound of approaching footsteps from somewhere out of Ralph's sight. Billy's face lit up suddenly.

"Unc' Anton!" he cried. "Unc' Anton. Daddy'th here thomewhere. Daddy'th here!"

He was toddling across the floor, suddenly was running with little, clumsy steps, his chubby arms stretched out—running away from where Ralph, pale-faced and horror-struck, was tearing at the obdurate wall with frenzied hands. "He'p me fin' Daddy, Unc' Anton!"

He passed from sight and the footsteps of the other stopped as if the little fellow had reached him, as if he were picking him up! Consternation rocked Ralph, horror stabbed his heart and twisted its reeking knife. He was too late, too late! Anton—the Thing that had Anton's form—had come back for Billy, was taking him away. . . .

"Come sonny," It said, "we'll go call mother. Mother is looking for you. . . ."

"Oh God! *Let me through!* It's taking my son away! Can't you see that It's taking my son to that other Thing so that They can suck his blood? *Let me through!*"

The maddened father hurled himself at the unyielding rock. He fought the granite, bit at it, gouged it. Almost as if it were a thing alive it battered him, slashed his flesh, stripped the skin from his knuckles. At last sheer failure of breath stopped his cries. He heard a tiny voice, far off, "But I want my Daddy," and silence.

Dean whirled, snarling. If God wouldn't help him he would help himself. He would run back to the other end of this tunnel, would head them off.

He plunged into blackness, whizzing through a darkness that was clammy now with horror, that snatched at him with noisome fingers and tried to stop his hurtling passage. But he was going too fast for them, too fast. He laughed triumphantly. Anton couldn't run as fast as this. The devil himself couldn't. He was going to catch Anton, he would snatch Billy from him and then he would tear Anton apart. There wouldn't be anything left of him to prowl the night and steal babies from their cribs, there wouldn't be enough left of him to tell what he had been. Pointed stakes through unresting hearts! Bah! He, Ralph Dean, knew something better than that. *An unquiet soul could not use a body that had been ripped to fragments!*

And then he'd find Myrtle and do the same to her. Their real souls would thank him, he knew that, would thank him because he had given them rest at last.

He was out of the tunnel, was crashing through the underbrush screen that he had surmised had masked it from discovery, was running blindly through a dripping wood that the storm had left. He was banging into tree-trunks, tripping over creepers, thudding headlong into noisome mud—picking himself up and running again in an unseeing, unfeeling, berserk rush death alone could stop.

EMPTIED clouds, huge-winged and black, drove across a sky graying with the first cold light of false dawn. Storm-riven trees strove to straighten themselves, groaning, and Lake Wanda muttered around her island, muttered of the destruction she had wrought and the pigmy human she had driven mad. Ralph Dean lunged through the last of the underbrush into the clearing about the old house, staggered, sprawled into a pool of storm water that had not yet seeped away.

Instinctively he pushed himself up out of the frigid puddle, pushed himself up to all fours and stayed like that. The icy douche had quenched the fever in his brain, thought functioned again, though haltingly.

Memory crawled back, horror, and despair. They had Billy, he had been chasing Them through the woods, had lost Them. He must find Them, must kill Them and save Billy. But where were They? It was almost dawn. They had to flee from the light, had to be back in Their graves, in the bottomless chasm beneath Lake Wanda's surface, before day broke. *Had They taken Billy with Them?*

Still looking down at the muddy water, Dean shook his head violently, trying to clear it. The sense of hurry, of imperative demand for haste, swept up in him once more. He lifted to his feet.

The house was before him, silhouetted against the gray-green glimmer of Mount Toran's sky-reaching mass. The downstairs windows still glowed. Strange that the fire had not gone out, he had last thrown a log on it hours ago! Ralph's bleared eyes squinted as he tried to remember when.

Something was moving stealthily in the shadows where wall and ground met!

Now the radiant rectangle of a window was dented at its sill by a black arc. It grew to a semi-circle, to the black profile of a head, peering in. A fisted hand came up, something long and narrow jutted from it, something that came to a point. It looked like a knife; a knife whose edge was cruelly jagged.

Ralph chuckled to himself, soundlessly, and his muddied face twisted in a crafty smile. They hadn't all gone back to the lake yet—that was one of Them. It was one that didn't know Ralph was not in the house and It was looking for him.

There was a little plashing noise as Ralph got out of the puddle, but the prowler at the window was intent on something It saw inside and didn't hear him. After that Ralph made no sound; he stalked his prey as silently as any Indian. He grinned at the thought. The Thing at the window must have the body of an Indian.

Good! The body was very old then, almost worn out, and would be easy to tear apart. Ralph's fingers curled, tingled with anticipation. He could feel them already clutching the rotted flesh, could feel the ancient ligaments pull apart like oil-eaten rubber. The bones would snap brittlely like dead twigs. He was right on top of It, in seconds. . . .

THE other grunted, whirled! Startled, Ralph struck at a dark face, between deep-sunk eyes that were like black flames. His knuckles thudded against bone, a stab of pain shot up his arm. The knife glinted redly as it darted at him. Dean dodged; the edge seared his shoulder like hot iron. He managed to grip the wrist before It could strike again. Queer! The flesh he clutched was solid; sinews like whipcord strained within his palm as the other fought to release that knife arm. Perhaps bodies didn't decay while They were using them.

Ralph's other fist pounded at a taut belly, beat an unavailing tattoo on banded muscles resilient as pliant leather. A hand flashed up past his face, clawed for his eyes. Dean caught it just in time. The two swayed, straining, breast to breast, in a back-breaking deadlock. There had been no sound, as yet, except the one surprised grunt It had emitted, the involuntary hiss of their agonized breathing, and the slap of Ralph's fists on the unexpectedly stalwart torso.

Dean's neck corded, sweat poured from his forehead. Sweat and blood, for his wounds had opened. Blood dripped across his eyes so that he could not see. His body was bathed in blood and his muscles were pulling from their sockets. He gritted his teeth and held on.

The other grunted again; the low sound It made was shuddersome in its utter malignity. Sweat oiled the palm with which Ralph clamped Its knife-hand, and the bony wrist was slipping, was twisting and sliding out. Panic clenched Dean's fingers and the slow menacing movement stopped. But he knew he could not hold out much longer. Black mists swirled within his skull, mists of exhaustion, of supernatural fear. He could no longer see his antagonist's malevolent eyes, could see nothing. . . .

But he felt a clammy-cold forehead press against his cheek, felt slobbering lips search his neck—*felt pointed teeth nip the skin of his neck! Oh God!*

Supernal terror galvanized Ralph with new strength. His taut body snapped like an uncoiled, gigantic spring, lifted the Thing that sought his blood and soul clear of the ground and crashed It against the house-wall!

Then Dean whirled and ran. The black and dripping woods received his plunging, gore-spattered, fear-winged form. He thudded into a rough-barked tree trunk, bounced off, lunged on—unfeeling, un-seeing, knowing only terror and the desperate need for escape.

Interlaced leaves of the forest roofed his path, shutting out the sky that was a kaleidoscope of gray and rushing black. From behind him an eerie cry keened through the blackness. Thunderous pursuit drowned the crash of his own passage.

Dean hazarded one harried backward glance, saw a lithe form slipping through the trees, saw an arm upraised and a jagged knife silhouetted against a momentary opening of the tree-screen. He leaped to impossible speed, twisting between the thick boles of the forest, fighting the myriad tendrils of the underbrush that slashed his body and his face with their wicked thorns.

Then a pallid shape glimmered ahead of him, just ahead! He could not stop; impenetrable brush kept him from swerving to avoid it. Light broke through a thinning of the arboreal canopy, brushed the white form's face. *It was Myrtle!*

A scream came from her bloated lips, the shriek of a damned soul, and a huge club lifted in her little hands. It arched down at Ralph's head!

He left his feet in a frantic dive that took him under the sweep of the cudgel. His flailing fist thudded into soft flesh and he crashed atop the woman-Thing's down-crashing form. He twisted instantaneously to scramble up and resume his flight.

A dark figure loomed above him! The light was a nimbus about its head and Dean saw a wan countenance, a pointed black beard and glittering eyes. "Anton!" he screamed. "Oh God! *Anton!*"

The underbrush crashed somewhere as the third of the living-drowned arrived. Walder made a swift movement. Blinding light exploded within Dean's skull and a single thought slid through Ralph's brain. "They've got me. They've got me at last!"

Anton's face danced in front of his eyes, blue lips pulled back from pointed teeth. Then merciful oblivion engulfed the broken man.

CHAPTER SIX

Voice of the Dead

THEIR voices were uncannily hollow, reverberant. But of course, they were dead for only a week and the Things that had taken possession of their corpses had probably not yet learned to use them with ease. The one that was using Myrtle's voice seemed to be angry. *"No!"* It said. *"I won't leave them. Not while the blood is still in their bodies."*

She wasn't satisfied, Ralph thought dazedly. Queer. When Myrtle was alive she ate very little but her corpse seemed to require more than the others. Now it was Anton, whose appetite had always been gargantuan, who was arguing with her. *"We've got to go, Myrtle. I can't wait any longer. You've got to come with me!"*

Returning consciousness brought full realization, and tingling horror swept Dean's recumbent form. He was bound, helpless. He lay on something soft and his eyes were closed. He was weak, terribly weak from exhaustion, from loss of blood.

From loss?

From the *theft* of his blood by that unholy pair who disputed now as to whether they should consummate their grisly banquet!

"I tell you I cannot wait any longer. I've waited too long already. I've gone through too much for you to leave you now. The sun is rising; it will be too late soon, you must come with me or...."

A wave of nausea took Dean, blotting out the end of the sentence. What would happen to Them, he wondered, if They did not get back to their graves before day broke?

"What have you gone through for me?" the woman flung out, bitterly.

"What have I...? Hell itself! Look at this! The Indian did this. Look at it!"

They'd been fighting among themselves! There wasn't enough blood for all of Them in the living left on the island and They were fighting over the nepenthe in his veins, his and Billy's.

Billy! Where was Billy, what had become of him? Was the youngster still alive?

"You didn't get that for me. He attacked you and you fought over Ralph's body. If I hadn't come to and tripped him just as his knife started to tear you, you would be lying out there and not he. I shouldn't have done that. I should have deserted you and saved myself as you deserted Sonia...."

"For you. I couldn't get you both loose from the canoe...."

"So you chose me!" The hysterical voice broke into a shrill, demoniac laugh. *"Out of the goodness of your heart you preserved my body and killed my soul! You ghoul! You vampire! You...."*

Ralph forced his eyes open. The chamber seemed oddly familiar. He turned his head and saw that he was in his own bedroom, on his own bed! The debris of his chaotic search still strewed the room, but it was empty; beside himself nothing else moved here. Yet he still heard the boom of those disputing voices.

"That is not true, Myrtle! It was the Indian! He took you away, he made you drink that devil's potion of his and...."

The words came from right beside him, yet he could see no one! Were They phantasms after all, had the coming day made Their stolen bodies invisible, left only their voices to betray their presence? *Could they hold him if that were so?*

Ralph sat up. He was not bound!

These strips of white cloth that wound his legs, his arms, his neck and his head till he must look like a mummy were blood-stained bandages! They had wanted to preserve his life-fluid for their sucking lips and had stanched its flow, but they had not thought to bind him! Ralph stifled a grim laugh, swung his legs to the floor, tensed to meet an attack from his phantom captors. And nothing happened.

Anton's voice was still sepulchral, but its accents had taken on the foreign flavor they assumed only under the stress of the strongest excitement. *"By the ikon of St. Pavel, Myrtle, you push me too far."* Ralph's skin crawled as the bodiless speech seemed to come from beneath his very feet. *"I know how to make you come. You'll follow if I take Beelee weeth me. . . ."*

"Not again, Anton. Not again." Her laugh was wire-thin, mad, but triumphant. *"I've put him where you can't find him. You won't do that again!"*

The thick rug that had always lain here was a shredded heap in a corner and the floor was strangely warm to Ralph's soles. *"You she-devil, you haven't. . . ."*

THEIR talk went on, the talk of those ghastly presences, and did not halt at Ralph's movements. They could see him, then, no more than he could see them. Yet he felt eyes watching him, hostile eyes, and his scalp tightened. His own eyes searched the room for a weapon, saw a poker peeping out from under the bed, where he had thrown it. He started to bend to it, slowly.

"No! Billy is alive and he is in the house, but he is where you cannot lay your filthy hands on him. He. . . ."

Ralph stiffened. Billy was alive and he was in the house! Oh God! Oh good God! If he could find him, get him out of here—he'd get to the mainland somehow, if he had to fight a host of vampires and swim the mile-wide, frigid strait.

Where was Billy, where could he have been hidden? Dean's aching eyes searched fearfully. That venomous gaze was still on him; some sixth sense warned him its owner was waiting for his chance to pounce. Who was it, who could it be?

A vague scratching sounded, too faint for Ralph to tell its source. It came again. . . .

Ralph dipped quickly, snatched, still without looking, at where he thought the poker was. His fingers touched metal, flat metal; it was not the round shaft of the implement he sought.

"Then I'll carry you, by God, I'll carry you away with me," Anton shouted.

A scream ripped the air, a scream of sheer terror, and sounds of a fierce scuffle were all about Dean. A blow thudded and he dodged it involuntarily, though it was incorporeal as the voices themselves.

The movement brought his eyes in line with the window. A face peered in at him, distorted, mad eyes gleaming from a gory mask—and a bloody palm was pressed flat against the pane!

Ralph looked down, grabbed up the poker frantically, hurled it at that fearsome visage. Glass crashed, and the face was gone. Dean started toward the aperture; but something that he had seen while he stabbed for the poker stopped him, pulled his glance back to the spot where he had been standing.

A flat plate, pierced, was sunk into the floor there, where it had been covered by the rug, a convoluted grating of wrought iron, ancient as the house itself. Its meaning flashed on him. The floor was pierced to let warm air rise from the room below —those voices were coming from that room—the big living-room! Mytle and Anton were not up here, were not invisible. They were down below, and the sounds of struggle were coming from there.

"Help, Ralph! Help!"

That was Myrtle screaming. Myrtle! Dean twisted to the door, started for it. Stopped. It wasn't Myrtle, it was something else in Myrtle's body. The other Thing that looked like Anton was fighting with It and It was calling him because It thought to use him to defeat Anton. Then It would turn on him. . . .

"Oh God! *Ralph!*"

The man's hands fisted and he bit his lips. A new thought came through the maelstrom of his mind. *Whatever she was, she knew where Billy was hidden! If Anton won, took her away, or destroyed her, the child would be lost forever.* He started for the door again, got his hand on its knob. . . .

And he froze as a tiny voice cried, "Muvver. Don't hurt my muvver!"

THAT was Billy's voice. Billy's! But it hadn't come from down below. It had been muffled, not clear and distinct as were the sounds from the living-room striking up through the old register. Ralph jerked open the door, yelled "Billy" into the hall. "Billy! Where are you?"

"Daddy! Daddy! Someone's hurtin' muvver." The response came from behind him. Dean whirled. The room was empty, stark, staring empty! And yet . . . "Daddee!" Ralph pulled a shaking hand across his eyes. Dulled as it was, that frightened appeal of his son's had come from within the room itself!

"Billy! Billy!" Oh God! "Billy, where are you? Tell daddy where you are."

Smashing furniture below drowned whatever answer there might have been, furniture smashing, the growls of an infuriated man, and Myrtle's scream, *"Ralph! Save me!"* Dean shook his bewildered head as if to shake the sounds from his ears. He licked dry lips with parched tongue and called again:

"Billy! Son! Daddy hears you but can't find you!" Then, with a memory of childish games: "I give up. Come out, come out, wherever you are."

A ripple of gleeful laughter. It seemed to come from the very wall itself, from the fireplace. "I'm here Daddy, but I can't come out. I don't know how."

What was that depression in the ashes on the coal hearth? Dean's head thrust out, peering. Surely—it was the mark of a bare foot, a small foot that could be only Myrtle's! Suddenly Ralph recalled the flicking of a white form into this very room, and its vanishment. A long stride brought him to the brick-lined and blackened mantle. "Son," he called, excitement quivering in his voice. "Son. Call again."

"Daddy! You're warm. You're hot."

That was right here, right behind the wall itself! A great light burst on Ralph. "Billy," he said, quietly, "what did mother do when she put you in there? How did she open the wall?"

He held his breath, his body shaking to the pounding of his heart. Had the child noticed, would he remember?

"She pushed a brick, Daddy, thomewhere high up."

Dean's eyes shot to the horizontal courses of brickwork that made the mantle. "Which one, son? Can you tell? Which one?"

"The one I hit wiv a 'pitball f'om my beanshooter. When muvver cleaned it there was a dooah in the wall opened. But she made me promithe not to tell. She thaid we'd play a joke on you and Unc' Anton and Aunt Sonia thometime."

"Good Lord!" So that was how. . . This must be the one, where the soot was smudged, showed a lighter spot.

Ralph's hand darted to it, he pressed in—and nothing happened. Sidewise then. Wood grated against wood, and a crack showed in the wall alongside the fireplace. It widened. . . .

"It'th opening, Daddy. I can thee you. . . ."

Dean got his fingers into the crack, threw his weight against the panel. It creaked wide. A small bundle leaped out from a dark hole in the thick wall, leaped into his father's arms. "Daddy! I wath thcared, it wath tho dark in there."

His father was covering the sooty little face with kisses. "It's all right now, little man. It's all right. There's nothing to be scared of any more. Daddy will—"

"Stop it, Anton. Let me go! Oh God! Let me go!"

Myrtle's voice had stabbed from below, lanced Ralph's heart. If only . . . Billy squirmed from his arms. "I fo'got. Thomeone'th hurtin' muvver. Come on Daddy, we muth he'p her." The tot was almost at the door in his stumbling rush.

"Wait, Billy! Wait." Dean's mind was made up. "You stay here and daddy will go stop the man that's hurting mother."

He dived for the youngster, but the child was out in the hall and a wind gust slammed the door. Ralph grabbed for the knob. It jammed. . . .

"Daddy," Billy squealed. "The Injun—"

His scream choked off. Ralph got the door open, plunged out. A horrific figure loomed before him, a tattered, gory figure, whose face was the bloody mask he had seen at the window. The child was caught up under one of the man's arms, his other was upraised, and a jagged-edged, cruel knife was poised over Billy's throat!

"Stay back or I kill," a hoarse voice growled, and mad eyes leered at Ralph. "Stay back, white man, and put hands up high."

CHAPTER SEVEN

Mongo's Choice

DEAN reeled back against the door that he had automatically shut as he came through. His mouth worked, but fingers of fear were clamped about his throat and he could not make a sound.

Murky shadows brooded in the long corridor; but the nursery door, between Ralph and the invisible stair-head, was half-open and a vertical beam of morning light poured through it to invest the fearful group with its lurid luminance. The red glow added the last touch of macabre horror to the taut, quivering figure, painting its nude, cadaverous torso so that even the curving shadows of its protruding ribs were the hue of clotted blood; sharpening still more its ancient, incredibly wrinkled face that was a hatchet blade of aboriginal savagery and unutterable cruelty, skull-like as death itself; searching out the orbs deep-sunk in abysmal eye-sockets, to be reflected back as twin lanterns of insane blood-lust and unquenchable, age-ripened hate.

The uplifted arm was that of a skeleton in a tight coppery skin-sheath; the ruby-glowing, serrated blade gripped in its bony fingers seemed to thirst with a malevolence of its own for the blood of the tiny, blond-curled babe hanging limply over the apparition's other arm.

"What—what do you want?" Dean managed to squeeze out. "What do you want from me?"

The leathery lips twisted in a grimace. "From you nothing except go. Go from island belong my tribe, leave Mongo in peace with shades of his people till he join them in long sleep."

A little hope stirred within Dean, though he was past coherent thought. "Of course—we'll go. Right away. We'll go at once." His arms started to drop, to reach for Billy. "Here, give me the boy and we'll get right out."

The other's knife dipped warningly and Ralph's hand stretched up again.

"No!" Swarthy eyelids narrowed and the eyes behind them were reptilian. "Papoose stay. Mongo make papoose like him. Soon Mongo must go to lodge in lake, no one left drink blood white man who come island my people's dead. Papoose do that so Mongo can rest under lake-water."

The slow, guttural accents dripped from the fleshless leering lips—dripped horror and despair into Ralph's tortured soul.

"Oh God," he squealed. "You can't do that. You can't! Take me. Take me and let the little one go. I—my body is stronger, my teeth are bigger, sharper. I can drink more blood than he. Do anything you want with me but let him go!" He took a spasmodic step forward, stopped, his guts twisting as the monster's knife lowered swiftly till it pressed close against Billy's throat. "You're making a mistake in choosing him!"

"No." The hoarse syllable was a sentence of doom. "Make mistake before. Bowl of Wanda not strong enough, not last with white squaw. Sure not last with white man. White papoose weak, Bowl of Wanda last with him. *No!*"

Words that had no meaning slid over the frozen surface of Ralph's anguished mind. He understood only the "No," the immutable, damning "No!"

And suddenly he knew what he had to do. His burning gaze clung to the keen point of that knife; close, so close against the white skin of the lad's stretched throat; and his muscles tensed. Though the leap he contemplated was lightning-fast, that steel must plunge deep before he could reach Mongo; but death, any death were better than the immortal horror that otherwise confronted the child he loved. Yet he hesitated, for a fleeting instant, and some other part of his mind was suddenly aware that the turmoil below had subsided, that the house was deathly still. . . .

"Go, White Man, or stay till I come to drink your blood." Mongo started to glide toward the open door of the nursery.

NOW! Now or never! *Goody-bye Billy! I'll follow you soon enough!* Dean sent the death message to his legs, weak and trembling. They were sluggish in response. . . .

Abruptly, then, a dark shape bulked in the dark behind Mongo, a white arm snaked over the bronzed shoulder and a hand closed around the knife blade, twisting it away from the babe's throat! Ralph saw red blood spurt from the white fingers. He sprang and his crashing fist obliterated the mad fury contorting the death-face.

The knife hilt darted up, caught Dean's chin, smashed his head back, sent him reeling against the wall behind. His skull crashed, light burst in a coruscation before him. But through the blaze he was aware of a whirlpool of action, of a pale figure snatching up Billy's falling little form, of a darker one materializing to plunge again at Mongo.

Tottering, trying to gather his scattered senses, Ralph saw the jagged knife sweep up, dart downward, saw the gleam of its blade quenched in blackness and heard the sickening sough of its stab. The dark figure surged forward, its fingers came into the red beam, clutching the copper throat of the savage. A head followed, a lip-lifted snarling face—*Anton's* face.

The two thudded down to the shaking floor. A scream ripped from the heaving, intertwined mass, a scream that burbled, was suddenly cut off—was answered by another scream—Billy's. *"Daddy!"*

Dean twisted. White draperies streamed out from a tall figure, dashing down the hall. Billy's face stared at him over its shoulder, mouth open. "Daddy!"

The long hair that swept across the child's face matched his tight curls in their blondness. Realization burst on Ralph. Myrtle had the child, Myrtle, its transformed mother with her appalling thirst for her own son's blood!

Ralph shoved himself away from the wall, took off in a frantic dive, plunged down the hall after the fleeing figure. It was almost to the stairs when his reaching hand touched Its shoulder, clutched It.

It shrieked—a thin, weird sound compounded of bafflement and terror—whirled around. Its eyes were twin orbs of rage and Its free hand lifted, clawed. Dean's fist swept up, checked as the fury was gone from Myrtle's face and a sudden light irradiated it.

"Ralph!" she cried. "It's you, Ralph. Oh thank God!"

This wasn't Myrtle, the vampire. This was *his* Myrtle! A tingling current of oneness born of their years together flashed between them, told Ralph that his wife had returned before even he saw the glow in her blue eyes.

His fist continued its sweep, but it went around her; his arm was about her, was drawing her close to him as his lips sought her now roseate ones hungrily. Billy's warm form was between them, but did not separate them, it was flesh of their flesh, blood of their blood. Tiny arms went around their necks, a gleeful voice prattled, "Daddy. Muvver'th back. I to'd you muvver'd be back thoon."

A groan quivered through Billy's prattle. Still holding Myrtle in the curve of his arm, Dean turned. The red had gone out of the sunlight that streamed through the nursery door; its white radiance fell across two still forms on the hall floor. "Oooh," Billy yelled, "Unc' Anton'th killed the Injun. Unc' Anton'th killed the Injun!"

RALPH lifted the boy down. "Run downstairs, Billy-boy," he said quietly, "and see if the rain has stopped." Then he was walking up the hall, but his hand clung to Myrtle's as if he would never again let her go.

A swift glance showed him that Mongo had indeed passed to the lodge of his vanished people; but Anton moved a bit, groaned again. A bubble of blood formed on his hirsute lips, burst.

"Ralph. Forgive me . . . old fellow. Always . . . loved her. Canoe wrecked . . . could save only one . . . saved her. Then . . . went crazy . . . I guess. But . . . no good. Do you f-for—"

Breath and life went out of him with a hiss. Ralph did not have to answer.

Dean lifted, turned to Myrtle. "What was it all about? What's happened? Tell me, dear."

"He had overcome me, was carrying me out of the door when we heard Billy scream. That seemed to bring him to his senses and we turned back. We heard you talking, crept up the stairs and down the hall. The two of you were so absorbed that you didn't notice us till we got near enough to jump the Indian."

Ralph pulled a shaking hand across his forehead. It seemed cruel to press his query, but he had to know. "No. That isn't what I meant. Myrtle—queer things have been happening. I thought you were—" His voice dropped to a whisper— "a vampire. . . ."

"Ralph! What an idea! How—"

"I caught you nipping Billy's skin, under his ear. You—"

Myrtle's eyes widened with horror. "Oh, God! I thought I had dreamed that." Her fingers went to whitened lips. "That was what the Indian did to me, when he made me drink the mess he called the Bowl of Wanda. He said he was going to make me like himself. . . ."

Ralph gasped. "Then he *was* a vampire, come back from the dead. We've got to get a sharpened stake, drive it through his heart, or he'll rise again. We've got to. . . ."

"Wait, Ralph. Wait. You're wrong. He isn't really a vampire, though he did drink blood. A lot of it comes back to me, a lot of his talk when he stole me from the cave."

"The cave. What cave? What was all that Anton said about his saving you stead of Sonia?"

Myrtle put a hand on his arm, smiled bleakly. "I had better start at the beginning, then it will all straighten out. When the storm caught us, the canoe was smashed on a rock in Skull Cove. Anton was pitched free, but Sonia and I were both caught so that we couldn't get loose.

"I came to on a pallet of leaves, in a cave. Anton was pacing up and down like a wild man, and Sonia was nowhere to be seen. When he saw I was awake, Anton began raving. He told me that the storm had been a heaven-sent miracle, that he had always loved me and married Sonia only in a fit of pique when I chose you. He could save only one of us—I was the one he had chosen. God had given me to him and he would not reject the gift. I must go with him, away from you and Billy, go somewhere where we could begin a new life, and so on.

"I told him he was insane, demanded that he take me back to you. He swore that he would never do that, that he would keep me there in the cave until I consented to do as he wished. He tied me up, so that I could hardly move, and kept talking to me till I was almost as crazy as he. The only times he stopped talking were when he had to go out and find water and berries to keep us alive. That's all we lived on, water and berries. . . ."

"Poor girl. No wonder you looked like a corpse when I found you."

MYRTLE went on. . . . "During one of his absences I awoke to find a terrible figure bending over me. It was that Indian. His knife was poised, he was about to strike, when a sudden idea seemed to cross his mind and stop him.

He sheathed his knife, picked me up and took me to another cave close by."

"Very close; in fact, he could watch you from the other." The thing was clearing up for Ralph; he remembered the cave to which he had been taken a prisoner and from which he had watched Billy run to Anton.

"When he got me there he told me that Oldun Island was sacred to the dead of his tribe, that it was their Happy Hunting Ground. His family had been hereditary guardians of the island; he was the only one left and for years had driven all white men from its sacred precincts by terrorizing or killing them. He insisted that he was centuries old, that he had prolonged his life by drinking the blood of his victims. But now even that would not avail; his time was coming, and he must recruit a new guardian from the hated palefaces. I was the one he had chosen.

"I begged him to let me go, to get me to you. But he only laughed at me, toying with his knife and bending over a cauldron in which he was stewing some unholy broth.

"Finally he made me drink the concoction he had brewed. It burned as it went down . . . and I knew nothing more till I awoke suddenly to find myself bending over you in Billy's nursery, with my teeth against your neck. You jumped up, looking so wild that you frightened me terribly. I ran out, ran into our room and remembered the concealed niche I had found beside the fireplace. I got in there and fainted."

"I had left you by the fire, tied up. Your lashings were cut when I got back. Who did that? Anton or—"

"It must have been Mongo. I was his creature; naturally he would release me if he found me tied. I know it wasn't Anton; he told me what he had been doing in the meanwhile. The breaking storm had driven him back to the cave. He had found me gone, and went out again into the woods to look for me. After a while, he decided that I must have found my way to the house. He peered in through a window and saw me lying by the fire. He didn't dare enter, but his crazed brain conceived the idea of kidnaping Billy and using him to lure me out again. He climbed up the outside of the house, got the child out and got him to the cave. Charity was lying on the cot, apparently sound asleep."

Ralph fitted in another piece of the jigsaw. "Mongo must have got in in the same way and killed her right after Anton had climbed down. Then he came back. . . ."

"And threw a blanket over your head just as you were about to jump at me. I had recovered consciousness and was trying to find you. He tied you up and chased me, but the delay gave me time to get into my hiding-place again. I stayed there a long time, till I heard someone come in downstairs, and heard Billy talking. That brought me out.

"Anton had brought Billy back. He told me he had found the Indian trying to kill you and had rescued you. In spite of his desire for me he loved you, also. That was before he kidnaped Billy. He had left the child in the cave, had gone out to get word to me somehow in order to consummate his mad scheme, had heard the yowling of an enraged wildcat and decided that it was dangerous to leave the boy alone in the cave. So he had gone back and fetched him to the house. I persuaded him to let me take the boy upstairs and put him to bed, and that was when I hid Billy in the fireplace niche."

Ralph felt hot tears burning his eyes; in his weakness he could not hold them back. "Poor Anton. He must have been torn for years between his infatuation for you and his love for me. No wonder he went mad at last."

"I'm sorry for him, too. When he saved you again, in the woods, I kissed him, and he thought I had yielded to him. We carried you back here, bandaged you up, and went downstairs, where he started the old argument over again. . . ."

"I know the rest, darling, I think. . . . Come, we'll get downstairs and take care of Billy. And after that, we ought to be able to signal the mainland for help."

"Yes, Ralph. And we three still have one another. We must try to forget all the—the rest."

FROM the summit of Mount Toran, Lake Wanda still looks like an eye, a brooding eye of mysterious evil glaring ominously at the sky. But the old house on Oldun Island, that is the eye's green pupil, is untenanted, and will soon moulder into the ground. Charity and Anton are buried on the mainland, but Mongo's withered body was consigned to the lake whose shores his people prowled before ever there were white men in the land. The people of the region insist that on moonless, stormy nights, they can hear his triumphant whoop howling down the wind, proclaiming to the ancient gods that even in death he still maintains his eternal guardianship of the sacred isle.

THE END

Another Soul-Chilling Novelette, by

ARTHUR LEO ZAGAT

In the December Issue   **Out October 25th!**

Madman's Mate

By
G. T. Fleming-Roberts

(Author of "The House Where Horror Dwelt," etc.)

What sinister horror lurked behind the high-walled mansion of the Loups? What kind of thing was John Loup's wife—was she woman, beast or walking dead? . . .

H E ARRIVED at dusk. Few in Ogden saw him come. He walked very slowly down Acres Street, avoiding people, then turned into the back road and walked east with the shadows towards the Loup's house. No one knew who he was. His face was covered with a black veil!

One who saw the man with the veil was Tom Atwood, sheriff's deputy. When he learned the direction taken by the stranger, Atwood went home, got the whiskey bottle out of the medicine chest, and drank three fingers straight. He needed that whiskey to warm blood that was already beginning to chill at the thought of the Loups and the veiled stranger.

They were mad—the Loups. Everyone in town said so. Of course, Ogden was a small place and not backward with talk. But the Loup family had always had a bad reputation, even in its best days; and now that the estate had dwindled and there seemed to be no one to build it up again, John Loup, the last of the line, had become a bogey with which to frighten children.

Atwood knew he was duty-bound to do something about the Loup House. There had been stories in and about town of queer goings-on at the old house—strange lights, strange sounds. Some said that John Loup, who was a confirmed bachelor, had a woman up there at his house. That story had gone around because packages were continually coming through the mail addressed to Mrs. John Loup.

Who was she? Where had she come from? Ogden was full of such questions. Tom Atwood, as deputy, ought to do something about it.

It was queer, too, with all the gossip and speculation no one asked what John Loup's wife was.

The knocker of Tom Atwood's front door clattered, then rapped out three times. Atwood ran his fingers through hair that was stringy with sweat. Even before he opened the door he had a vague premonition that his visitor was the man with the black veil!

Without an invitation, the man walked into the hall. He was tall, heavy about the shoulders, built very much like Tom Atwood. He wore a cheap, ill-fitting black suit. Attached to the band of his felt hat was a black silk cloth knotted, at its lower extremity, about his throat.

"Tom," he said in a deep voice that the veil robbed of resonance, "you've got to lock me up, do you understand? Get me into jail, for God's sake!"

Atwood couldn't answer. He stared back at the black veil trying to imagine what kind of a face it hid.

His visitor spread his big hands out so that Tom could see rough palms. "They're clean," he muttered. "Clean hands. I want to keep them like that. But unless you lock me up, there will be blood on them tonight! Loup blood! God knows I don't want to be another Cain!" The man brushed his hat from his head. The veil dropped.

When Atwood saw the face, he uttered a sharp cry of horror. One side of it from ear to chin was raw-red and wrinkled like the skin of a scalded tomato. The other side was dead-white by contrast, and the skin was stretched so tightly that his right eye seemed to be *on* his face rather than in it. The man passed his hands over his forehead and down across his face as if his fingers were feeling his hideousness. "I—I forgot," he whispered out of the corner of his twisted mouth. "Just seeing *her* made me forget. You don't know me. Nobody would. But I am Frank Loup."

ATWOOD leaned heavily against the back of a chair. He needed support. Frank Loup had been dead since the war. Yet here was a man with Frank Loup's body and the face of no God-fashioned creature saying that he was Frank Loup!

The man came closer, grasping Atwood by the coat sleeve. His eyes fixed Atwood with their earnestness. "I didn't die," he whispered. "Hell wouldn't have me. I'm alive. I was alive with half a face after that shell burst. They grafted on skin and all that. But when they sewed my scalp up, they did it all wrong. It makes my eye stick out like that.

"I've been in Italy since then, working and trying to forget. I didn't think I could come back and face Mary looking like this. Then, I couldn't stand it any longer. I had to come home even if I couldn't see her."

"B-but," Atwood stammered, "your wife, why—" How could he say it with the poor devil looking at him with eagerness in his eyes?—"Why, Mary's dead," he finally blurted. "Died four years ago."

Frank Loup nodded his head. "I know. My brother wrote me. He was the only one who knew that I was alive. He used to send me a little of *my* money. He told me Mary was dead. I sent flowers—" He choked. "Now I'm back because when I die I want to be buried in the same soil—"

Suddenly, Frank Loup tightened his grip on Atwood's sleeve. Tom could feel his arm throb so tightly that the cloth stretched. "But Mary *isn't dead*," Frank Loup gasped out. "I've seen her! She's up there with my brother John. That's why you've got to lock me up. If you don't, I'll—" He stopped, biting off his sentence with his teeth. "Listen," he whispered, "do you know the origin of our family name? It's French."

Atwood shook his head.

"It—it means 'wolf'," Frank Loup said huskily. "It's an old, old family. There's tainted blood in our veins—madness, the insanity of lycanthropy! It always becomes apparent in at least one child in every generation. One of us always becomes fixed with the illusion that he is a *beast*. Perhaps I am that *one*." He shuddered. "If John has tricked me, if he has my wife up there in his house, I—I think I shall tear out his living heart with my own hands!"

"Wait a minute," said Atwood, trying to steady the man, though his own voice was shaking. "Get a grip on yourself.

Mary's dead. I saw the death certificate, saw Dr. Winthrope sign it—"

"But where is Dr. Winthrope?" Frank Loup shouted. Atwood knew the doctor was dead. "That's it," Frank Loup went on as if he had divined Tom's thoughts. "Winthrope is dead. You didn't know him as I did. The Loup money would always buy anything. Winthrope would have come cheap!"

"But there was a funeral. . . ."

"Did you go?" There was a crafty grin in Frank's voice if not on his ugly face. "You didn't. A private funeral—and at night! I tell you, Mary is not dead! I went up there this evening as soon as I got in. John didn't want to see me. He said my face made him sick. John always was an artist—sculpturing and the like—and he's got a weak stomach for some things. But I'll swear I saw Mary pass the door while I was talking to John. He said I was mad, but he wouldn't let me in. I told him I'd be back for him tonight. And go back I will! If he has Mary up there, by heaven, I'll kill him!"

Then Frank Loup's rage passed. He began pleading. "You'll lock me up, Tom. You won't let me murder my brother? You'll put me in jail?"

Tom Atwood took out his keys and jingled them reflectively in the palm of his hand. "Yes," he said, "I think that's best. You'll be made comfortable, and if you're not better tomorrow, I'll see about getting you a doctor. And to-night—" Atwood drew a long breath—"tonight I'm going up to your old house and have a talk with your brother."

Frank Loup shook his head. "I can't let you do that. John has changed. He always was queer. Now, he—he's damnable!"

Tom succeeded in laughing. "Well, come along. I'll let you know if I learn anything. . . ."

TOM ATWOOD remembered John Loup as a remarkably tall, thin man —almost emaciated. He had the air about him of a man who knows more than he dares tell and thinks of many things that are not good for him. There was no doubt about him being artistic in an erratic sort of way—painting a bit, modeling small statues, even writing morbid verse.

After he locked Frank Loup in the jail, Atwood turned his car up the back road that ran behind the Loup estate. He stopped, half a mile from the town, at the ten-foot iron fence that encircled the place. He climbed over the fence and started across the back lawn.

Atwood sighted the family burial vault, standing as it had for years beneath a mammoth willow tree. It had been a place for raising goose pimples on him when he was a boy with a whistle on his lips for every churchyard he passed. Tonight he felt the old chill returning.

As he approached the vault—for he would not give in to his desire to avoid it—the wind, like a spectral hand, brushed the thin veil of clouds from the face of the moon. In the ghostly light, the old, mournful willow cast splotches of moving shadow on the roof of the tomb.

In front of the gloomy, black marble vault, where the heavy bronze door closed over the crypt, was a statue known about Ogden by the name of Stone Eyes. It represented the life-size figure of a woman, robed and hooded, with one hand extended as if beckoning to all the old bones sealed up in the vault. There was something about it that reminded you of the Loups—the same thin features, the same stern aspect. But the eyes—lidless, unsleeping, vacantly staring! Atwood felt a shudder twist up his spine as he glanced over his shoulder at old Stone Eyes.

It actually seemed that those lidless eyes glared at him, measuring him for a shroud!

Atwood recalled the legend: At midnight, Stone Eyes was supposed to come to life, knock at the door of the vault, and enter to speak with the dead! Atwood spat smoke disgustedly. He was an ass! Yet all the way up the path to the house, he kept turning to look back. . . .

THE house was square and scrofulous-faced where white paint was peeling from the brick. Huge pillars reached from the piazza to the slate roof. The structure was topped with an ugly cupola.

A green lamp burned in the hall, the only spark of light Atwood could see through the leaded door-glass. He stood there for a moment, hand on the brass knocker. From inside came a sound like the sob of a child, yet there was something of a puppy's whimper about it.

Instead of knocking, Tom Atwood twisted the door knob, found the door unlocked, and noiselessly entered the hall.

Lolling in a chair, was Michel, John Loup's big deaf-mute servant. He was not a pleasant sight at all, with his coarse, black hair, his broad nose, wide open mouth, and ivory colored teeth. And as Atwood stepped inside, Michel cried in his sleep like a dog.

Atwood was startled. His indrawn breath hissed through his teeth. The deaf-mute stirred slightly. Atwood moved quickly, taking shelter behind drab velvet curtains that hung over the living-room door. Looking between the curtains, he could see the servant stand up —six feet six inches of brute brawn— look around, and sniff like a hound. His short thick fingers quirked around something in his belt and came away locked over the handle of a long-bladed knife. The servant walked slowly, parted the curtains, and passed through the door as if he had not seen Atwood. Suddenly, he turned, leaping straight at the curtain which shrouded Tom Atwood. His knife ripped through the cloth, narrowly missing Atwood's throat.

Atwood smashed out with his right fist, a blow that only slowed the deaf-mute for a moment. When the knife thrust came again, Atwood was ready for it. He held in his hand a leather shot-sack that he had carried ever since he had been deputized. The fingers of his left hand stopped the man's wrist in mid-air, while with his right hand he clubbed down on the servant's skull—a dull *plump* of a blow. Michel uttered a little gurgling sound, reeled, pitched noisily to the floor.

Tom Atwood listened intently, tongue between his teeth. He thought he heard bare feet pattering on the floor above. Then everything was silent.

Breathing heavily, he crept up the stairs.

In the upper hall he could hear no sound except the imaginary crackling within his own ears. A greenish glow of light seeped into the gloom from one of the wide-open doorways. He tiptoed to the curtain and looked in.

A whispered oath tumbled from his lax lips. Never had he seen such a room. It was unclean, *ungodly!* In each corner of the room was a heavy bronze urn filled with brown, withered flowers. The room stank with their rotting stalks. Except for the bed, there was not another stick of furniture in the place. The huge bed was of carved ebony, and spread with black sheets and pillows. A green lamp hung from the ceiling, tinting the occupants of the bed a sickly shade. The occupants! John Loup and—

"God! What a sight!" Atwood muttered. Was it a woman, or. . . ?

Her face—for a woman *it* appeared to be—had the blue-greenish shade lent by the lamp. Her features were sharpened, nose knife-bridged, lidded eyes sunken. Her thin, bony fingers were crossed over a withered lily that lay on her breast!

The hideous truth— Here was a woman, once beautiful. Here was the woman who had once been Mary Loup!

But what was she now? A dozen ugly conjectures crowded into Atwood's brain. A mad sort of cry, getting the better of Atwood's tightened throat, retched out.

John Loup sat up stiffly and opened his eyes so that they caught the green light and gleamed balefully at Tom. Unnaturally crimson lips tightened back from white, wolfish teeth. His voice was cathedral-toned. "I knew you would come back as you said you would."

What did the madman mean?

John Loup went on, smiling his ghastly smile: "I wanted you to see her as she is. I've kept her for you, kept her from the grave four long years. But I shall *kill* you before I will let you take her from me. You're not jealous?" He laughed, a rippling sound like that of a stream flowing beneath December's ice.

Then Atwood began to understand. He remembered that he and Frank Loup were built very much alike. In the half light near the door, John Loup couldn't have seen his visitor's face. John had expected Frank Loup. That explained why the servant had guarded the door with the intent to kill.

"You see, she was so beautiful," John Loup went on. "I could not bear to think of her in the cold vault, in the realm of the worm. So I brought her to my bed. You can't be jealous now, Frank. Embalmers' pencil-painted lips are cold— cold—cold. . . ."

"Merciful God!" The thought drummed in Atwood's fevered brain: John Loup slept with the dead! But though his mind was afire, his body was frozen with horror. Mary Loup, four years dead, preserved by some embalmer's art, lying in the black bed—

ATWOOD staggered back into the hall. Suddenly, John Loup sprang from the bed—so suddenly that the head of the corpse beside him rolled on the pillow. "Who are you?" he shouted. "You're not Frank!" He started for Atwood, striding along, his bare bony feet flashing in and out of his black night robe. His claw-like fingers were extended, hungry for the feel of Tom's throat. His red lips parted—gleaming teeth gnashed with rage. He got just close enough to Atwood so that the deputy felt the long fingernails rake across the flesh of his throat. Horror became terror. Tom was knocked from his trance. He uttered a dry sob, and fled on leaden legs.

Tom Atwood never knew how he got out of the house. He forgot about everything until he found himself in his own room. For an hour or more he lived again and again through each second of horror. That black bed! The unshrouded corpse! John Loup—a ghoul!

Suppose he told others what he had seen? He could hear people whispering behind his back: "There goes Tom Atwood. He's as crazy as the Loups!"

Atwood sighed. He would have to go to the jail and tell Frank Loup what he had seen. He took another bracer of whiskey and started out.

A dusky shadow crouched on the steps of the jail. The young Negro, Jim Haleck, who acted as turnkey whenever the jail had a tenant, was sitting there holding his head in his hands.

"Well?" Atwood's nerves gave a knife-edge to the word.

Jim groaned. "Mistah Atwood, I'm near kilt. The man with his face half tore off broke out and bashed in mah haid!"

After some moments of questioning, Atwood got the story out of Jim. A little while before Atwood arrived at the jail, John Loup's servant came with a message for Frank Loup. By means of pencil and paper, the mute inquired as to where Frank might be found. Jim Haleck delivered the message at Frank's cell, whereupon Frank was stricken with violent madness. He got his hand through the bars, seized Jim's throat, and forced him to give up the key. Once out of the cell, he knocked Jim in the head, and ran off into the night.

Atwood turned into the empty cell. There he found a slip of paper, evidently the one brought by the deaf-mute. It read:

> Meet me tonight in the vault, darling. I will come to you. Your wife in this world and the next,
>
> Mary.

Tom Atwood knew that Frank Loup was just mad enough to do what the note suggested. Heaven and Hell would not prevent him from keeping that rendezvous—and with a corpse! Atwood couldn't quite grasp the depth of the plot; whatever it was, he knew that it could come to no good. He ordered Jim to drive him at once to the Loup place.

Outside the iron fence, the Negro brought the car to a stop. "Wait here, Jim," Tom ordered curtly.

Having climbed the fence, Atwood saw Frank Loup walking about a hundred yards ahead of him. Frank was shuffling along through the tall grass, his head bowed as if in deep thought. Then the shadow of the great willow swallowed him.

Atwood ran to a grassy mound that overlooked the scene, and dropped down on his belly. From there he could see the door of the vault and old Stone Eyes standing there with hand outstretched. Frank Loup stumbled past the statue, and Atwood could hear the tinkling of his keys as he sought out the one that fitted the lock. The door yawned open. Frank Loup entered the realm of the dead.

It was midnight. Wind brought the chime of the clock up from the village. Atwood counted every stroke, and with the twelfth came a strange sense of impending disaster.

His heart grew cold. Every hair on his scalp prickled up.

Either the insidious hand of madness was meddling with his mind, or the statue in front of the vault had moved. The beckoning hand dropped stiffly. Then without apparent effort, Stone Eyes glided into the vault!

Midnight silence was shattered by a hoarse cry that throbbed with terror, that shouted up from the mouth of the vault.

Atwood was on his feet running towards the vault, though prudence told him to run the other way.

But there were no more cries—only the dull, sickening sound of blows striking dead flesh!

Ten feet from the vault, Atwood slowed up. He could see something white moving within the dark interior. He stepped to the door, fumbling for his flashlight. Then *it* came! The white thing seemed to move on the cold, dead-smelling draft from the door of the tomb. Atwood thrust out stiffened arms to stop the thing, but as it glided into a moonbeam, he saw the face—the white, immobile face of Stone Eyes herself!

But the moonlight pointed to something else. In the white hand, that extended from beneath the folds of the white robe, was a long knife. Its blade was bathed in blood!

Atwood fell back before the gliding statue. He saw the knife raised as if to strike. His arm went up, a puny shield against such a foe. The blow came—but from behind him! Yellow lights flashed before his eyes. He lost his senses.

CONSCIOUSNESS returned gradually. For moments he lay there, half stunned, eyes closed. It seemed that far in the distance he could hear a strange, screeching noise, followed by a hollow thump—then silence.

He opened his eyes, staring straight up into the branches of the willow tree. The moon pushed an oblique column of light through the foliage. His eyes followed it and lighted upon an extended arm. He watched the arm, expecting it to move, to strike, *to kill!*

But it was as still as stone!

"Mistah At—wood!"

That was Jim calling him. Tom Atwood picked himself up and shouted back. Then he staggered over to the statue—for it was Stone Eye's arm he had seen in the moonlight. He turned his flashlight full upon the white stone face. The vacant eyes stared unseeing. His fingers trembled all over the stone surface. Terror beaded his brow with clammy sweat. The sinister dread of impending madness possessed his brain. Minutes ago, he had seen that statue *move.*

But it was stone, cold stone!

He stepped back shuddering.

"Wh-what's goin' on here, Mistah Atwood? You've been gone mos' half an hour!"

Tom swung around. The sight of Jim gave him a new grip on his flurrying senses. However, he had good reasons for not answering Jim's question just then. He needed human companionship as he had never needed it before. "Wait here, Jim. I'm going in there." He nodded towards the vault.

Atwood took his flashlight, turned it on, and entered the tomb. The place reeked with the smell of old bones and new-let blood. Frank Loup lay on his back in the center of the floor. Face and chest were raw with rage-driven knife slashes—enough wounds for a dozen deaths!

For a moment, Atwood stood there trying to piece the puzzle together, to permit himself to believe what he had seen spelled madness. There was something he ought to have remembered—some sound. He walked to the door of the vault. Wind was playing through the branches of the willow. He could see Jim shudder with every whispering sound. Atwood looked up into the tree. Some sinuous shape dangled above his head. Suddenly, it returned to him: while he had been lying there on the ground, he had heard a shriek and a dull thump.

"Come on, Jim," he said grimly. "We're going up to the house."

"Not that crazy house?" There was awe in Jim's whisper.

"Well, there's a murdered man just inside that vault. If you'd rather stay here, you can."

"G-guess I'll go along with you, Mistah Atwood."

They crossed the lawn, rounded the house, and quietly approached the front door. It was part way open. They crept into the hall.

Above, Atwood could hear slow, measured footsteps pacing across the floor. Beckoning to Jim, he crawled up the steps. In the hall upstairs, he could see the same greenish light coming from John Loup's room. Atwood peered in.

The blinds of a huge window had been thrown back. Moonlight poured through the pane, augmenting the glow of the green lamp. Standing in the window was a figure clad in voluminous white robes and wearing a white hood. It might have been a statue of stone except that it swayed slowly back and forth while rocking in its arms a long, stiffened bundle.

Atwood stepped quickly into the room. His groping hands found the main light switch near the door. He pressed it on and stood waiting.

THE white figure glided around. Under the hood, Atwood could see the high cheek bones, the wide, wise brow, and baleful eyes of John Loup. Lying across his arms, like a great stiff doll, was the body of Mary Loup!

John Loup's lips jerked back. "Why have you come?" he droned.

"I've come," said Atwood slowly, "for you. I charge you with the murder of Frank Loup, your brother!"

John paced to the bed, tenderly placing his gruesome burden back on the black sheets. "Sleep well, darling," he murmured. "I shall yet awaken you." Then he faced Atwood. "You, too, have come back from the dead. I told Michel to kill you."

Atwood laughed harshly. "My skull is pretty thick. It takes more than a blow on the head to kill me. But I'm not so dull that I can't prove you killed your brother! You didn't want him to return and take over the management of the estate, did you? So you posed tonight as a statue in front of the vault after you had ordered Michel to haul the real statue up into the willow tree with a block and tackle. You sent a note to Frank, in order to get him to the tomb. He passed you, as anyone would have, thinking that you were the statue. You followed and stabbed him to death. As you left the vault, Michel came up from behind me and knocked me in the head. You thought I was dead. Michel then lowered the statue back into place. I heard the squeal of the pulley and the thud of the statue striking the ground. And there on the bed is the proof!" Atwood pointed to a white, plaster mask that lay on the black sheets. It was an exact replica of the face of Stone Eyes modeled by John Loup's mad artistry.

John Loup shook his head. "I do not care for the estate. I did not want Frank to come here and put my darling—" with a mournful glance at the embalmed body on the bed— "back in the cold tomb.

Someday—" he droned dreamily, "on a night when the moon is full, I shall be able to bring her back—back to this life again. It was that I did not want Frank to interfere. He never loved her half as much as I did!"

Atwood sickened at the thought. Strange, distorted jealousy—jealousy for a corpse! "You're mad," he shouted.

A crafty expression stole over John Loup's face. "Not so mad but what I look behind me before going forward!"

Atwood spun around—stared straight into the muzzle of an automatic held in the unflinching hand of Michel, the deaf-mute. But there was something else—a black shadow moving in the hall outside. A small form it was—a very frightened but very brave boy. Jim was creeping up behind Michel.

"Shoot, you fool!" shouted John Loup, forgetful of Michel's defective hearing.

Atwood saw two black hands seize the deaf-mute's knees. Michel was taken by complete surprise. His legs jack-knifed, his gun fired at the ceiling. Atwood leaped, leading a smashing blow with his right fist. Michel collapsed, falling over Jim's kneeling form. Jim squirmed from beneath the giant, and got to his feet. Atwood pivoted in time to meet John Loup, as the latter attempted to get through the door. He seized the madman by the throat, threw him screaming to the bed.

But John Loup wasn't resisting. He was laughing—a hideous little cackle that mounted higher and higher until it became an hysterical giggle. He clung to the corpse, covering cold, dead flesh with burning kisses. Words sobbed out with his laughter. "They'll never separate us, sweetheart! Never!"

* * *

When at last they had handcuffed John Loup and his servant and locked them both in jail, Atwood, Jim Haleck and several townsmen returned to the Loup house. They wanted to search for the woman Frank Loup claimed to have seen. They could not find her. But, of course, Frank Loup was as mad as his brother!

However, in one closet they found all the packages that had been sent through the mail addressed to Mrs. John Loup. Each one contained some bits of feminine finery. All were unopened.

Jim Haleck rolled his eyes and declared that John Loup knew devil magic and could make a zombie out of the corpse of Mary Loup. He had, Jim declared, purchased clothes for the trousseau of his undead bride.

They scoffed at Jim and joked about his Negro superstitions as they left the house. But Tom Atwood knew there wasn't a man among them who would sleep with his lights out that night. Tom knew that he was to spend many a restless hour wondering—trying to convince himself that the next time John Loup slept with the dead it would be until eternity. . . .

In the December Issue

G. T. FLEMING ROBERTS

writes another of these tales of eerie mystery and terror

Out October 25th!

RIVER

By Wyatt Blassingame
(Author of "Village of the Dead," etc.)

For centuries the bones of the Flat Head tribe had lain untouched. . . . Bill Bruce smiled at the curse upon those who disturbed them. But when hideous, grinning death walked the night, when his own skull was a tightening, fiery thing that burned the flames of hell in his anguished brain—then he ceased to smile . . .

THE three men in the excavation atop the Indian Mound were afraid. Bill Bruce could see it in the tenseness of their sallow, dirt-smeared faces, the jerky nervousness of their movements. Gradually their emotion had begun to communicate itself to him, making the muscles of his lean, tall body stiffen slowly, grow cold. Almost suddenly he realized that he too was afraid of what one of those shovels might turn up at any moment—afraid of the curse laid on the man who disturbed the bones of the Flat

OF PAIN

*Novelette
of
Nameless
Fear*

Head Indians which had lain here untouched for more than two hundred years.

Bruce laughed harshly, shook off the feeling. But the laugh died quickly and

lines of worry showed at the corners of his black eyes. His full, good-natured mouth pulled thin as he stared off to where September sunlight made a glittering ribbon of Moore's creek set off by the dark green wall of the oaks and pines beyond it. Then he looked back into the pit and silently cursed the luck which had made him hire these inexperienced farmers as archeological assistants. If Wade Martin, who owned the property on which the mounds stood, had not forced him to pay such a damn stiff price he could have brought along a skilled helper. Now he *had* to find relics, and worthwhile ones too, or he was ruined financially. Everything he had was sunk in this venture.

The men in the pit worked silently, fearfully. For years weird stories had circulated about these mounds. Persons in this remote and superstitious section left them strictly alone. Bruce had been hard put to it to find workers. Two of his helpers were middle-aged, half-starved farmers, who were willing to do anything to earn a few dollars. The third was Zeke Norman, young, sandy-headed, a bit more educated than the others. But now even Norman was nervous.

Jake Peters was digging rapidly as though he wished to get the thing finished. He was a tall, gangling man with faded blue eyes and thin, colorless hair. He drove his shovel deep into the earth, flung it back over his shoulder. Something white gleamed under the clay, then disappeared as loose bits of earth trickled over it. Peters jerked frightened eyes toward Bruce. Before he could speak, the archeologist was in the pit beside him. Crouching, Bruce began to remove the earth with his hands.

Every man in the excavation stopped work. They leaned forward, half frightened, half curious, to watch the slim, hard fingers scoop away the earth. Again

there was the dull white gleam of bone through the red clay.

Jake Peters' nasal voice was husky. "That's them. We found 'em."

"I hope they're dead," Norman said. He laughed, a bit nervously, but the other two farmers did not join. Part of a white skull peered up from the red clay.

Bruce dragged away more earth, revealing the whole skull, the top of the spine and bony fingers resting on white breastplates. The top of the skull was flat, rounding sharply into the forehead. Bruce knew how this tribe of Indians had bandaged their children to give them flat skulls. Without looking around, he said, "Jake, you get here by the skull and keep the dirt back." Bruce moved carefully, clearing the rest of the body. Zeke Norman was standing close to Peters.

The tall, middle-aged farmer knelt at the head of the skeleton, staring at it. His tobacco-stained lips were parted and his breathing was loud against the tense stillness of the afternoon. Slowly Peters reached out a clay-grimed hand, touched the flat skull.

The thing happened without warning. Absorbed in his work, Bruce had forgotten the men about him. Abruptly Jake Peters made a gasping sound, said: "What the hell?"

Bruce looked up. Peters was staring at him, but the faded blue eyes were wide, puzzled, unseeing. Then as if a spring had broken, the man flung himself backward, slapping both hands to his head. He shrieked, a high, throat-splitting, terrified scream that seemed to rip the afternoon quietness and set it vibrating with horror.

Peters struck the ground flat on his back, rolled with the wild fury of a cat to his feet. His dirt-covered hands were pawing madly at his head. His mouth was wide open and cries vomited from it in a shrill, agonized stream. With one leap he gained the top of the excavation.

Still crouched in amazement beside the skeleton, Bill Bruce heard the rapid beat of Peters' shoes as he raced down the mound into the woods that circled it.

Norman's breath was whistling through his nostrils. He whispered, "His head . . . what. . . ? The Flat Heads. . . !"

The other farmer stood motionless, his face weirdly white under the dirt and sweat.

Bill Bruce's long, hard muscled legs flung him erect. "Come on, Norman. We'll catch him," he snapped. He raced up the side of the excavation, paused. Behind him Moore's Creek lay shallow and glittering in the sunlight. In front, tall oaks made dark shadows on the rocky hillside. Jake Peters had already vanished into the trees, but a sharp, high scream came from the woods to Bruce's right. Evidently Peters had cut back toward the small creek. As suddenly as they had begun, the cries clicked into silence.

BRUCE went down the mound with a rush, plunged into the woods. The ground sloped sharply upward on his left, on his right it went downward to end in a sheer bluff above the creek. Behind him as he ran, Bruce could hear the pounding steps of Zeke Norman.

At the Creek's edge Bruce paused, glancing down at the shallow water thirty feet below. Little pebbles glittered on the bottom. Occasional boulders raised jagged heads above the surface.

"Hey, Jake!" Bruce shouted.

The words rang through the clear sunlight, echoed dully off the mountainside, and faded into silence. There was no answer and Bruce started downstream, along the bluff. He had gone less than twenty feet when Zeke Norman caught his shoulder, jerked him to a stop. The countryman's face was bloodless, his mouth working. He raised his left hand and pointed.

Ahead of them the cliff dropped a sheer thirty feet to the water, and near the cliff was a tangle of big rocks. Motionless on the rocks, face down, was the body of a man. Beneath his head was a nasty mess of blood, and a dull red stain streamed off with the water. He couldn't see the man's face. He didn't need to. It was Jake Peters.

Bill Bruce felt then a touch of the fear which was to follow. He was not conscious of being afraid as he searched a place where he could climb down the cliff, but there was an odd, heavy feeling in his chest, and his hands quivered slightly as he lowered himself from rock to rock. Zeke Norman followed close behind him.

When they reached Peters, Bruce rolled the man gently on his back. The countryman's nose was broken, his cheek scratched. His eyes stared wide open and sightless. Looking at the man's head, Bruce went sick at his stomach. The top of the skull had been crushed, mashed flat.

Bruce swallowed the lump in his throat. "He must have run off the cliff," he said, "and fallen on this rock, head down."

Norman gulped. "His head's flat and . . ." The words seemed to have burst from his lips and he stopped them suddenly.

Bruce turned slowly, dark brows knitted over black eyes. "What do you mean?"

The countryman looked down at the body. His eyes skidded away, came back to Bruce. "That's what everybody said would happen if we dug up them Indians. They were Flat Heads, and they. . . . Well, folks say that a long time ago somebody bothered with them mounds and their heads got mashed flat one way and another. They all said we . . . said *you* would get your head mashed flat. But now. . . ."

Bruce clenched his fists, leaned wide shoulders forward. "You don't believe those stories, do you?"

The countryman shifted uneasily. His eyes twitched toward the body on the rocks, swung back to Bruce. "What did happen to Jake? Maybe he fell off that cliff, but how come he jumped out of that hole yelling 'bout his head?"

The words struck Bruce like cold water. Why had the man run screaming over this cliff? Bruce's jaw shifted nervously, then set. "I don't know," he said. "But, by God, I'll find out. If anybody's trying to break up my work. . . ."

He stooped and lifted the body of Jake Peters and said: "We'll carry this back to my cabin."

He went up the sandy bank where it dropped low near the Indian mounds. The place was deserted. Bruce turned his head toward Norman and asked: "Where could Eddie have gone?"

Norman cleared his throat huskily. "He . . . he's probably gone home. Probably he ain't gonna work anymore . . . now."

Bruce knew the meaning of the countryman's tone, and his finger tips whitened as they mashed against the body he carried. He'd sunk everything he possessed in this venture. He *had* to get those relics out. He said quietly, "Are you going to keep working . . . after this?"

Norman did not answer. He shifted from foot to foot, his eyes on the ground. Bruce said, "All right. You cut off across the hill to Jake's home. Tell his folks to send after the body."

Still carrying the corpse, Bruce turned upstream toward his cabin.

CHAPTER TWO

The Skeleton Walks

THE cabin was some two hundred yards above the Indian Mounds. About halfway between the two, and across the narrow creek was the small shack where old man Wennie Jenkins lived. Bruce knew the old man would be sitting on the front porch dozing. He never did anything else. He'd see the body when Bruce passed with it. Well, no point in trying to prevent him. Everybody in Blount County would know what had happened.

There was a small clearing directly opposite old man Jenkins' home. When Bruce reached the clearing the old man was sitting as he always did, legs stretched along the top step, his head drooping toward his chest, a corn cob pipe dropping from his mouth at the same angle. Bruce was half across the clearing before the old man saw him and the body in his arms.

The pipe fell from Jenkins' mouth, rolled down the steps. He moved with the jerkiness of an old man as he got to his feet and, leaning on his cane, tottered across the little yard. "Hey!" he yelled at Bruce. "Hey! What you carryin'?"

Bruce did not stop. The body was heavy in his arms, and he didn't feel like gossip. "Jake Peters fell off the cliff into the creek," he told Jenkins.

The old man made a grunting sound, kept coming. "Hurt bad?"

"Dead," Bruce said. He was in the woods on the other side of the clearing now. He could hear old man Jenkins trying to cross the creek on the rocks and shouting after him.

His own cabin showed up through the trees, and he made a whistling sound of relief. The body was heavy. Bruce's arms were beginning to ache, and sweat was running into his eyes, burning them. But he wasn't thinking of the discomfort. He was trying to find some reason for Peters' actions. Zeke Norman had been close to the farmer, yet he had seen nothing. Peters had nearly reached out and touched the skull. Then. . . .

BRUCE was within twenty yards of his own front porch, his eyes on the ground ahead of him, when he heard the woman's voice. It was clear and startled, and it jerked him to a halt, snapping his mind away from Peters' death. "Oh! What . . . what's happened?"

She was standing on his porch, wearing a simple, white linen dress that brought out the red glint of her hair. She was tall, slender and curvesome. Her lips were red and soft, parted now in horror. Bruce bit his lips, cursed silently. Who was she and why the devil had she come here?

He reached the porch, climbed the steps. The girl stumbled backward, but her eyes followed him. Bruce went inside, put the body gently on the bed, spread his handkerchief over the face. Then he went back to the girl on the porch, and said: "Jake Peters fell off the cliff. It killed him."

The girl nodded. Her eyes were a greenish blue and set far apart. The linen dress clung softly to the curves of her body. She asked: "You're Mr. Bruce?"

"Yes."

"I'm Mary Marshall, the school teacher over at Clarence. I heard you were excavating some Indian mounds, and I came over to see the work. I . . . Mr. Peters was one of your helpers?"

Bruce said: "Yes." He meant to stop there. It was none of this girl's business how Peters had died. But the thing was boiling in his head and before he knew it, he was explaining to her. "It means I can't get any help. But it doesn't mean I'm going to stop. I'll finish alone."

Something stirred in the girl's green eyes. "But why did Mr. Peters. . . ." She stopped, staring past Bruce.

Bruce turned, saw the men coming into the little clearing about his cabin. Two of them were in front, followed by old man Jenkins who was talking in his high, cracked voice. Bruce knew them. Wade Martin, from whom he had bought the contents of the Indian mounds, was a big, square-faced, black-headed man. His mouth was square and cruel, his eyes narrow and close-set. The short, stomachy man beside him waddled when he moved. His skin was almost ochre and dirty. He wore dirty, bright-colored clothes and moccasins. Bruce had seen him in the small town of Clarence and heard that he lived with his family in a tent somewhere near the Birmingham highway. His name, he said, was Flat Rock, and he claimed to be one of the Flat Head Indians, but looked more like an American gypsy. On two occasions he had warned Bruce against disturbing the gods of his fathers, threatened him with disaster if he continued. Bruce had laughed.

Now the Indian waddled straight forward, stopped in front of Bruce. His voice held a slightly foreign accent, "You stop now! Quit insulting the burial grounds of my fathers!"

Bruce said quietly: "No. I'm going to finish my work here."

Wade Martin reached out his big hand, caught Bruce on the shoulder. "If I was you, I'd give up. The folks around here won't want any digging after . . . after what's happened."

"They can stay away," Bruce said. He was getting angry now.

Flat Rock waved his pudgy arms. The gesture was awkward, almost funny, but the man's face was sinister. "Touch one of those bodies and the destruction will fall on you!"

Bruce opened his mouth to answer, snapped his lips shut again. He turned toward Mary Marshall. "Perhaps you'd like to come down with me? I'm going to bring back the first skeleton now. These men can stay and help Jake's folks when they come. His body's in the cabin."

TWILIGHT was a dusky blueness outside the cabin, but inside the gloom was thick. Bill Bruce looked down at the skeleton which he had assembled on the floor. The first one. Tomorrow he'd keep on with his work. The success of this venture meant everything to him, a job if he won—money, a name among archeologists. Failure meant ruin. He didn't intend to fail.

Bruce turned, looked at the bed where the body had lain. It gave him a queer feeling in his chest. For the thousandth time he wondered why Peters had rushed like a madman from the excavation. If he could only figure that out. . . .

From the dresser he took a bit of soap, and stepped outside. The creek was the only tub he had. He bathed, went by the spring back of his cabin, drank deeply, then returned to the front porch.

Just when the thing started, Bill Bruce never knew. Perhaps he dozed, sitting there in a rickety straight chair, his feet propped up against a post, and his head began to hurt while he was asleep. When first he became conscious of the pain, it seemed that the long aching and hammering had been going on forever within his skull.

He knew that he was sleeping, or at least dozing, yet the pain was a black and living thing within his head, growing worse. He tried to fight himself completely awake, thinking that perhaps he should go inside the cabin for an aspirin. Sleep clung to his eyelids, dragging them down, holding them shut, but it did not shut out the pain. It was always there, hammering at his skull, crushing down upon the top of his head. Growing worse, worse. . . .

His eyes opened slowly. There had been a sound somewhere, though he couldn't be certain that he had heard it. His brain was reeling, aching like that of a drunken man. His eyes were straining in their sockets, but seeing nothing except a moving, twisting blackness.

At least he knew that his eyes were open and staring into the night. The full moon had not yet come up, and the darkness was pitch thick. He could scarcely see the post against which he had propped his feet earlier . . . and the post was wavering before his eyes like something seen through a mist. His head seemed to swell until it was on the point of bursting. Then it began to contract, the top mashing down upon his brain.

And then, in lone long, horrible moment, Bill Bruce thought he recognized the pain. Something was crushing down upon his skull—mashing it *flat!*

He scarcely heard the choked cry of terror that leaped from his throat. He tried to raise his hands, grip his forehead, feel his skull and relieve the wild fear that had touched him. He thought his hand was rising—and suddenly he knew that it had not moved. It lay still on the arm of the chair.

Bill Bruce tried to curse then in a wild paroxysm of fear and pain. His eyes bulged, staring through the darkness to where his hand rested on the chair arm. The hand showed dully in the darkness, and the pain behind his eyes blurred what he could see.

Then he heard the sound. Through the roaring agony within his skull, the sound crawled horribly to strike at his aching brain. It was a low, clinking noise. The dry, slow clink of bones!

Somehow Bill Bruce turned his head. The muscles stretched and groaned in his neck. He had the weird impression of watching his own head turn slowly, painfully, as though it were no part of his own body. He was conscious of himself sitting there in the chair, stiffly erect, unable to move.

Then the head had turned far enough

to see the blacker shadow that was the door of the cabin. And again the sound came, the dry, dead clanking of bones!

Something moved in the darkness beyond the doorway. The bones clanked again, closer now. Abruptly the torture under his skull ceased and he was frozen with horror—held motionless and unbelievingly terrified in every fibre and blood drop in his body.

Standing in the doorway was the skeleton. He, William Bruce, had brought it here, a few bones at a time, and laid them loosely on the floor. But now it stood complete, erect, glaring at him from eyeless sockets.

The thing took one long stride forward, straight toward Bill Bruce. The bony feet clanked on the floor. The fleshless fingers swung, tapped gently against the dully-showing hip bones.

Bruce heard the cry that ripped from his lips. Furious agony lashed through his head again, blurring the vision of the skeleton.

He staggered half way up, wavered, crashed over backward. He heard the smash of his chair, the dull thud of his head striking the floor.

The pain lashed like a red whirlwind, and went out.

CHAPTER THREE

Return to the Grave

THE pain returned first. Something was hurting, hurting terribly. Bruce heard someone moan, saw this strange person roll feebly in an effort to shake off the agony that gripped him. Then the pain was nearer, more vivid, and Bruce could see it like a black flame.

He rolled over, raised a hand to his head. The motion cleared his brain somewhat, though the aching kept on. He knew now that it was his head which was

hurting, that it was he who had moaned and rolled over.

Bruce ran his hand over his head. It was wet with perspiration. He struggled to a sitting position, stared with glazed eyes around him. He was on the porch of his cabin, the overturned chair beside him.

"That damn thing couldn't have walked," he said aloud. "It couldn't even have been carried all together." Abruptly he recalled the horrible clarity of the skeleton in the doorway. He cursed himself for a fool. "Well, I'll go look at it," he said at last.

His knees buckled when he tried to get to his feet. Catching the post, he pulled erect, stood holding to it for a moment, blinking. The exertion had set the pain throbbing wildly in his head, and it was nearly a minute before he was able to walk. He dug a match from his pocket, found the lamp just inside the cabin door, and lit it. He turned toward the corner where the bones had lain. The yellow light flowed through the darkness, across the floor, and found the corner.

The skeleton was gone!

For a moment there was nothing but sheer disbelief. The skeleton *had* to be here! This was the wrong corner. Perhaps. . . . Then slowly it occurred to him that he had known the skeleton would be gone—he hadn't really expected to find it here.

Bruce tried to laugh, but the sound was harsh and unnatural. He couldn't believe that the skeleton had walked out of his cabin. That was impossible. Yet—his laugh jerked to a halt—he had *seen* the thing go!

He turned and stumbled from his cabin, wild sensations confused within him. A skeleton couldn't walk back to its grave, but Bruce could not sleep until he knew.

His legs felt watery, and the pain in his head was an unending throbbing as he walked the path toward the excavation. Twice he stumbled and fell, got painfully to his feet. He cursed himself for a fool, and kept going, in his chest cold dread of what he would find.

He came out into the small clearing opposite old man Jenkins' place and stopped. A light was glowing back of a shuttered window. Funny, he thought, that the old man should be up at this hour. Then he remembered that he had no idea what time it was. The moon was still low and it couldn't be late. He turned suddenly toward the creek and the large, flat rocks on which the old man crossed.

HE WAS still ten yards short of the creek when there was a movement on the porch. A figure showed black against the shuttered window. Jenkins' cracked voice rang out, "Stay where you are, there. Don't come no nearer!"

Bruce stopped short. He was still half in the shadows of the trees, but along the small creek and in the yard of the cabin moonlight lay softly. He stood there, motionless, dazed, the pain in his head making his thoughts hazy. At last he called out: "It's Bill Bruce, Mr. Jenkins. What's the trouble?"

He thought he heard the old man snort. Then the bent figure came pegging down the steps, a double-barrel shotgun in its right hand. "Well, come on over." There was something tense, shaky about the man's voice.

He crossed the creek, met the old man in his yard. The thin, lined face was quivering, showing dully in the moonlight. The lips were sucked in over toothless gums. For a minute neither man spoke. They stood there, staring into each other's face. The old man's eyes wavered, passed over Bruce's head. Then the eyes stopped moving and the old man almost staggered, his face creased with wide amazement, horror, disbelief.

Bruce asked fearsomely: "What is it?"

The old man didn't answer, but he kept gazing at Bruce's forehead. At last his eyes wavered, his sunken lips quavered. "You . . . you look sorta sick."

Bruce swallowed hard, almost choked on the fear that had clutched him. Why did the old man look at his head that way? His voice was jumpy. "I've had a pretty bad headache all night."

Jenkins' gaze flickered back to his head. He licked his lips. "Reckon it's the moonlight. And I'm sorta upset tonight, myself. But your head looked . . . kinda funny." He paused and Bruce could see that his withered fingers were whitening about the shotgun. His voice was cracked, frightened. "Must be gettin' old. Seein' things. Twice tonight."

Fear jumped into Bruce's chest. He leaned forward, the muscles in his back and shoulders rigid, cold. "What things?"

The old man shifted restlessly. He said, "You got one of them skeletons up at yore place, ain't you?"

The indrawn breath hissed through Bruce's teeth. He heard his voice, strange and unnatural, asking: "Did you see it, walking back this way?"

Jenkins' old body shuddered like a leaf in the wind. "I thought I seen it, but. . . ."

"Which way did it go?"

Jenkins pointed with the muzzle of his gun. The barrel wavered as he raised it toward the excavation. "Down there."

Bruce shook himself. His head was throbbing, making his thoughts wild and eerie. He had to get himself under control, settle this thing. He set his jaw.

"I'm going to find out." He turned and went back across the creek, along the path toward the Indian mounds.

THE mound loomed gaunt and dark in the moonlight. The top was black with the shadows of the great oak on the left; silver flecked the right side, adding to the darkness of the top. A low wind was stirring now, making a soft whispering noise among the leaves. To the right, Moore's creek puttered along its pebbles. The tiny sounds seemed only to add to the thickness of the silence and the wildness of the scene. Bruce had the weird impression that he was some primitive savage in a primitive land; the pain in his head was a wound, and he was going now, as the Indians went hundreds of years ago—toward the place where he was to die, where his bones would whiten and molder. . . .

He fought off the feeling, started up the mound. Half way up he stopped. He was cold with fear. He took four long steps, reached the top of the mound, and looked down into the pit.

"God!" he said aloud. "It's here!"

It was dark in the excavation. The red clay of the bottom showed black, and against it the bones were a dull white. A skull glared up out of its eyeless sockets, and bony fingers were folded across dull white breast plates. The rest of the bones were buried beneath the clay.

The skeleton lay exactly as it had when he first uncovered it—when Jake Peters had leaped screaming from the pit to run madly to his death.

Bill Bruce stumbled back down the side of the mound. He was unconscious now of his aching head. At his cabin he flung himself exhausted on his cot. It was impossible that these things could have happened. Utterly impossible. Yet he had seen them.

After a while he found that the hammering within his skull had diminished, his mind worked clearer. He began to review the events of the night, one by one, trying to find an explanation.

"After the skeleton had gone," he thought, "I followed, stopping at Wennie Jenkins' home. The old man looked at me. . . ."

"God!" the word broke from Bruce's lips. What had the old man meant when he said Bruce's head looked funny? What had caused all this pain, that curious, flattening sensation?

He felt sick at his stomach, and it took an effort to get erect and reach the lamp on the table beside the door. Slowly then he went toward the mirror which hung against the far wall. The yellow lamp light skidded across the room as he moved, across the small bed, over the old chair and the empty hearth. His shoes sounded loud, ominous on the boards.

The lamp light glinted in the mirror before he reached it. He stopped, pushed his head close, holding the lamp beside his cheek.

The sound that he made was sickening, as if something had struck his belly. He staggered backward and almost dropped the lamp. For a minute he stood there breathing like a trapped animal. Then he fought himself back to the mirror and peered into it again.

There could be no doubt. The shape of his head had changed! Only slightly, but changed. The angle above his forehead was sharper. The skull was flatter!

CHAPTER FOUR

Head of Fire

BILL BRUCE set the lamp on the table and went out on the porch. The wind had freshened. It felt cool and good against his hot skin. He stood there, holding to the post and muttering aloud: "I'm sick. That must be it. I've got a fever and I'm seeing things." But there was no confidence in his words.

He remembered what the Indian had told him that afternoon: "Touch one of those bodies and the destruction of the Flat Heads will fall upon you!" Two men had touched them. Now Jake Peters was dead, and Bruce. . . .

Abruptly he remembered the girl. She had helped him bring the bones to his cabin. What had happened to her? "Oh, God!" His hands gripped the post until little splinters dug into his fingers. If anything had happened to her. . . . He remembered the look in her green eyes as she had said good-bye, the sound of her voice. He had sworn then he would see here again, often. If he had brought this horror upon her. . . .

His throat felt dry and parched. He walked through the moonlight to the small spring back of his house, drank deeply and bathed his head. The water was cold and tasted good. He went back to the cabin, pulled off his clothes and flung himself on his bed.

Sleep came quickly, but with it the pain in his head began to grow again. He was conscious of it mounting higher and higher, even beneath the lethargy of sleep which held his mind and body. Then the dreams came—weird, eerie, dreadful. Twice he woke, wet with sweat and crying out against some horror that faded with wakefulness. Before dawn the dreams ceased, and he slept quietly.

When he awoke again, the little alarm clock on the mantle showed ten minutes to nine. His head was still hurting, though not so badly. He swung his feet over the side of the bed, sat up.

He had awakened with one thought in his mind, and now, slowly, fearfully, he turned toward the mirror. He could feel a nerve twitching at the corner of his mouth. He raised a cold hand, rubbed it across his head. The shape felt natural enough, but yet. . . .

He reached the mirror, stopped. His breath, his heart, his brain, seemed suspended during the long moment that he raised his eyes. Then he saw his reflection. A long sigh came from his lips. The shape of his head seemed natural enough. He peered closer. Yes, his head was all

right, unless. . . . He shrugged fiercely. His head looked natural. It had always been a little flat on top, but not more than some other persons. He must have been seeing things last night.

Turning, he took soap and walked naked to the creek, bathed and came back feeling better, though his head still throbbed. He was eating and thinking of Mary Marshall, praying that nothing had happened to her, when he heard her voice.

BRUCE jumped to his feet, almost fell as his weak knees buckled. She was smiling as he came through the door, but when she saw him the smile vanished. A look of wonder and fear came into her face. She said, "What . . . what's happened? You look so sick."

Bruce said, "You're all right?"

She stared at him. "But why shouldn't I be? And you. . . ."

He stood for a moment without answering. Not until he heard himself speaking had he realized that he believed in the Indian curse. In daylight the whole thing seemed foolish. If he told her, she'd merely laugh at him.

And yet, as during the afternoon before, he found himself explaining. She stood watching him with those green, level eyes, her soft lips barely parted. "You don't think I'm crazy?" Bruce asked.

"Of course I don't think you're crazy," the girl said. She came close, put her finger tips against his cheek.

Bruce stood and looked at her. No, she didn't believe his story. But how could she? She probably thought he'd been drunk and had a siege of the D. T.'s.

"Would you like to go to Clarence and see Dr. Moore?" she asked.

Bruce's hands went out and caught her shoulders. "I'm not crazy!" he said furiously. "You've got to believe me. Come down to the mound and look."

"All right. But I walked across here

from the road, and I'm thirsty. May I have a drink of water?"

"Surely." She went with Bruce to the spring, knelt beside it and drank. Side by side, they started toward the excavation.

Wennie Jenkins was sitting on the porch of his house, legs stretched along the top step. As soon as they came in sight he creaked his body around toward them and asked: "What did you find last night? I thought that skeleton had you, way you come back by here, staggerin' and payin' me no heed when I called."

Bruce said that he had found the skeleton, and kept going.

They stopped at the top of the mound, looking down into the pit. The skeleton showed exactly as it had when they began removing it the afternoon before. The eyeless skull, thick with clay, looked up at them.

Bruce's voice was slow, heavy: "You believe that I'm not crazy? Now, run on home and leave this to me. No need of you getting tangled up. If I'm. . . ." he paused, took a deep breath. "If I'm all right next week, I want to come and see you."

The girl put both hands against his chest, clenched them. Her green eyes glinted. She said: "No, I'm going to stay with you, see this thing out. It can't be supernatural. We'll. . . ." She stopped. A puzzled look had crossed her face, and she rubbed her temple with her fingers.

"What's the trouble?" Bruce's voice cracked with anxiety.

Mary Marshall smiled faintly. "Nothing. This sun gave me a touch of headache." She turned toward the pit. "Let's get those bones out again."

Bruce pulled her back. "Please go home. If you've got a headache, it may . . ." he left the sentence unfinished.

She shook her head so that the sunlight quivered along her red hair. "It's noth-

ing." She started down into the pit toward the skull.

FOR the second time, Bill Bruce carefully removed the dirt from the skeleton. Mary was kneeling beside the skull. Bruce said: "Maybe I should take pictures of it this time. It might. . . ."

The girl's short, frightened gasp interrupted him. His head jerked upward. She was still kneeling, her hands fluttering at her breast, her mouth open, eyes wild and startled. In the same instant her face changed. Fierce pain showed in her eyes. Her hands jumped to her head and she staggered erect. She made a short, sobbing cry.

Bruce reached her, careless of the skeleton. He caught her in his arms. "What's happened? What is it?"

Bill Bruce did not feel the thing at first. He was holding the girl close, glaring about trying to find the thing that had hurt her. Gradually he began to realize that the very top of his skull, above the throbbing ache, had grown icy cold. And then, abruptly, his hair seemed to burst into flame. His whole head was like a wall of fire.

Catching the girl by the hand, he drove up the side of the pit, raced down the mound toward the creek, his one thought to bury his head in its cool waters. The girl was sobbing as she stumbled along beside him.

They sloshed knee-deep into the creek, and stopped.

Instinctively both ducked, thrust burning heads into the water. Bruce felt the cool dampness strike his scalp. For just one instant the touch of the water was comforting—then the whole creek seemed to turn to acid, searing his scalp more horribly than before. The girl cried out, jerked erect. Bruce jumped, his right toe struck a rock and he went sprawling, rolling downstream under water. Furiously, he scrambled to his feet. He and the girl fell heavily on the bank.

Gradually the burning sensation left Bill Bruce, but the ache in his head kept on. It was a dull, unending throbbing, a hammer beating ceaselessly against his skull. He sat up and bits of the clay bank stuck to his wet clothing. Mary Marshall sat with her hands against her cheeks, her face drained of color, the skin under her eyes taut and pale.

She bit her lip to still its quivering. Then she said, "My head doesn't burn like it did. But it's beginning to ache, terribly. Like something mashing down on it, trying to . . . flatten it."

Bruce reached a hand toward her, stopped. He cursed savagely behind locked teeth. He shouldn't ever have let her in for this. He said huskily: "You rest here until you feel better. I'm going and look around."

The skeleton lay as he had left it, almost completely uncovered, the skull in the sunlight, the feet in shadow. Through the thick leaves of the oak he could see the glint of the sun. He circled the pit, went down the mound on the other side, around the oak. He didn't know just what he was searching for. But there *had* to be something, some clue to what had happened!

He climbed the mound and into the excavation again. On hands and knees he searched the pit. There was nothing to show that the bones of the Flat Head had been touched since his tribe buried him hundreds of years ago. At last, feeling sick and weak, Bruce went back.

"I can't find anything to show what happened," he said simply.

She looked up and he gasped at the paleness of her face. Her lips parted, shut tight again, cutting off the words.

Bruce shook his head fiercely and the motion made the aching greater. "It

can't be that!" he said. "There's got to be an explanation!"

After a moment, Mary said: "Let's go back to your cabin. I . . . I feel sick."

Bruce helped her stand. "I'll go get the doctor."

"No-o," she said the word slowly. "If we told him, he'd think we were crazy."

WADE MARTIN was standing spraddle-legged on Bruce's porch when they came into the little clearing. When he saw the girl his black eyes narrowed, his square mouth tightened. He stared from her to Bruce and a flame jumped into his eyes as he watched them come toward him. "Don't neither of you look so spry today," he said. "Been falling in the creek?"

Bruce helped Mary to the small chair, sat down wearily on the floor, back against the wall. Martin swung his big body around to face him. "You still plan to dig up them bones?"

Bruce raised his aching head. What if he gave up the project? It would ruin him financially, hurt his name in archeological circles. But if he refused to give up, what then? He had seen that his skull was flattening slightly. He had seen it in the eyes of persons who looked at him, and he had seen it for himself. Why? There was only one answer and even now, gritting his teeth, he refused to admit this. Anger suddenly swelled in him.

He said: "You're damned right I plan to finish my work."

Martin's square face flushed. "You don't look like you're doing it. And you're getting this here lady all mixed up in it! Round here we don't like for. . . ."

Mary Marshall said shortly: "He's not getting me mixed in anything. He warned me. I went of my own accord."

Martin swung to face her. He took a deep breath before he spoke, and Bruce thought he saw fear in the farmer's eyes. "What happened?" he asked.

The aching under Bruce's skull was continuing. It was driving him crazy, he thought.

"What the hell is it to you?" His voice cracked.

Martin took one angry step forward, stopped. His scowl relaxed slightly. "You're fixing to die," he said. "Why don't you give up this fool idea and get outa here while you can?"

"And leave you with all the money I paid for these mounds, with every cent I could get my hands on. Hell, no!"

The farmer's big mouth jerked open, shut again. He said: "All right, then. I'll give you back yore damn money. We'll break the contract."

For a moment Bruce sat there, back pressed against the wall, staring up at Wade Martin. Thoughts came to him through the slow aching of his skull. With his money back he could make a start somewhere else. He couldn't live like this much longer. The pain was driving him crazy. Perhaps if he went away it would cease. The curse that went with these mounds wouldn't follow. . . . He checked his thoughts suddenly. His breathing was heavy. Sweat stood on his forehead. By God! He'd never admit *that* was the cause. He said: "No, I'm staying."

Anger flamed in Martin's face. "I'm makin' you one last offer. Anybody can look at you and tell you're dying. I'll give you yore money back and a hundred dollars to get outa here. If you don't . . ."

It was the unvoiced threat that made Bill Bruce angry. He hurled words through the mist of pain that enveloped him. "I told you I was staying, and damn it, I am!"

The farmer's big body grew tense. He said: "All right. Stay and see what happens. You'll get yore head flattened."

He turned and stomped down the steps.

Mary Marshall asked: "Why does he want you to leave so badly? I never heard of *him* being worried about anybody's health."

Bruce was breathing heavily. He said: "I don't know, unless. . . ." He paused, thinking hard. "There was another group after these mounds. They had more money, but weren't willing to pay. Perhaps they've decided. . . ."

He sank down on the floor again, grunted and rolled over to one side. Digging his right hand into his wet pocket, he pulled out several pebbles, dropped them out on the floor. They were small, heavy. "Must have got these when I fell down in the creek," he said. He leaned forward to examine them more closely.

Abruptly his head jerked up and he stared with fevered eyes at the girl. His lips were parted, pulled hard. His dark eyes glittered. "I think I know what it is," he said slowly. "And it's killed a lot of men before this. It'll keep on."

"What do you mean?" she leaned forward, hands gripping the arms of the chair. "You mean that curse killed. . . ?"

Bruce said, "You might call it that. It's. . . ." The words broke sharply. At the edge of the clearing he had seen a shadow move. But in that second, he had recognized the Indian, Flat Rock.

CHAPTER FIVE

The Living Are Buried

THE afternoon passed swiftly. Nightfall was needed to determine Bruce's plan. Even then he might fail. Both he and the girl dozed, and awoke at twilight. Bruce stood up. His knees were weak, throat dry, but the aching in his head was less.

The girl smiled. "I think I'd better do the cooking. But I'd like some cold water to drink." She stood up, swayed and almost fell. With one lunge Bruce reached her, caught her close to him. Her body felt soft and yielding in his arms.

"You're sick," he said. "Keep still."

Gently she pulled away. "Just a little dizzy. I'm all right now."

Bruce went inside, lighted the lamp, then went to the spring for a bucket of water. When he came back she had already started a fire, and pulled plates and dishes from his cupboard.

Later they sat on the porch, waiting for the moon. As he sat there, back against the wall, Bruce felt the strange lethargy of the previous night coming over him. His eyelids tugged down, and the whole inside of his head seemed to be filled with a rolling, throbbing blackness. Fear gripped him suddenly, fiercely. Was the skeleton coming back tonight? Was his head going to flatten again? He had to stay awake, had to fight the pain, keep conscious. He strained at his eye-lids like a man lifting a weight. Every fibre in his body was aching, filled with pain. Under his skull a hammer beat dully and furious pressure mashed on his head

Slowly his eyes came open. Through the mist of agony he could see the girl. She was leaning forward in the chair, eyes tight shut, her face twisted and contorted by pain. Bruce had to fight the words from his lips. "Mary! Don't go to sleep. It—it's what I did last night."

He could see the white blur of her face in the darkness, see the muscles twitch. Her head came up slowly. Her eyes were glazed when she looked at him. "What?"

Bruce tried to jump erect. His body went half up, crashed down. He caught himself on his hands and knees, crouched there a half minute while the pain in his head beat like terrific waves of blackness. Then he crawled to the girl's side. "Keep awake," he said. His throat was sore and he could scarcely talk.

How the next hour passed he never knew exactly. He kept his hands pressed against his temples, trying to keep the weight on his skull from crushing it, flattening his head. And after a while the pain became less, though the hammering against his temple remained. The moonlight filled the little clearing.

Mary Marshall was conscious now, though her breathing was loud and painful. She said: "It's time to go now. The moon's up."

Bruce shook his head and the motion seemed to shake the hammer harder against his skull. "You're not going. I'm going with you to your car, then come back. You've been through enough."

She said fiercely, "I'm going with you. If you don't take me, I'll follow."

Bruce suddenly knew that he wanted the girl to go—and at the same instant fear of what might happen to her swept him. He got to his feet slowly, holding to the post. He was breathing through his mouth in short, deep breaths. He swayed as he turned from the post, went in the cabin. He came back carrying a .38 automatic.

The girl was erect now, watching him. "That won't be of much use if. . . ."

Bruce laughed shortly, without humor. The laughter hurt the muscles of his throat, made his head spin more. He thrust the gun inside his shirt. Together they went down the steps . . .

THEY did not follow the path, but went upstream along the creek bank for nearly a quarter of a mile and found nothing. They turned then, and still keeping close to the bank, went back toward the cabin and the Indian Mound beyond.

They crossed the clearing opposite Wennie Jenkins' cabin without being haled by the old man, plunged into the woods again on the other side. There was a strip of bank here where moonlight showed plainly. Willows grew thickly along the opposite bank, overhung the stream, making it a tunnel of darkness.

Bruce took two steps on the sandbank, jerked short. His breath made a furious, whistling sound as it tore from his nostrils. His eyes jerked in their sockets, and terror struck a cold knife in his bowels. "Oh, God!" The words were ripped from his throat.

"What is it?" The girl's hands caught his arms. Bill Bruce knew that she had seen.

Where the creek was blotted out by the inky shadows of the willows, the thing showed dully. The white skull was a pale blur; the spine and ribs were almost invisible in the darkness, but Bill Bruce knew the thing that stood knee deep in the water, rocking with a spectral ghastliness from side to side.

The skeleton had left its grave!

The cold knife of fear in Bruce's stomach suddenly broke into flame. A wild torment of horror, of panic, swept up to burn his heart and lungs, to reach and envelope his brain. To make him for a moment into what was almost a gibbering, terrified maniac.

Then his nature asserted itself, and the fear lashed into terrific, unreasoning anger. He hurled himself forward.

The skeleton straightened stiffly, stopped its eerie swaying. For one moment the eyeless skull gazed through the darkness at Bruce. Abruptly the thing turned and went in an awkward, jerky race for the shore—directly toward the mounds.

Bruce cut to the left, meaning to head it off. By God! If he could get his hands on that thing! Skeleton or no skeleton. . . .

The skeleton had reached the bottom of the mound when Bruce slipped and went headlong in the sand. He twisted, rolled to his knees. He saw the skeleton reach the top of the mound—leap, and vanish into the pit.

Snarling, half mad with rage and long-drawn agony, Bruce raced up the mound. It'd be hand-to-hand now. He'd settle the thing if he died!

He reached the top of the mound, took one fast step toward the excavation—and stopped. To his aching head the whole world had been spinning, but now it stopped, froze in sheer disbelief. The snarl died into a slobbering whimper.

At the bottom of the excavation, half covered by earth, lay the skeleton. The bony fingers were folded on the breast bones, the eyeless skull stared upward!

BRUCE did not know what he had expected to see, but the very immobility of the thing below him, the utter permanence and motionlessness of the bones was horrific. Bruce raised his head slowly, awkwardly, looked across the mound to where the oak tree grew, and beyond that to the wall of trees. The skeleton couldn't have reached them in the slight time it had been out of sight. Neither could it have buried itself. And yet. . . .

Through the cold fear that held him, he heard the click of Mary Marshall's shoes coming up the mound behind him.

Thought of the girl loosened the muscles of his body. Without looking at her he circled the pit, went to the edge of the woods. Nothing but darkness beneath the trees. Nothing could have reached them in that time, anyway. He turned and went back to where Mary Marshall stood at the top of the mound.

Pain had made dark circles under her eyes, and fear fluttered tiny pulses within the circles. The sight of her drawn face hurt Bill Bruce more keenly than the hammering within his head. The girl did not look down at the skeleton as she asked, "Is—is that it?"

Bruce said: "I don't know."

"But he couldn't . . . the thing can't

. . . why. . . ." Her voice trailed off, and the silence that followed seemed to Bruce to be part of a world of death, a world without life or motion or sound, a world in which he was only a carven and spiritless image. He and Mary stood with their backs to the trees, staring off toward the sandbar which was only a silver line drawn across the black, limitless hand of death.

The sound was not loud, and yet it broke the silence as a pin may explode a toy balloon. It might have been a twig cracking. It might have been bones.

Bruce flung himself around. The motion seemed slow, endless. He felt like a man turning in a pool of molasses, moving with infinite reluctance.

He saw the thing out of the corner of his eye. The white, eyeless skull was less than a yard away. The bony arms stretched above it, bony fingers clenched together. He saw the dark shadow of the thing they held. Then the fleshless fingers whipped at Bruce's head.

All the agony of the last two days seemed to explode beneath his skull. He pitched backward into a sea of blackness filled with glittering, blinding lights. From somewhere far off through the darkness he heard a woman scream in terror.

THE words came before he knew their meaning. They were like the lights, circling, roaring, senseless. There was another sound, wild and crazy.

The lights began to fade and Bruce fought through darkness into clarity. He saw the moonlight on the side of the mound, knew that he was lying where he had fallen. A man was speaking "—hit him if he hadn'ta turned around so quick like. Thought maybe he was gonna shoot me or some'en."

He knew that voice. Wennie Jenkins!

Bruce twisted. Mary was crouched back against the edge of the pit. Her face showed ghostly white in the darkness, terrified. To one side of her was the skeleton, and as Bruce turned it raised a shotgun in bony fingers and said: "Jest lie where you are. If I kill you here I'll have to tote you, and you're too heavy."

Bruce lay still, but a long sigh of relief oozed from his mouth. He knew now what this thing was. His head ached fiercely, but now that he was only a few feet away he could see clearly enough. The skeleton was nothing but white paint on a black suit—and inside the suit was old man Jenkins. Beyond Jenkins he could see the oak tree with the big hole in its trunk, the bark covered door which would lock like a part of the tree when closed. So that was how the skeleton had vanished!

Jenkins reached out a hand, jerked the girl between him and Bruce. There was a ripping sound as her dress tore, and Bruce caught a glimpse of breasts more soft and white than the moonlight which showed them. Jenkins slapped her, and as Bruce came snarling to his feet, his pistol forgotten, the old man yelled: "Keep still, damn you, or I'll blast you now!"

Bruce choked the roaring fury within him. He couldn't do Mary any good by getting himself killed. He said: "You needn't hurt her. She's never harmed you."

"Oh she aint' heh?" The old man spat the words. "If it wan't for them goldamned school teachers nobody'da ever bother round these here mounds." He slapped her again, hard, and she staggered back under the blow.

Bruce's muscles were quivering, jerking with fury, but he kept his feet flat, far apart. Maybe talking to the devil would make him stop striking the girl. Bruce said: "You'd like for them to leave you alone here to pan gold, wouldn't you? Oh, I know there is gold in Moore's Creek. I got a nugget in my pocket when

I fell in this morning. You wouldn't like for Wade Martin to find out, since he'd run you off the land and pan the gold himself."

"I knowed you'd found out," Jenkins said. He came one step closer, out into the moonlight at the foot of the excavation. The old man paused for a moment, leering above his gun. His voice had a nasty, chuckling sound. "But don't nobody else know. And you and that gal ain't gonna tell 'em."

Mary Marshall caught her breath sharply. Bruce felt Jenkins' words like cold steel in his belly. There was no doubting what the old man meant. Bruce said: "Sure. We won't tell anybody."

Jenkins chuckled again. "Shore you won't. Dead folks don't tell nothin'.

The girl made a whispered, choked sound. Her hands caught at Bruce's left shoulder. He could feel her body shrinking close against him.

Bruce said, "Sometimes dead men do tell. When they find our bodies there'll be an investigation. The whole thing will come out then. Your damned gold won't do you any good in the electric chair!"

The old man rocked back on his heels, swayed forward again. His lips which caved in over toothless gums were grinning evilly. "They ain't gonna find you," he said. "I got it all figured out. Folks 'round here been 'spectin' you to die, foolin' with these here graves. The way you looked the last day ain't been too healthy. When you jist disappear folks'll think them Flat Heads got you."

There was a cold lump in Bruce's chest, and cold sweat was running across his forehead to cluster in his brows. "You can't make a body disappear. You can't. . . ."

THE old man was laughing again. "Turn 'round," he said, "and git on down there to the creek."

For a moment Bruce hesitated, gauging the distance between him and Jenkins. If he could get his hands on that gun. . . The old man stopped. A bony finger curled around the trigger. "Git on!" he snapped. "Or I'll blast you down."

Slowly Bruce turned, started circling the pit. Mary kept beside him and he tried to catch her eye, tell her to move to one side. If he could get his pistol from under his shirt he could turn, maybe drop Jenkins before he could fire. At least get him before he could kill Mary.

"Git yore hands up!" Jenkins said.

Bruce cursed under his breath, raised his hands cheek high, thinking it best to wait until he got a break. This close to Mary a shotgun would touch both. Side by side they went down the mound, across the sandy strip toward the creek.

"Git in that creek on this side and start wadin' down it," Jenkins ordered.

Bruce had almost forgotten the pain in his head now, but his brain was still slow, dulled by the agony which had held it for so long. He tried to think of some plan, some way of escape as they started wading through the calf-deep water. Behind him he could hear Jenkins plodding along. Maybe if he got the old man talking. . .

Bruce said: "So you're the one who's been pulling all this ghost stuff on us since I started digging, trying to frighten me off so I couldn't find out about your gold."

"If you'd gone away you'da kept living. I reckon the curse did git you."

"How'd you work that trick last night? That skeleton walking and my headache and the flat head and all?"

There was mirth—and madness—in the old man's laughter. "Wasn't that great! I had some pizen I learned about in yore spring. You nearly caught me puttin' there, but it give me a chance to slip back to yore shack and change that funny mirror I'd put there to make your head look flat. When you drunk the water you passed out fer awhile, woke up with that headache. You can't see plain after that stuff. You couldn't even see I had you tied to yore chair. While you was asleep I carried off the skeleton. Then I come walking out clinkin' a couple bones and wearin' this suit. You shore did turn over hard. All I had to do was untie you 'fore you come to again."

"And you climbed up that hollow tree, poured something on our heads to make them burn?"

"Golly!" Jenkins kept laughing. "I didn't mean for that Jake Peters to kill his fool self. He shore did run."

Even as the old man spoke, Bruce was circling the big rock on which Peters had crashed. It was probably hydrogen chloride, "high life," Jenkins had poured on their heads. That was the reason it had burned more when thrust into the creek.

For a full minute the three waded down stream. Their shoes made loud slushing sounds in the water. The moon was almost directly behind them now, so bright that they flung dark shadows along the silvered water. Far off an owl began his dolorous question. The girl shuddered.

The left bank was getting lower, shelving off gradually to where a sandbar, overhung by willows and elder bushes, poked out into the creek. The bushes were low over the sand, and Bruce swung right to avoid the bar.

"Keep right on across that sandbar," Jenkins said. "Push them willows out of the way and go right across it."

Sudden hope flamed in Bruce's chest. When he was half hidden by the bushes, hands down to push them out of the way he could whirl, and. . . .

He was right on the edge of the bar now, Mary beside him. He took another step, reached for the willows. Mary was slightly behind him now. He heard her gasp. Her hand caught at his arm, and he didn't quite reach the willow. She was pulling on him, and his feet were sinking deep in the sand. He tried to pull them out, lunged, lost his balance and plunged forward, pulling the girl down with him. The sand gave with a slushy, oozing sound and his body sank deep. Quicksand!

THE girl screamed in sudden terror. She floundered, tried to get to her feet. The motion made her sink deeper, hands, feet, knees. Bruce had squirmed, tried to get up. The muck sucked at him, dragged him down. It gripped his legs, tugging at him. He was being buried, buried alive, dragged gradually into an oozy, muck-filled grave!

The willows were close overhead, their tender, slim twigs drooping downward like a woman's hair. Bruce lunged upward. His fingers touched the leaves, clutched. There was a soft crack as the twig broke. His body fell down, and the sand made a yawning noise, sucked him deeper. He went nearly to his waist. No chance to reach the twigs now. In one, two minutes his shoulders would be under, then his neck, his chin, then mouth and nose and eyes. He twisted, saw Mary lying on her back, legs and hips already beneath the sand. She had ceased screaming, but her mouth was open, jerking in terror.

"They'll play hell findin' yore bodies now." the old farmer was standing at the very edge of the quicksand, waving his shotgun. "Don't nothin' ever come outa there!"

The sand pulled Bill Bruce deeper. He tried to prop himself with his arms and they sank to the elbow. He could feel the sand sucking like tiny mouths, swallowing him into its black, wet depths to choke the life from him. To fill his mouth and lungs and eyes.

The idea came to him like the sudden cracking of a whip. Not much hope, but a chance. At least there was revenge. He jerked at his right hand, pulled it from the sand. Wet muck clung to it. He was waist deep when the hand flashed under his shirt, swung out the gun.

Jenkins saw the gun glimmer in the moonlight. He bellowed, jerked his shotgun. The crack of the pistol was drowned by the roar of the gun. Wet sand spewed like a geyser into Bruce's face.

The shotgun slid from stiff fingers, splashed in the creek. The old man pitched forward.

Bruce lunged, tried to reach the man. His fingers scraped on the blue shirt, slid off. The motion drove him deeper. There was a terrific weight pulling on his legs now. Jenkins, face down, was half buried by the force of his fall and sinking slowly. Even if Bruce caught him, it would do no good. They'd both go down. And Mary. . . .

The sand pulled at Bruce. Wild terror blinded him, burned like cold fire through his body. To be buried alive! God! It was better to die as Jenkins had done. But he'd dropped the pistol. His eyes glinted as he looked for it.

He heard Mary's half-choked sob and twisted his head to look at her. She was almost gone, only her arms and face and throat above the surface. The sight flung a furious strength into Bruce. He twisted toward where Jenkins lay, and almost tore himself from the sand in one great effort. His fingers touched the blue shirt, slipped, caught again. He jerked, tried to pull himself up. He rose slightly, but Jenkins went deeper. He'd never be able to crawl over the dead body. Even if he did, Mary would be gone before he could help her.

A low wind came down the creek, stirring the willows overhead, making the shadows shift along the sand. Sudden hope flamed in Bruce. He dug his fingers deeper in Jenkins' shirt, tugged, flung his left arm high.

The fingers brushed the willow leaves, held. Then as he started sinking, the willows bent under the pull. One leaf broke. He clung to the others. The slender twig bent more, more. . . .

With furious slowness Bruce worked his hand along the twig, caught the slender limb. He tugged on it, pulling straight so that it would not bend and break. The sand kept sucking downward.

He worked his hand six inches higher on the limb, tugging gently, fearfully. Jenkins' body was almost buried since Bruce had shoved on it. If the limb broke there'd be nothing left. Nothing but death. His hand slid higher. He began to fight the pull of the sand.

Twisting his head he called out to the girl, "Catch my belt. Hold on." Her hand floundered along the top of the wet sand, almost missed, caught. Bruce put more weight on the limb, pulled harder.

The next few minutes passed with the dragging slowness of prison years. The slender willow limb was the one thread of life which held Bruce and the girl. Very gradually he fought his way along it. At last his body, then hers was on top of the sand. And finally they were on the bank.

When the girl had stopped crying and raised her head from Bruce's wet chest, she looked quickly at the sand, then back. "He . . . he's gone," she said.

Bruce said: "Yes. Some of our children may dig up his bones a few hundred years from now. But, he won't put any curse on them."

THE END

If Thy Right Hand Offend Thee...

By
John Flanders
(Author of "A Night in Camberwell")

He knew not whence that hand had come nor where its pain-torn owner went; but of the leering, lingering death that came with it, he knew . . .

LIGHT after light went out along Central Avenue. The brilliant street was slipping back little by little into the darkness. Gumpelmeyer the jeweler gazed out at the black sky, the scintillating pavement, the oily, silent house fronts. He thrust his hand cautiously out of the door and jerked it back with a startled gesture. It had been bitten by an icy rain that felt like some corroding acid.

He decided that there was no possible profit in leaving the shop open and pouring a flood of neglected light into the wet darkness of the Avenue. Optimistic and imaginative as Gumpelmeyer usually was, he no longer dreamed this evening of a loudly got-up young woman accompanied by an escort in large-check tweeds who pulled out of his pocket a great roll of bank notes; nor of a taxi pulling up at his curb and disgorging a sharp-featured young woman of the world and a frightened old codger, stupid, reluctant and three-quarters drunk; nor of the cautious appearance of a citizen in large spectacles, who would distrustfully withdraw from the inside pocket of a moth-eaten jacket a bag of gems worth an Emperor's ransom and offer them for sale for little more than nothing.

The jeweler turned two or three buttons and transformed the glittering fairyland of jewels into a gloomy tunnel, faintly visible still in the cautious green triangle of light from one small portable lamp which was powerful enough to cast a vague glimmer over the gems and gold displayed in the front window.

This done, he stood in the door and breathed a few heroic mouthfuls of the night air—then he stepped back and seized the lever which controlled the ponderous steel shutter—edged at the bottom like the knife of a guillotine—which protected his palace of treasures from the dangerous poverty of the streets.

At that moment, without warning, a shadow fell across the sidewalk in front of him. For an instant, Gumpelmeyer saw nothing but the shadow. Then he realized that a hand was thrust out toward him.

Was it a threatening movement or a gesture of entreaty?

The jeweler had no opportunity to decide which, but neither the one nor the other pleased him. His cautious soul recoiled with loathing from beggars and with abject terror from robbers. Half angry, half frightened, he growled: "Get out of here! Leave me alone!"

But the hand came nearer and nearer. Gumpelmeyer stared at it in horror: "Get away from here, I tell you!" And with a mad impulse he threw himself on the lever with all his weight and strength.

There was a thundering crash of falling metal, followed by a cry from outside. But the cry was lost in the reverberation of the enormous machine, whose hasty fall echoed through the whole great building.

Then Gumpelmeyer noticed a ghastly object on the wire mat in the front of the door—a mangled, bloody scrap of flesh and bone—a severed human hand. . . .

HOW long did he stand motionless, staring at the wretched thing?

He never knew.

He seemed to have lived through an agonizing dream, tortured with cries, groans, imprecations reverberating up and down the street, and filled with streams of blood, red blood from a mutilated arm. . . .

But when he recovered a degree of self-control, he realized that all of this had been a dream and nothing more. Outside the iron wall, the silence was absolute.

Away back in the long shop, a clock began to strike, hesitatingly at first, it seemed. Then in unison, all the timepieces in the clock section proclaimed the hour. Ancient wall-clocks, Flemish chimes, majestic weight-clocks, mysterious luminous dials, artistic little boudoir clocks, all of them weary of counting the steps of time in silence, broke out at once into noisy calculation, biting the silence of the night with their metal teeth.

Gumpelmeyer prevailed on himself to peer through a break in his shutter into the silent and deserted street. The rain was still beating the pavement. He heard no sound but the moaning of the wind which crept in from the sea.

"It was certainly a robber," he told himself. "If it had been anybody but a robber he would be lying there now in a faint. Unless he had strength enough to bawl for ten thousand dollars damages!" His accommodating conscience was very ready to be placated. "He was trying to rob me, and I shouldn't wonder if he would have killed me!" he added.

Then he saw a vision of himself lying on his back on the shop floor, his throat cut from one ear to the other, while about him the showcases were emptied of their treasures. And with the indignation of a virtuous citizen who has been shamefully mistreated, he walked to the severed hand, which lay almost against the door, and kicked it out into the middle of the shop.

"To the garbage with it!"

He had planned to drive the thing, with his foot, the length of the shop and on into the inner court, where there was an opening into the sewer.

He counted the strokes.

"One, two, three, four . . ."

He worked his way through the shop, across a branch office, into a corridor. Why did he see himself at that moment as a child again, playing with the other children in a back alley?

He remembered how, by dint of prudent thefts, of economizing, of shrewd trading, he had managed to buy a wonderful red-and-gold ball. That was certainly the finest ball ever made. It would bounce and leap as if it had a fantastic life in itself.

Ah, there it was again, lying in wait in a corner—a touch of his toe, and it zigzagged down the steps. Where had it hidden itself? Ah! it was still moving, rolling demurely along the narrow corridor—ha! there, he had it again, the tricky thing—and zip—it leaped clear to the ceiling—oh, horrors! The naughty rascal had soiled the clean white wainscoting—dirty mud—

No, it was not mud—it was a splash of red blood—it was—

Gumpelmeyer was no longer the ragged gamin of the back alley, but a wealthy jeweler on Central Avenue. And it was not a thirty-cent rubber ball that he was kicking in front of him, but an amputated hand, blood-stained, drawn up into a ball, clenched into a hateful threatening fist. . . .

At the end of the corridor the bloody scrap seemed to take an uncanny life. It rolled off down the stairs into a cellar, in a different direction from the one in which Gumpelmeyer's toe had aimed it.

It took him an hour to find it again and to bring it to the surface, clutched in a pair of pincers made of two sticks.

On the linoleum floor of a little waiting-room which opened on the inner court, the hand seemed to come maliciously to life again. At every kick it would roll under some article of furniture, it would dart from one hiding place to another like a hunted rodent. At last a desperate swing of the jeweler's foot drove it six feet into the air, and it fell on the open keyboard of a piano. And as it fell the fingers struck the keys in a dismal discord.

Gumpelmeyer dropped limply into an arm chair. He gazed at the lugubrious object with the fixed stare of a madman. In the bright light from the chandelier he studied its details with a sick, stubborn attention which he wondered at but had no power to change.

It was a very unusual hand, extremely small, but so long that it seemed deformed. It had clearly not been washed for days, but the unwilling keen gaze of the jeweler caught here and there the breaks and discolorations of an ugly skin disease—and he observed that another disease, even more mysterious and horrible, had eaten away the ends of the fingers, deformed the thumb, and twisted the nails.

Then, in a sudden gust of rage, his self-control completely gone, Gumpelmeyer flung open a window and seizing the pitiful carrion firmly in his bare hand, he flung it out into the dismal night.

ONE morning as he was serving a customer he found it necessary to lay down the ring which he was holding up between his fingers. There was an intolerable itching in his right hand. He called his clerk to complete the business with the puzzled purchaser, and retired to examine the suffering hand. He could see that the skin was lifted and broken here and there by little reddish craters.

An hour later he was in the office of Dr. Nathaniel March. The Doctor prescribed certain salves and ointments, and dismissed him with an air of uneasiness and disgust, begging him to leave his five-dollar bill on a specified marble table-top in the outer office.

When Gumpelmeyer had consulted his twentieth physician, he was wearing a black glove which he never removed in public, his shoulders were falling forward, his eyes avoided other eyes as those of a hopeless drunkard do, his belly had shrunk in, and he would sit for hours staring at a dusty corner of his street door. Moreover, his business was going to pieces with incredible rapidity.

* * *

One night the rain was lashing the city with a million wet whip-thongs.

And the cowardly populace had fled from the mud of the streets, and were feverishly making merry in their splendid electrically-lighted amusement houses, where the noisy orchestras were drowning the hiccoughs of the city's drunkards and the groans of the city's violated and murdered.

Central Avenue was nearly deserted. A man came crawling through the rain, very, very slowly. He was so frail and miserable that he looked more like an unsteady shadow than a man. He had rung the bells at fifty doors—he had held out his hand to a hundred pedestrians.

"David Kroon, give me something," he murmured. "I am Gumpelmeyer."

At the sound of his voice, David Kroon uttered a startled cry and plunged hastily into the door of his shop.

Gumpelmeyer dragged on in the rain. He gave up all hope, and fully expected to die the next day. Suddenly he felt an impulse to see his old building.

One shop-front, and only one, was still lighted in the row of shadowy fronts. It was Gumpelmeyer's own old place. He stood and gazed a long time. All at once he noticed that the light from the window fell on his hand.

The disease had distorted it strangely, making it curiously long and thin, twisting the nails, eating at the fingers, scattering scaly ulcers over a skin which it was impossible to wash clean. All of a sudden a scene from the past came before Gumpelmeyer's eyes. He saw another hand, dropping out of another rainy night.

And bending his head forward, he prayed to God for forgiveness. . . .

Then he was startled out of his dream. The lights went out in the shop, and a man came to the door.

Gumpelmeyer saw the man lay his hand on the lever which governed the shutter, he heard a click—the iron wall began to descend. The old jeweler rushed forward —and a moment later he staggered to his feet, a thousand flames of suffering burning in his brain—a thousand darts of pain in the bleeding stump from which the hand was missing.

* * *

Two months later, as he was leaving the hospital, he heard some one call his name. He turned around and recognized David Kroon.

"I am sorry that I left you in the lurch when you were down and out. Open another shop. I'll finance it for you. I am sure you can make a go of it."

Gumpelmeyer knew beyond any possibility of doubt that he could "make a go of it." He knew that his old strength had come back to him, that his shrewd business sense had come back, sharper and more enterprising than ever. And the future opened up before him like the dawn of a new day, for he felt that before God and before man he had paid his debt.

Novelette
of
Eerie Terror

In all the desolate Northland waste there was no other haven for Philip Rollins and his young bride. Yet death in the muskeg would have been better than the terrors which lay in wait for them, in that bottomless hell that spawned its ancient tortures . . .

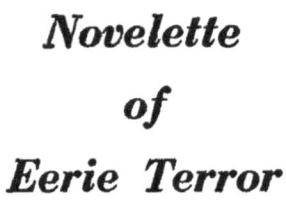

Monsters of the Pit

By Nat Schachner

PHILIP ROLLINS and his bride of less than a month stumbled wearily through the limitless muskeg of northwestern Canada. To the right, twenty miles off, was the Slave River, bearing in its sullen depths the shattered remains of their canoe and most of their supplies. The Great Slave Lake, their objective, was still a hundred miles to the north, sole outpost of civilization in ten thousand square miles of swamp muskeg and barren tundra. No Indian or wandering trapper ever traversed these desolate wastes.

Rollins turned with anxious tenderness toward his young wife. She was good to look at, Kay was, even with weariness and the tearing weight of her knapsack bowing down her slim shoulders. She caught his glance and smiled bravely. Good kid, he thought remorsefully, not to complain. The whole crazy idea had been his—this spending their honeymoon in the great northern wilderness, drifting in a canoe right up to the Arctic Circle.

At that it had been a glorious adventure, until disaster met them among hidden rocks in swift rapids. They had reached the low swampy shore in safety, but Great Slave Lake was far away, and the banks of the river were impenetrable swamp. So with a grin on their lips and fear in their hearts—carefully concealed from each other—they had struck inland, into unexplored country of which the Indians at the last trading post had spoken with ashen faces and muttered warnings. Not even the timber wolves, they said, were to be seen in its brooding vastness —yet there were shapes and things . . . and then they took refuge in studied evasions and vague trailing words to all of Rollins' half-mocking questionings.

"Tired, darling?" he asked.

Kay smiled wanly. "A bit," she admitted, and would have fallen if he had not caught her. "I'm sorry," she gasped, "but I—I can't go any further."

Phil looked desperately around. The sun was slanting to the west, a grimly bloody orb. Night was skimming the tangled brush with swift-pacing shadows. Black flies and clouds of mosquitoes rose from the swamps with voracious hums. Night in the muskeg, without shelter, without protection, could prove a terrible thing.

His eyes lit on a low rolling mound to the north, a slight elevation that nevertheless stood out as a landmark in this dreary mixture of bog and underbrush.

It was wooded, too, thick with tall waving trees through which the expiring sun forced bloody darts.

"Thank God!" Phil said fervently, "we won't have to sleep in muck. Can you make it, Kay?"

"Of course," she answered. Supported by his broad shoulder she limped and stumbled the intervening half mile. They stood on the edge of the slope a moment.

"Queer," Kay murmured. "I've never seen trees like that before."

Neither had her husband. They were not pine or hemlock or spruce or maple or oak or any other normal and familiar tree of the northlands. Rather they were —and Phil groped blindly for similes— something lush and tropical, like gigantic ferns, with green smooth bark and high waving fronds that swayed in regular dance even though there was no breath of stirring air.

Something tugged at Phil's consciousness, some vague, half-remembered trailing mention by the Indians of a hill in the muskeg. He had not paid much attention to what they had said, and now he was sorry, for he remembered distinctly the ripple of fear that had undulated like a wave over those ordinarily impassive countenances.

But he was too tired now to flog his memory, or wonder at the fantastic growths. Nevertheless an uneasy feeling pervaded him, made him strangely reluctant to enter those dark, tangled depths.

"Perhaps, darling," he suggested, "we had better camp right here on the edge."

His wife slapped unavailingly at darting, biting insects. White vapors rose in miasmic layers from the quivering, rotting muskeg. Already their faces were puffing.

"We'll be eaten alive," she said. "Let's climb to the top. It should be dry and comfortable up there."

Phil shook off his strange forebodings.

Kay was right. It was the only sensible thing to do. Those weird fern trees? After all, his knowledge of botany was limited. And Indians were notoriously given to savage and barbaric superstitions. He shrugged them off with a laugh that sounded hollow in his own ears.

"Let's go," he said firmly.

TEN minutes of slow climbing toil and they stood on a level patch. A sharply defined clearing, exactly circular, and hemmed in by tall, monstrous growths. The fast failing light gave no evidence of what was directly beyond.

Kay sank to the ground with a little moan. She had used up the last ounce of her waning strength. Phil forgot his vague, increasing fears in ministering to his adored bride. He flogged his wearied limbs to action, made her a clumsy bed of intermingled grass and smooth, fallen fronds. She smiled at him gratefully and was instantly asleep.

Rollins tried to force his clinging eye-lids open, but they seemed weighted with lead. He began to dream that he was in a dank, impenetrable jungle, running for his life, pursued by strange monsters. Already he felt the foul furnace breath of one searing his face, a steel-clad claw reached out and ripped the flesh from his arm. He screamed—horribly.

He awoke, bathed in nightmare sweat, trembling. It was dark, and a thin moon made more intense, rather than lightened, the thick shadows of the waving tree-ferns. The cry was repeated. He stumbled to his feet, gasping. It was not he who had screamed twice.

"Wh-what is it, Kay?" Sleep still clogged his swollen lids.

The girl was a dim, shrinking shape in the filtering light. Her slim figure was taut with fear, her eyes were pools of terror, her cheeks were chalky white.

She pointed. "Over there," she whispered, "I saw something move."

Phil turned a drowsy head. There was nothing but solid shadows and whispering sibilances from the frond-like branches.

"You were dreaming," he said. "Go back to sleep."

He put his arm around her. She was trembling violently—so unlike Kay.

"I—I saw it, Phil," she insisted in a small voice. "I wasn't dreaming. I awakened suddenly. Someone was watching me, I was sure of it. You know that feeling one gets." Her husband tightened arms around her and nodded. He remembered his own dream—or was it a dream?

She shuddered. "There were eyes out there—behind that tree—red, glaring eyes like saucers. I screamed and twisted my head away. And beyond—to the right, were more eyes. Then suddenly, they were gone."

She buried her head on his shoulder. "Let's get out of this horrible place," she wailed. "I'm afraid. I'd rather sleep out in the muskeg."

He fondled her golden, shapely head. "They must have been animals of some kind or other," he comforted. "They won't bother us if we leave them alone." Yet even as he spoke small drifting recollections came to him of what the Indians had mumbled under their breath, back there at the trading post, whispering as if fearful that they would be heard, even at that distance.

"But the eyes were high above ground," Kay said shakily. "About six feet. And these trees are smooth and branchless almost to the very top."

Phil felt a chilling sensation thicken his blood, but he only answered: "You are tired and overwrought. Try to sleep."

At last her trembling ceased, her head drooped back, her eyes closed, her breathing became regular.

Phil watched her with anxious tenderness. The half-heard stories rose to plague him. Stories of the foolhardy hunters who crossed to the hill, and had never been seen again—of the birds of the air who swerved out of their courses to fly with swift-beating wings along the river.

He had listened to many tales told in the disjointed fashion of the Indian. They had seemed idle enough back in the trading post, in front of the heartening glow of the log fire. But now—they took on shape, form, solidity, made this strange wood and its stranger trees a thing of blood-draining nightmare.

He grinned wryly in the darkness. He was ashamed of himself, ashamed of his fears. He was deathly tired, yet he intended keeping watch the night through. If only he had a gun, a weapon of any sort. But then, he thought, he had never shot a lethal weapon in his life. His had been a singularly peaceful existence thus far, except for the breathless adventure of marrying Kay, and this crazy honeymoon of his. He looked at her wan loveliness in the pallid light. He caught his breath sharply. If anything happened to her. . . .

WHAT was that? A thin rustling sound in the looming trees, their long outlandish shapes silhouetted against a coppery sky? Nothing else! He shuddered and swore at himself, striving to stir up courage. He had been positive someone was watching him, someone whose eyes had bored into the back of his head.

It was damned silly. He knew there wasn't another human being within a hundred miles in any direction. Even if the stories told by the Indians were not old wives' tales, no man, red or white, ever dared set foot in this fabulous territory. Yet no animal's eyes would have given

him that sensation in the back of his head.

Kay stirred in her sleep, moaned uneasily. Her lips parted, little strangled sounds issued. She was dreaming, and the dream was not pleasant. Her cheeks were flushed now. She looked feverish. Rollins put a shaking hand to his own brow. It felt very hot. His mouth was dry, his eyes were like molten lead.

He laughed shakily. That then was the explanation. They were both a bit under the weather—a touch of swamp fever, delirium perhaps. Even that was better than. . . .

Oh God! There was that same feeling in the back of his head. Eyes boring into him. It was the fever, he told himself angrily. He must not turn, must not give in to his imaginings. Yet the blood pounded in his veins, drove pulsing through his skull. Something was pulling him, forcing him to turn around. Slowly, irresistibly, his head moved. It did not seem to be a part of him any more.

Two round balls of fire glared at him out of the darkness. They were spaced some inches apart, and glowed, disembodied, almost six feet from the ground. He shook his head to clear the fever. The eyes remained. His tongue was thick and furred. He said desperately to himself: "They're *not* human—they're *not* eyes."

A shriek bubbled and racketed through the night. Rollins jumped—his temples throbbed insanely. Kay!

His wife was sitting upright. Fever made two red spots on otherwise paper-white cheeks, her eyes were wide and staring. She clutched at his hand, held tight with a death grip.

"The eyes! There they are again!"

Out of the darkness, out of the gloom of the weird fern-trees, red disembodied orbs floated, closing in on a horribly constricted circle. Orbs that caught the coppery glow of the moon, and reflected it with pitiless, yet strangely human glare. Nearer and nearer they came, soundless, blood-chilling, terrible in their slow advance.

Kay tottered to her feet, biting her lips until they crimsoned with blood to keep back the desperate shrieks that tore at her throat.

"Oh God!" she moaned, "What are they?"

Rollins held her tight. His teeth chattered. He was going mad. Had he seen aright as the moon's rays lanced through a break in the thick fronds to show huge, shaggy, crouching bodies in a dim, glaring circle, only to merge again into unrelieved blackness?

He spun desperately around, seeking escape, anywhere except to remain in that slow, terribly tightening circlet of eyes. Wild hope flared through him, poured strong life into his frozen veins. Directly ahead, into the flat waving fronds, there were no hideous orbs. A sudden swift dash, and. . . .

He hung back a moment, chilled, as a thought struck him. That way, if the Indian tale were true, lay the place from which no one ever returned. He tried to pierce the black gloom. The trees obscured all sight.

The disembodied eyes were closer now, picking up speed, hemming them in on three sides, driving them remorselessly, purposefully, in one direction.

"They're only animals," Rollins lied. "We had better run for it, Kay. This way!"

Through the lush grass they fled, leaving their packs scattered on the ground, into the weird cathedral heights of smooth green trunks and Stygian gloom. On and on, stumbling, smashing into unseen boles, gasping for air in tortured lungs.

And always, at an even distance behind, keeping pace on three sides, slowing when they stumbled and fell, increasing speed when Rollins tried a desperate spurt, floated the disembodied eyes, round and red in the blackness, deadly silent.

Panic swept over Rollins. He heard Kay's teeth chattering with fever and fear. They were being herded, like cows for the slaughter, toward an unknown fate. Yet he dared not turn and face the menace of those baleful orbs.

The strange trees thinned, cleared suddenly.

A great cry burst from Kay. Rollins tried to dig his heels into the soft turf, to brake their swift-rushing flight.

It was too late! The ground gave beneath their feet in a long steep slope. Down, down they tumbled, rolling and grasping with fear-stiffened fingers at the strangely smooth and glassy sides, faster and faster until their senses whirled in revolving dizziness. Rollins caught glimpses of the rushing world as he went over and over.

They had fallen into a great conical depression that plunged deep into the bowels of the earth, through which thousands of white columns of steam plumed in slanting spears. Their wet warm breath blasted hot and clammy on Rollins' fevered face. The eerie glow of the pit made ghostly wraiths of the falling couple.

Down, always down! God, would it never stop? Death, terrible in its finality, awaited them at the bottom. No one had ever returned, the Indians said. Their bones would join the moldering heap of other unfortunates at the bottom of the slide, there to rot through all eternity.

Kay's agonized face flashed past him. He reached out a frantic hand, missed, and kept on rolling. Then he stopped, suddenly, crushingly—the universe seemed to have fallen on him. Black waves rushed over his head. Was it delirium or the smash-up of his senses that made him hear a long, weird ululation of triumph from a hundred animal throats before he passed out?

CHAPTER TWO

Down to Hell

ROLLINS groaned and struggled weakly to a sitting position. His head and body throbbed with exquisite tortures. Where was he? What had happened?

The world around him was a weird glow, interpenetrated with white lances of smoke. Beneath him was a soft, yielding moss-like material. He marshaled his swaying senses, tried to think. Dimly it all came back to him—the baleful eyes, the remorseless herding, the swift descent. The moss had saved him from death. But there was something else, something important that his fuddled senses tried to grasp, and that kept on slipping away. He tried to focus his aching mind, yet only a blur remained.

There was a soft slithering stir beside him. He sat stiffly, heart trip-hammering. A gigantic shape, irradiated into enormous proportions by the drifting steam, almost brushed his shrinking body in its noiseless passage. It stooped in the wavering light. For a single instant red saucer-eyes glared at Rollins. Then with horribly silent tread the monster vanished into white mist.

The veil dropped from Rollins' blurred senses. He sprang gasping to his feet. Cold sweat poured from his face. His clicking teeth formed one frantic word. *"Kay!"*

That shadowy monster had flung her on his shoulder, had carried her off! He peered desperately into the eerie haze, a great fear within him. He started to run, aimlessly. He must find her before it was too late. He shouted again, reckless of the consequences.

"Kay!"

Far off, like a dying echo it seemed, came an answering call. Frantic, urgent, gasping: "Help, Phil. Help!" Then, heavy blanketing silence, as if a great hand had clamped down on her struggling mouth.

Rollins rushed like a madman in the direction of the voice. The steam suddenly swirled to one side. Far ahead, dim in the eerie glow, a rounded arm waved convulsively, seemingly out of the ground itself. Then it sank swiftly beneath the surface.

Rollins leaped ahead. His foot caught in a fumarole—he tripped and smashed into the ground. Cursing and sobbing he staggered to his feet again.

Before him was a solid wall of steam— and no sign of Kay or her monstrous captor. A dead blanket of silence enveloped him. He flung himself madly into it, heedless of tripholes, heedless of floating eyes or the strange denizens of the pit. One thought only obsessed him with terrible singleness.

He must find his bride, his darling Kay!

He called again and again into the smothering steam. Dull echoes returned to mock him. He ran again, blindly. The mist coalesced into a looming solid. He smashed into it full tilt. A guttural gasp exploded in the night. The form staggered and was resilient, like rubber—or flesh.

Rollins was beyond fear. He was a yammering, raging cave man, whose mate had ruthlessly been torn from him. He rammed into the obstruction with both fists flailing. There was an answering yelp of pain, as his fist sank into a yielding body. Then something lashed out of the darkness and crashed into the side of his face.

The next instant both combatants were rolling over and over on the turfy ground —gouging, kicking, biting, ravening beasts. Steam, emerging from vents in the soil, scalded them both, blinded them with damp exhalations. A fierce blood-lust sang through Rollins' veins. His fists thudded into an unseen face. The stockbroker was gone—in his place was primitive man battling with unknown monsters. He raised his hand to smash down again. The hand poised in midair, motionless, frozen.

FROM the white-streaked blackness beneath him, from the inert lump of flesh he was pummeling, came a string of curses, obscene, choked, furious, but civilized in all their implications.

He had been grappling with a human being in this pit of terrors!

"What the hell!" Rollins ejaculated, and jerked to his feet.

The steam clouds wavered uneasily away, to disclose a man, ragged and torn, limp on the ground, staring up at him with fear-swept eyes.

"Who are you?" Phil demanded.

The man struggled to his feet. He held his throat gingerly. A black stubbly beard covered his chin and almost hid his red fleshy lips. His nose was curved like a scimitar and his eyes glinted from under bushy, matted hair.

"Me?" he muttered in a hoarse choked voice. "I'm Judd Wilson. But you—a human being, here, in this horrible place! Tell me," he babbled on imploringly, "you're not—one of them. God, what they did t'me afore I was able to escape!" The man shuddered with what seemed a palsy of fear. "Ever since I fell in, while a-huntin' fer wolves, they had me. They tortured me until—" He stopped short, sank his quivering face into his hands— long, lean and clawed they were—and sobbed great dry sobs.

Rollins felt glacial cold steal over him. Kay was in their hands now. Good God!

If . . . He shook the trembling man harshly.

"They—they have my wife. For God's sake, man, pull yourself together. You must help me. We must get her away. We must all get away. Do you hear?"

Wilson shrank from him. His eyes were crafty, half-mad. They shifted strangely to the background of glowing steam.

"I—I dassn't," he whispered. He thrust his jaw closer. His voice rose to a scream. "This place is Hell—the kind the preachers usta talk about. They're devils, I tell you." Light froth gathered at his bearded lips. He turned as if to make a sudden dash.

Rollins caught him by the collar of his ragged shirt. Pity flooded him for this man, manifestly unbalanced by the terrible experiences he had gone through. But he needed him, needed every possible help to find Kay, somewhere underground in the grip of hideous beings who moved soundlessly, and whose eyes shone in the night like those of nocturnal animals.

He forced himself to speak slowly, as to a child, trying to penetrate the man's cracked understanding. "Judd Wilson," he said earnestly. "We must help each other. Find my wife for me, and I'll help you get away. Otherwise, all of us will die."

Wilson surveyed him craftily. Suddenly he cackled: "Heh—heh! We'll fool those devils yet. I'll show you where they go—down into Hell, but I won't go, I tell you." He was screaming again. "I'll never go down there no more."

"Hush!" Rollins whispered apprehensively. "I'll go myself—just you show me the way."

Without another word the man trotted off into the enveloping smoke. Rollins trod almost on his feet in his anxiety to keep sight of him. All around was steam, great billowing clouds, jetting up from the ground in a thousand strong spurts, overlaying the whole infernal pit with its hissing white glow, hiding the fumaroles, the vent holes, the contour of the ground. Overhead boiled the steam, like soup in a fiery cauldron. Beneath, the earth was hot to the touch and quivered with incessant low rumbles.

In the dim recesses of his consciousness Rollins remembered having read of places like this—fuming pits fed by subterranean fires that antedated the ice age —place of refuge for strange plants and stranger animals while solid mile-high glaciers obliterated all the rest of the northern hemisphere.

But just at that moment Rollins was not interested in erudite scientific explanations. One overpowering purpose burned like a clear flame in him—to find Kay and escape from the weird monsters of the pit.

Judd Wilson stopped suddenly. His stubbly face twitched fearfully. His clawed fingers pointed to a yawning hole directly ahead. In the steamy fog he seemed the wavering shadow of a nightmare vision.

"They live down there," he whispered hoarsely. "Devils! In Hell! I ain't agoing, so help me, I ain't. . . ."

Rollins stared into that ominous smooth round hole. The entrance to Hell! He felt the ridges of his spine bristle and arch under the impact of nameless fears. Memories of childhood rose to plague him, of preachers who thundered of hellfire and devils. This place, those eerie, half-seen monsters, were like illustrations to those implacable homilies.

He was tempted for an instant to turn and run—to scramble up those glass-smooth sides, to perish alone in boggy muskeg, rather than face the unknown terrors of that yawning pit. But the thought of Kay brought him up with a jerk. He set his teeth hard to still their chattering. His wife, the beautiful girl he had married, with whom he had envisioned a lifetime of happiness, was down there, suffering nameless tortures. The thought of her white body subjected to defilements. . . . He groaned and said: "Wilson, I'm going down. You wait here."

The man quavered eagerly: "So help me, I will. So long's I'm outa their way."

Rollins bent over the cave-like entrance. It was round and smooth and steeply slanting. White puffs of steam blew out into his face. With an inward shudder he thrust a leg over the edge.

A scream knifed through the billowing smoke behind him. A jittering blood-curdling scream. Wilson's voice, agonized, hoarse with terror.

"Look out! They. . . ."

Rollins twisted desperately. A dim bulk loomed overhead—something descended with crushing force on his head. Light blazed in his skull, quenched into blank darkness.

KAY struggled vainly in the arms of her captor. Her small fists beat futilely against the great shaggy breast, the shrieks that tore out of her throat seemed curiously muffled, as if by confining walls. The stench of the encircling beast was overpowering.

"Oh God!" she moaned. If it only were the fevered nightmare of delirium—if only she would awake to find a white, starched nurse, cool and competent, leaning over her and saying: "There, there, child, you must rest. You have had a bad dream." She grasped at the thought, played with it. Her head was hot and feverish, her body shivered with malaria. Dear God, it must be so!

But the stench was sharp and acrid, the steamy passage clammy against her skin, and the huge shaggy arms that tightened round her slim form hurt her with coarse bristles.

Down, down, until time itself seemed to lapse, until the very center of the earth seemed near. The tunnel was getting more and more close and fetid, the vaporous exhalations hotter and hotter. Perspiration poured in rivulets from her quaking body.

Then suddenly motion ceased. The mist swept away magically. The air became clear again. A huge vaulted cavern loomed around her, its walls green-glowing.

Her eyes went draggingly to her captor. She felt smothered in his tightening grasp. Huge red eyes, lidless, inflamed with bestial hate and cruelty, glared down at her. The face—dear God—a nightmare out of Hell! Squat, deformed, brown-haired, with broad, flaring, red-rimmed nostrils, low, retreating forehead, and two yellow tusks that protruded from a grinning, slobbering mouth.

The head bent over, the mouth opened, and foul rank odors enveloped Kay in a miasmic haze. She shrieked and went limp.

As the sound of her cry went racketing through the vaulted echoes of the cave, hundreds of man-beasts, similar in bestial foulness to her captor, spewed like devil's spawn out of innumerable clefts in the fused rock walls. The cavern swarmed with misshapen things, converging on their fellow and his captive.

He crouched against the wall, showing his fangs in a soundless snarl. He held the limp body of the girl in one great arm, her white body arced over, head downward, the framing gold of her hair sweeping the rock floor, the fever burning two red spots in her pallid cheeks.

The man-beasts swept on in ominous silence. Foam dripped from their bestial lips, lust burned redly in their rimless, saucer-like eyes. The lone captor gripped Kay tighter. His huge mouth opened and he emitted a roar of defiance:

"Oom—pah—loo!"

The strange savage syllables excited the onrushing mob into a veritable frenzy. The great cavern echoed frightfully to their answering roars:

"Mem—say—ga!"

Kay had not fainted. Yet she could not move. Terror had paralyzed her limbs, frozen all her vital functions. Her throat was held in lockjaw tightness, her arms and legs were leaden tons. She could not shriek—even that relief was denied her.

She lay in seeming stupor, held captive by one, surrounded by a thousand others —horribly like men, yet not men—the furious lust in their eyes only too evident —about to dispute for possession of her frail body in gigantic primeval combat. If only, she prayed soundlessly through stiffened lips, she could faint, if only they would tear her limb from limb, before. . . .

The circle converged. Great brown bodies sprang forward with howls that sounded like words. Her captor suffocated her in his encircling grip. He shouted defiance. Neanderthal men, misfits in the twentieth century, beast-men who never evolved, cut off in this strange underworld pit thousands of years before by great glaciers!

Kay tried to shut her eyes against the horrible sight. The plunging beasts were almost upon them. Already she gagged at the accumulated fetor of their bodies. A great hairy arm lunged out, caught at her trailing arm. Her captor snarled, knocked off the grip with a battering sweep.

Then they were overwhelmed. Furious dark bodies overlaid her, snatched with greedy paws at her limbs. Racking pains shot through her slender frame—in seconds she would be dismembered. Lungs filled to bursting with stark fear, shriek after shriek released her strange paralysis.

She felt herself falling, snatched at, clutched, grabbed anew. Eyes, mouths, fangs, stench, filled the universe. She was passing out.

A shrill whistle pierced the frightful din, pierced her failing consciousness like a sword. A single syllable followed:

"*Room!*"

Kay gasped dizzily. A second before she had been under a smother of furious pawing bodies, now she was sprawled on the cold stone floor—alone!

The man-beasts, monstrous, gigantic, had gone back in an ebbing wave. They crouched in a great circle around her, panting, snarling, bestial faces turned in one direction, sullenly obedient to that guttural word.

The blood rushed back into the girl's limbs. She sprang to her feet, pressed gasping against the wall.

A strange figure approached from the opposite end of the cavern—a solitary fantastic figure. A thousand eyes watched his steady, unhurried gait, a thousand fearstruck, shuddering eyes.

Kay pressed her hand weakly to her head. She moaned. She could stand no more. Terror, sheer, stark, ravening terror, had unhinged her mind. She was definitely and irrevocably mad. For the Thing coming toward her with even, stealthy pace was not like the others. It was slighter and shorter, and its shaggy skin crinkled in loose folds on the slender frame. From the ape-like shoulders reared a rigid, corpse-white head with conical hairless dome and horribly bulging forehead. As if a freak of evolution had forced vast brains into a skull too small for their expansive pressure.

Her eyes quested frantically around. She must clear her aching head of this frightful fantasy, this thing born of delirium. But the great cavern and its swarming denizens refused to change. The creature strode through a respectful gap,

was almost upon her. His eyes gleamed with a frozen light—his hairy hand reached greedily out for her.

Kay swayed, shrieked, and fell. She had fainted.

CHAPTER THREE

The God of Pain

THE steam was hot and clammy. The heat was fast becoming insupportable. Rollins gasped for air. The vapor seared his throat. He groped through the swirling mist—he was alone in the room—seeking a way out. He must get out before he boiled alive. Horrible fear smote at him. He shouted in thick gulping tones.

Someone, far off, laughed mockingly. It had a fiendish sound. The terrible truth rushed upon him. He remembered now. Those red-staring eyes, that floating soundless step. Of course! Like a fool he had been trapped. He was doomed, and there was nothing he could do about it.

He shrieked, terribly.

That shriek awoke him. He found himself staring into nothingness—into blank white vapor. It was hot and clammy. It ran in acrid rivulets down his streaming face, made his clothes a sodden mess. Something warm and sticky, heavier in body, salty to the taste, ran with it.

He put his hand to his head. It bulged with pain, a long gash reached across his scalp. He extended his arm. It crashed into hard unyielding stone. The vapors of his nausea swirled around him. He was lying at the bottom of a vent hole, and the steam rushed past him from subterranean depths. Low grumblings and mutterings accompanied the hissing fumes.

Rollins got dizzily to his feet, and bumped his head sharply. The passage was low-ceiled. His head cleared. It all came back to him. He had been hit on the head and precipitated into the hole on the heels of Wilson's shouted warning.

Wilson was nowhere in sight—he must have died in the pit. And Kay?

The memory of the shriek which awoke him came back, flooding. It had not been his own voice. It had been Kay's. Then she was somewhere around, here in the bowels of the earth, in frightful peril.

He shouted into the gray mist!

No answer. Was she dead too?

A wave of recklessness swept over him. If she were dead, then he would also die. But first he would kill as many of these underworld monsters as he could. His hands were hot and dry, his throat a furnace. He groped unsteadily through the boling vapors. The passageway led down.

Age of interminable groping, heat that was scalding, air that made him choke with its acrid fumes. Rollins was at the end of his strength. His head hurt horribly. Then he found himself in a small rock-hewn chamber, where the air miraculously had cooled and a dull light pervaded the walls.

He staggered upright, and took deep grateful drafts. The chamber showed signs of habitation. In a corner was a bed of interlaced boughs covered with huge fern fronds. Close to it was a crumpled mass of something furry. Rollins stepped nearer to investigate.

As he did so, his eye came in line with a crypt in the rock. He staggered back with a cry, heart pounding madly.

In the crypt, glowing with a greenish, putrescent light, grinning at him with horrible grimace, was a skeleton—a human skeleton! The fleshless phalanges pointed straight at him with frightful gesture, the green-tinged jaw gaped widely, the eyeless sockets glowed with liquid flame.

A HIDEOUS snarl froze him to immobility. From behind the couch of boughs and ferns a shape rose. A great hairy shape with hate-filled eyes. Rollins shrank back in fear; he could not know that this was Og, the man-beast who had kidnapped Kay. Blood streaked slowly down the hairy arms. One pointed fang was broken at the root.

Rollins looked wildly around for a weapon. There was none, none that could cope with this strange monster from a bygone era. One heave of those powerful shoulders, and he would be a twisted, broken welter of bones like that skeleton in the niche.

The man-beast snarled again. Superhate distorted the bloody countenance. But not for the frightened man before him. His burning eyes were directed to the crumpled mass on the floor. He pounced, swept up the folds in a great paw.

Then for the first time he seemed to sense Rollins' presence. He shifted triumph-filled orbs in his direction. Clutching tightly at his spoils, dragging it along on the stony floor, he moved forward, soundless, sinister. Rollins pressed against the wall. He could go back no further. The monster was between him and the passageway. Escape was impossible.

Og came nearer, slobbering in anticipation. Rollins tensed his muscles for a last desperate hopeless dive. Already the man-beast's breath was foul on his face.

"Room!"

The single syllable echoed hollowly through the chamber. Og stiffened, jaw muscles twitching in unwilling fear. He looked hastily around. So did Rollins, heart pounding with imminence of death. There was no one in the chamber besides themselves.

Og licked his sole remaining tusk stealthily. Fear and ferocity struggled for mastery on his monstrous features. He swung his head from side to side. Silence! That one syllable had been all.

Rollins watched with a choking sensation in his throat. Somehow, he knew without understanding, his fate was trembling in the balance of the next few seconds.

Og snarled low, looked down at the furry thing under his arm. Fear faded into a grunt of triumph and satisfied hate. He lifted his head, crouched for a spring. Rollins knew then that he was doomed. He waited the onslaught with dull anguish. Memories of his short wedded life, bitter sweet now in their futility, passed through his mind in quick succession. He could see the man-beast's legs whip forward as though on steel springs. He thrust out a helpless hand to ward him off.

There was a strange click in the chamber. Og's snarl rattled in his throat, he teetered and almost fell forward. His jaw gaped, and froth gathered in his lips.

The skeleton in the niche was moving! The light in the chamber dimmed and the bony travesty of a man seemed to clothe itself in ghastly green flame. The fleshless hands went up and down, the long-boned legs flexed and unflexed in horrible walking strides. The grinning skull nodded in staccato time, and the jaw gaped with fleshless laughter.

Rollins was transfixed. He thrust a trembling hand across his brow. Even the attacking monster was forgotten in the horror of the living dead.

The jaw gaped wider.

"Room!"

The strange word rolled around the chamber, seemed to emanate from the bony mouth.

A howl of terror answered it. Og threw his bundle down behind the couch as though venomous snakes had basked in its fold. His great legs cleared the bed in one bound, and he was gone, into a

cleft that penetrated the rock behind it.

At once the skeleton ceased its ghastly approach, appeared to retreat into its crypt and shudder into immobility as the light once more grew brighter in the chamber.

ROLLINS turned to flee, the way he had come. He had had his fill. If he weren't mad already, he soon would be. And he had still to find Kay.

In the mouth of the passageway, he bumped headlong into something, someone running the other way.

"Oh Lord!" it gasped, and staggered into the light panting. It was Judd Wilson.

His bearded jaw waggled unsteadily at the sight of Rollins, his shifting black eyes stared as though they had seen a ghost.

"I—thought—you were dead!" he mouthed. "That devil, up there, choked me. Then he went for you. I ran away and hid."

"He hit me hard enough," Rollins said grimly. "But what are you doing down here? I thought all Hell couldn't drag you into this place again."

The man shuddered, looked around fearfully. He seemed possessed with the ague. Rollins could see him grip himself. His eyes lost their half mad light.

"You see," he said quietly, "I came down for that gal—your wife—you spoke about. You were dead—leastwise so I imagined, an' I didn' want to leave a gal with these devils to suffer what I suffered."

Rollins was surprised, and touched. He stuck out his hand.

"Thanks, old timer. Now we've *got* to find her."

They shook. "Uh-huh!" Wilson agreed. "But she ain't here. That means they must have her in the torture place, the big cave."

Rollins' face was sweaty and bloody. He had lost that round look which lent him dignity in the city. It was grim with desperation now. "What are we losing time for, then?" he cried.

"Right, pardner." Wilson moved hastily for the passageway.

"Just a moment," said Phil. He remembered that strange bundle of fur Og had been so anxious to seize. "What is that fur thing in the corner? Maybe it. . . ."

Wilson's face contorted with agony. "They're coming fer us," he cried. "Hurry, or we're goners."

Rollins followed his fleeing form into the boiling corridor, pounding along with crouched limbs from imagined pursuit. He called on Wilson to wait, to guide him through the steamy darkness. A faint, muffled voice, frantic with fear, seemingly far off, urged him to greater speed.

Rollins, lungs bursting, obediently ran harder. He smashed into unyielding rock, whirled, and felt great wet hairy arms tighten round him in bone-crushing embrace. He felt himself lifted, and carried along swiftly.

He was a captive, a prey to the beastmen of the underworld!

ROLLINS strained at the cruel leather thongs that lashed him securely to a jutting splinter of rock. The great underground cavern to which he had been carried was luminescent with a greenish glow that seemed to emanate from the walls. Its ceiling was lost in a high arch of drifting steam. At the farther end, set in what seemed a natural amphitheater, was a huge black shiny rock, foursquare and flat on top. A grotesquely sculptured figure, of the same black material, towered gigantically in the very center of the altar.

Rollins shuddered, yet could not drag his eyes away from that thing of horror. The workmanship was crude and clumsy,

there was no sense of anatomical correctness, and the graving tools had dulled and chipped rather than smoothly carved, yet the hewn colossus literally vibrated with a palpable shimmer of evil, of the compressed suffering and torture of worlds without end.

Its gargantuan limbs were twisted and deformed—one arm dangled shrivelled and broken, the other, immoderately long, swept almost to the surface of the rock, and terminated in five widespread cupping fingers, wide and deep enough, Rollins thought with a shiver, to hold a human form in clutching embrace.

The sculptured shoulders sagged as if under an unbearable weight, and the lolling head drooped forward and down as if to permit sight of the great cupping hand far beneath. But it was the strange contorted mask of features that held Rollins' breathless gaze, made him forget his own predicament, even the fate of his wife, in shuddering waves of nausea.

No fiend out of hell, no sinner expiating dire crimes in purgatorial fire, could ever have felt one half the suffering, the keen agony, the torturing pain, that were depicted on that awful graven face. Black stony eyes bulged in frightful similitude of horror, thick red-flecked lips twisted in terrible soundless scream, one cheek hung pendulous as if sliced down to a thread of holding muscle, a deep gash scarred chin and clefted forehead.

A God of Pain! A statue dedicated to Agony and Suffering!

The perspiration started on Rollins' clammy forehead. His eyes darted fearfully around the vaulted cavern. It was deserted, left alone to himself, a captive, and that terrible graven colossus on its sinisterly suggestive altar.

The man-beast who had captured him and bound him securely to the rock was gone. Yet something was brewing, something terrible, and inconceivable. He could feel it in the breathless hush of the cavern, in the twisted figure of the graven image, in the swift rushing plumes of smoke far overhead, in the constant quiverings and shudderings of the solid-seeming rock beneath. Was it fact or the mere rasping of tortured nerves that made the tremblors seem more violent than before, the vaprous jets against the arch more dense and billowy?

Rollins flung himself against his bonds again, and fell back, raw and bleeding where the unyielding thongs bit cruelly into his flesh. He was beyond fear for himself, but Kay. . . . Oh God, let her be dead, he prayed fiercely.

CHAPTER FOUR

Priest of the Beast-Men

HE LIFTED haggard, sunken eyes. Something slithered along the farther edge of the cavern. He looked again. More flitting, soundless shapes, in tens, in hundreds, in thousands, until to his fevered gaze it seemed that the walls had awakened to fetid, crawling life, that gigantic brown larvae had spawned from lifeless stone to fill the hollow with their bloated forms.

They swept by him in troops, huge man-beasts on silent pads, things out of nightmares, red eyes intent on the altar and its hideous god. They filled the amphitheater, squatted on haunches around the black basalt, thrust hairy heads backward in caricature of an expectant audience at an outdoor play.

Rollins felt his heart hammering in his bosom as if it would burst. For the front line of grisly spectators were horribly crippled figures, hobbling on dangling useless limbs, holding out withered stumps of what once were hands to the leering statue, jaws twisted and gashed, skulls flattened under tremendous pressure.

Pathetic beings, smashed in some great cataclysm, peering out of half blind eyes at the personification in immortal stone of all their pain and torture.

Rollins had to bite his lips until the blood ran to prevent a sudden scream. The whole phantasmagoria had fallen into a sinister pattern, infinitely horrible in its implications. Shuddering understanding had come to him. There was no doubt about it now. The rumblings and grumblings of the imprisoned giants of the earth were momentarily increasing. The ground shivered and heaved, and the huge vault swayed as in a storm. The steam ceiling was lower too; its clammy whiteness impenetrable.

A simultaneous ululation burst from a thousand throats, guttural, pregnant with terror and groaning despair.

"Room!"

Their hairy arms, sound and withered alike, went out in fierce supplication to the hideous towering God of Pain.

There was a low underground roar, and a wide irregular crack opened as if by magic in the wall closest to the bound figure of the man. Grayish smoke plumed forth.

"Room!"

Desperation mingled with anguish in the blast from a thousand man-beasts. It held a new, threatening note.

Rollins moaned at the sound. He shouted insanely. "Take me! Take me! Not her! Kay, you are dead—I know it—oh God, tell me she is dead! That they are waiting for me, not for here!" He shuddered into gasping silence. He felt strangely lightheaded.

But the squatting man-beasts paid no attention to his cries. Their eyes were glued fiercely to the altar. A figure was rising slowly out of a trap door in the rock, directly alongside the colossus of Suffering. The ground was a continuous rumble now. Another crack appeared, more blasts of steam jetted into the cavern, but the man-beasts were intent only on the rising figure.

Rollins stared at the apparition with the smaller body of a man-beast and the head of a nightmare. High and bald and gray it was, with a ghastly, putty-like texture, and the forehead bulged in a horrible curve. Black cruel eyes glared frozenly at the mute-stricken assemblage.

"*Room!*"

Half-sigh, half triumphant echo. The immortal creature whom their fathers and forefathers had followed submissively in his priestly ministrations to the sculptured Pain God, would save them from impending calamity. Prehensile fingers grasped a short, crudely hammered sword whose blade was dark with sinister stains.

In his anguish, Rollins noted that one man-beast alone who did not bow like the rest before the minister of evil. It was Og, the brute he had met in the chamber, who had been compelled to drop his vaguely seen trophy by the lifelike apparition of the skeleton. He crouched to one side, lips retracted from yellowed fangs, great paws clenching and unclenching, red-rimmed eye overflowing with hate and baffled fury.

The priest of pain lifted his sword. There was a stir behind the altar. All heads bent toward the stir like a field of corn before a storm. Rollins craned too, fearing what he would see. The underground convulsion was increasing in violence; the mutterings were becoming low roars, but not a head turned from its strange focussed intentness.

Two figures emerged, climbed invisible steps to the rear of the altar. They were carrying a third. The two were hairy brutes, Neanderthalers like the rest; but their limp burden was slim and khaki-clad.

"Kay!"

A great tortured cry burst from Rollins at the sight of his bride, her lovely golden-crowned head drooping over a hairy arm, her cheeks paper-white.

SHE raised her head at the anguished voice of her husband. She opened her mouth weakly and collapsed again.

They were on the altar now. The priest advanced, towering over her stricken charms. He made a gesture. The man-beasts placed her in the cupping fingers of the God of Pain. Her slender legs dangled over.

"*Room!*"

Exultation, fierce delight, swept the nightmare audience. There was but little time, but the victim was prepared, the priest skillful in his ministrations. Surely their god would drink with gusto the sufferings of the sacrificial girl, and ward off catastrophe from their underground world. Never in all the unimaginable antiquity of their dwelling in the pit had such a toothsome morsel been offered in vicarious sacrifice.

Rollins twisted and strained until the muscles corded on his body—and the veins bulged startlingly—futile, half-insane efforts, for the rawhide thongs cut only the deeper, and the knots would not budge. He shouted strange oaths in a voice he did not recognize for his own, he clamored frantically against the rising roar of the quake, yet the man-beasts paid no attention to his cries. The ceremony on the altar held them in fierce grip; only through it could they be saved from the inevitable.

The priest bent low over Kay. His curiously compressed mouth was close to her. Sounds, indistinguishable at a distance, issued. The girl looked up with horror-struck eyes at the apparition above her, and shook her head in repulsion.

The priest of the beast-men glared at her a moment, lifted his crude iron sword, and slashed suddenly downward.

Again and again he slashed, while Rollins, teeth clenched, eyes a red blurry haze, made strangled noises.

Khaki blouse, khaki breeches, woolen stockings, silken underthings, shredded away. The white slim body of his bride, virginally molded, lay utterly nude in the greedy fingers of the god. A great shout burst from a thousand throats. Red eyes glazed with lust and knowledge of what was to come. Og crouched lower and made little panting noises. His fierce stealthy gaze wavered between girl and priest.

Kay shrank from the strange baleful glare of the bulging skull above her. He leaned over again. His cold, putty-like lips made a clammy trail on her white bosom, brushed over a tender breast. Sounds issued that Rollins could not hear.

The girl shuddered convulsively with mingled fear and shame. Again she shook her head in desperate refusal.

The priest-creature reared back. Hoarse bellows of rage snarled in his throat. His sword swept down. Raw flesh ridged magically across a gleaming white shoulder. Bright blood spurted in fountain cascade over rounded limbs and thighs. Kay screamed—a high-pitched pain-shot scream.

Rollins pulled at his thongs with insane strength. The girl he loved was being tortured before his very eyes, a white vicarious offering to the bestial God of Suffering in place of the man-beasts of the pit.

The Neanderthalers were on their hairy legs, howling and roaring with hideous exultation. Soon, very soon, the anguished god would be glutted, even as he had been in the past, and the threatened whelming earthquake would subside.

But the whole cavern now was rocking on unsteady keel. Gray blasting steam poured from a dozen vents. The air was fetid with sulphurous stench. The man-

beasts wavered. They seethed in an agony of fear. In the murky haze they seemed like devils gyrating in a fiery cauldron. Their voices rose to a hideous roar. They surged toward the altar. Rollins sensed, even though he did not understand, the clamor of their guttural syllables.

The sacrificial victim was their only salvation. They mouthed at their priest, yelping with fierce fear.

Quick! There is no time to be lost. Torture the stranger, girl, make her to writhe with nameless agonies. Rip her! Tear her! Slice her apart! Offer the steam of her cries to the great God of Pain. Glut him with the warm spouting of her blood. Quick, before he visits us the terrors of his wrath! Already he roars his anger at us; we have been remiss in satisfying his lust for pain, for the joys of writhing limbs. He will feed on us instead, his worshippers and adorers. See, the walls quiver; the steam from his nostrils envelops us. Do not dawdle, oh priest of our forefathers, but smite with the magic weapon.

Kay's nude form lay limp in the obscene fingers of the god, white purity in a shambles of sight and sound. The hideous priest lashed down again. A gaping wound seared the other shoulder. Kay moaned feebly. The Neanderthalers leaped and mouthed gibberish. To their brutish imaginations the restless earth was already subsiding. Soon the god would have his fill of blood and pain and relapse into his usual somnolence.

Mercifully, Rollins was only partly conscious. He could bear the awful sight no longer. As in a clogging dream he saw Og, face a mask of hatred, jump for the altar and swing himself aloft just as the frozen-faced priest raised the dripping sword again.

Og went for him with a snarl of demoniac frenzy. The minister of suffering swung around. The gray bulge of his forehead bobbed insanely. The sword swung with him.

SUDDENLY the cavern filled with a swelling roar that drowned out the petty shrieks of the combatants, of the horror-struck Neanderthalers. The underground giant had aroused himself. Rocks ground on rocks. Great sections of stone tore loose from the walls to fall with great crashing sounds among the howling snarling man-beasts. Hot blasts drove pulsing vapor from a thousand crannies, filling the hollow with searing heat. Tongues of liquid flame darted forth, dripped molten lava on the quivering floor. They formed hissing pools that spread with horrible slowness over the tumbling rock. The whole world seemed to rend in ruining fragments—the din was indescribable.

The last thing Rollins saw was the priest of pain and Og locked in straining embrace. The short sword rose and bit in the great hairy shoulder. Og went down, and the priest of the beast-men snatched at Kay's naked form and seemed to disappear from view.

Rollins went stark mad. Heedless of biting pain he ripped at his bonds. Scalding steam hissed across his tortured body. Lurid flames enveloped him. Jagged rocks came hurtling to the ground, mashed into bloody pulps the shaggy bodies of the Neanderthalers. In the murky, red-shot haze they ran, stumbling and shrieking, in every direction. Their god had failed them, their offering had not been enough. He was glutting his lust for torture with them instead.

Rollins heaved again, staggered. The jutting splinter of rock to which he had been bound disintegrated into a hundred pieces. The leather thongs fell from him. He was free. With a gibbering cry that matched that of the beast-men themselves, he plunged into chaos.

Just how he found the opening in the altar was forever to remain a mystery to him. As was his miraculous avoidance of rocks and lava and steam and the blindly fleeing Neanderthalers. But find it he did—a quaking, shimmying smoke-filled cavity that led down into invisibility.

He plunged in without hesitation, running, thrown from side to side by stunning concussions, gasping in the acrid atmosphere, obsessed with one thought, to find Kay and the bulging-skulled priest before it was too late.

Flame lashed out behind him, hot tongues seared his shoulder as he staggered into a chamber. It was the cave in which he had met Og. Irresistibly his eyes turned in the green-glowing murk to the couch. On it was the white body of his bride, nude, screaming, struggling under the backward pressure of the priest of the beast-men!

With a snarl that was half animal, Rollins cleared the intervening distance. The creature sprang up. A hair-covered hand caught clumsily for the sword, slashed down in a sweeping arc.

ROLLINS did not attempt to duck. He felt the slicing of his shoulder as a thing remote from himself. His hands shot out, caught the hideous being by his neck. His clutching fingers were infused with a terrible strength. They tightened.

The priest gurgled horribly, while his putty-gray face and overtopping skull retained their frozen malignity. The iron sword made a wide gash in Rollins' arm. But he was beyond hurts. The struggles grew more feeble, more spasmodic. The sword dropped with a clatter. Rollins pressed harder.

The figure slumped. As it did, the shaggy, brown-haired skin parted and fell open. It slipped to the floor. The lolling head shuddered and rolled off. It shattered into a thousand clayey pieces.

Rollins opened his fingers and started back.

"Judd Wlson!" he gasped.

The man slid slowly down. His black-stubbled chin wagged feebly, his crafty eyes were dulled with the glaze of approaching death.

But Rollins sprang with little moaning sounds to the side of his wife. She smiled wanly up at him. The blood dripped slowly from her wounded body.

"I'm—all right," she whispered.

He caught up the shaggy skin, enveloped her tenderly in its clinging folds. Then he went back to the dying trapper, feet unsteady in the swaying of the ground.

"Well, Judd Wilson," he said harshly. "I knew the priest to the god was not one of the beast-men, but I didn't expect to find you tricked out in a mummer's skin and a plaster head."

The prone man twisted feebly and looked up. "I'm a goner," he said with difficulty. "I—I fell in here years ago. They tortured me with the sword—they're mortal afeard of that god of their'n. They usta draw victims by lot if no outsider happened to blunder in. They think that's the only way to keep him quiet."

Wilson groaned as the ground heaved again. "Fer centuries," he continued with slow laborings, "they had a priest fer the pain-god. Seems as though, long time ago, there was a wise man of their tribe. His brains grew so they bulged out his head. And he lost all his hair. He got the notion of the Pain God, and made hisself high-priest—claimed he'd never die. Of course he was a fake, but when he died, his son kept it quiet, and fashioned a skull of plaster so he'd look like his father. It's been handed down secret in the family.

"Afore I passed out, the priest dragged me in here—wanted me to last fer the next ceremony. I killed 'im with a rock. Then I skinned him, covered myself with his pelt like a robe, shoved the plaster skull on my head, an' fooled the whole gang—except Og. But he warn't sure, and the skeleton of the dead priest I rigged up with strings scared the daylights outa him."

He paused a moment, and Rollins was certain he was dead. But the mouth twitched, and words dribbled out painfully. "When—when you came, I was scared you'd be smart enough to expose me and take my place. Then—I wanted the gal—ain't seen a woman in years. You was in my way; so I tried to kill you, while pretendin' to help. But she—she wouldn't listen, even on that damned altar, and all those fiends screechin' fer her blood."

His head lolled, his eyes closed, his face was the color of death.

Rollins shook him fiercely. "Wake up." Wilson barely opened his eyes. "You've been a dirty rat," said Rollins. "Redeem yourself now. How do we get out of this Hell?"

Judd Wilson grinned pallidly. It was like a corpse laughing. "Easy," he muttered. "Ain't no use t'me no more. Found it a while ago, while exploring. Behind the bed's a hole. It widens later an' leads to the muskeg on the other side of the hill. The priest job made me feel important, so I didn't want to quit."

Far off a rumble started, like the swift approach of an express train over bumpy rails. It grew in volume until their ears were blasted with great concussions of sound. Then, a grinding crashing roar, followed, and the whole world seemed to collapse. Powdered rock dust swept into the chamber, and thin squirts of steam.

Wilson heaved himself up, supporting himself with sudden strength on both elbows. A ghastly grin split his face.

"That was the end. The cavern's

blown up, with all the beast-men—They an' their damn Pain God!"

The strength went out of him. He sank to the floor, shuddered and lay still. Judd Wilson was dead.

THE green glow was gone, but red flame, licking through the stone, made murky illumination. The earth, silent after its tremendous effort, started slow trembles again. There would be another and mightier quake soon.

Rollins caught up his wife. She had fainted. He fumbled behind the bed. A narrow hole showed blackly. He squeezed into it, went bumping and bruising through an interminable passage. Half way through there was another terrific crash. The tunnel collapsed behind him in a shower of flying rock and debris. The passageway to the pre-glacial world was forever barred.

An hour later he stumbled out into a vista of flat muskeg and buzzing mosquitoes. It was night.

Behind them there was a glow in the sky. The hill with its strange tree ferns was gone, levelled by the earthquake, heaped into the mysterious pit that had pierced its bowels. Kay stirred, lifted her lips. Rollins pressed them hungrily.

And ten days later, the trading post at the nethermost end of Great Slave Lake was startled to see two scarecrows come staggering in from what had been considered impenetrable, lifeless muskeg. Willing kindly hands caught them as they fell, nursed them through days of delirium and fever, through strange babblings of beast-men and Pain Gods, and tree-ferns and worlds in the depths of the earth. When the fever finally left Rollins and his wife, Kay, they were gaunt and wasted, but on the road to recovery.

Johnson, the chief trader of the small community, shook his head: "Ye be

mighty lucky, strangers. Ain't no one ever come through that muskeg alive. Where d'ye hail from?"

Rollins told him, in halting, gasping words—his strength had not returned as yet—knowing in advance he was doomed to disbelief.

Johnson did not disappoint him. He shook his head with a frown. "I know —I know," he said hastily. "Ye've both been babbling some while ye were sick, but then ye were pretty low wi' the fever when ye came in. That's what comes of listening to them damn Indian stories."

"But," Rollins argued weakly, "I tell you it all really happened. You can still see the remains of the earthquake."

Johnson grinned sheepishly. "I wouldn't go there fer nawthin'," he said. "It's —it's . . ." He fumbled for words, "it's too mosquitoey!"

Rollins should have known then and there that he was licked. The beast-man's skin was not good evidence. In the course of their delirious march, the dark brown hair had rubbed down to bare skin. Johnson maintained it was nothing more or less than the mangy hide of a timber wolf.

But Rollins tried again. "Know Judd Wilson?"

Johnson looked startled. "Sure," he said slowly. "He was lost in the muskeg several years ago. Died in the bog or starved most like."

"Judd Wilson," Rollins remarked evenly, "was the priest to the Pain-God."

For the moment he thought he had the sceptical trader. Then the strange, half-frightened look on the leathery face gave way to a broad smile.

"That there Wilson was such a damn liar when he lived, yuh can't even believe him when he's dead," he grinned.

Rollins turned blindly to his wife for comfort. There was nothing more for him to say.

THE END

THE CORPSE CARVER

By
Laurence Donovan

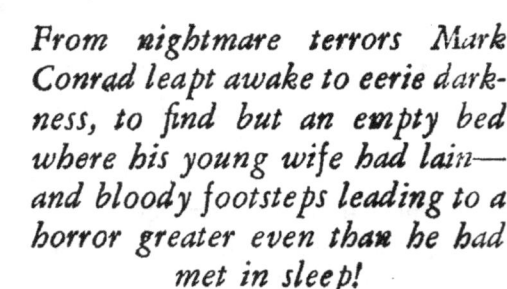

From nightmare terrors Mark Conrad leapt awake to eerie darkness, to find but an empty bed where his young wife had lain— and bloody footsteps leading to a horror greater even than he had met in sleep!

MARK CONRAD fought his way to consciousness. The strangling hold of the nightmare hand slowly eased its pressure. Awake, Conrad's long gulping breath inhaled a noxiously sweet odor. For a full minute the youthful millionaire sportsman struggled, with tense nerves and rigid muscles, to free himself of the strangling talons imbedded in his throat.

Gradually he became aware the hand was only imaginary. The thing which bore upon his heart and lungs with such crushing intensity had no material proportions. Yet it was definitely real, agonizingly painful. Even when he was fully aroused his brain was still at grips with tentacles that had no form or substance.

Yet before he succeeded in moving, in becoming articulate, Mark Conrad's steady mind told him he must have been the victim of a dream. The vision had been so nebulous it could not be recalled. Commonplace facts of his surroundings began to make themselves apparent.

Through the two tall narrow windows slanted the pale reddish glow of a low Everglades half moon. Somewhere outside a whippoorwill mourned with eerie cadence. Frogs below chanted a guttural chorus. Higher voices complained stridently from the swamp trees.

At the foot of the lawn that sloped from the great house with its red-tiled turrets to the spacious palm-guarded waterfront, the gurgling tide of the river sobbed through the mangrove bushes. The broad fronds of the Royal Palms moved in a light breeze with softly sibilant rustling.

Mark Conrad knew and loved these familiar night voices off the broad Caloosahatchee River. From the mystic great lake of the swamp to the blue and clean-washed gulf, he knew every foot of the river's reaches. But this was something else. . . As he succeeded at last in moving one tightly clenched hand, something beyond clear reason came over him with an engulfing, choking flood of terrified apprehension.

Having broken the nightmare spell, though that hellishly sweet odor still seemed to clog his throat and nostrils, Mark Conrad spoke. His words, he discovered, were painfully spaced whispers, barely more than gasping sounds. He forced his body upward from the yielding mattress, straining to make his words louder and more distinct.

"Linda!" he said. "Linda! You all right?"

But the sound of his own voice in the darkness reassured him; he wished now that he hadn't spoken. His lovely bride of a few weeks lay sleeping in the luxurious twin bed only a few feet away under the windows. If he awakened her, he was only letting himself in for a laugh at his own expense. The cool-nerved Mark Conrad, yielding to the boyish terror inspired no doubt by a bit too much of the excellently broiled quail that had been the high spot of their host's tempting dinner!

Mark Conrad at once attempted to relax, hoping his young wife had been sleeping too soundly to be aroused. The dim shape of her bed was outlined close to the window. It had been ridiculous, thinking any harm could come to either of them here. They were guests in the home of Professor de la Roque, who had come to the Caloosahatchee nearly a year before, renovating and refurnishing elaborately the isolated old Swearingen mansion a few miles below the lake on the river.

But Mark Conrad's bride had not replied. Against his will, his ears abruptly strained to hear her soft regular breathing that would tell she had not been aroused.

Then it came, the deeply sinister sigh, as if a woman's sob were being choked back into her throat. Mark Conrad came upright, the iciness of a new and inexplicable apprehension shuddering along his spine.

"Linda!" This time his voice was clearer. "Linda! Are you awake?"

The deeply breathed sigh had died to nothing. Within the high-ceilinged room with its massively paneled walls, the pall of silence was intensified. The night voices outside became mournful banshee wailings.

Again, "Linda! Do you hear?"

This time, as there was no reply, Mark Conrad's hand reached out to the opposite bed. The imprisoning thralldom of the nightmare that had held him was definitely broken now. As his hand sought the reassurance of his young wife's form, Mark Conrad swung from his bed.

Bare feet struck slippery stickiness of warm fluid. His pajama-clad body pitched forward, falling against Linda's bed. Utter madness forced a startled oath from his throat as he recovered his balance, hand groping for the little chain of the night light.

As he sought that elusive chain, Mark Conrad tried to fight back the horror sweeping with a wave of nausea from his floundering feet to the roots of his prickling scalp. This couldn't be! God! Where was that light chain?

One hand still reached for it. The other slid across the bed his bride had occupied, only to be drawn back with the revulsion of his clutching stomach muscles. For the bed was empty—and it too seemed covered with that same sticky warm fluid in which he had stepped!

ONCE more the deeply breathed, sinister sigh swept the room. Again it was as if a woman's sob had been choked back, gurgling in her throat.

His hand found the light chain. The dim radiance of the bulb in its little pink hood flashed over the twin bed with its coverlet of golden silk.

From Mark Conrad's constricted throat was forced a stricken gasp. For seconds he was paralyzed to inaction. This thing couldn't be! Nothing like this could be! It couldn't have happened to Linda!

His tortured eyes stared first at his hand and arm. They rolled to the rumpled silk coverlet. They took in the space between the beds and then his still disbelieving gaze went to the farthest shadows of the big room.

Mark Conrad was alone. Alone with this—this blood-bathed bed and the sticky, bloody trail along the deep rug. Frozen he was for half a minute to horrified inaction. Then he moved, trying to cry out, only to discover that his throat muscles refused to obey his brain.

The door of the bathroom was closed. Mark Conrad tried to keep his feet from the blood as he moved toward it, still vainly attempting to shout and bringing only animal-like moans from his vocal cords. And in his moving, he was finding nerves and muscles still bound by the rigidity he had believed to be a nightmare.

Again now he noticed that noxiously sweet odor that had assailed his nostrils on awakening. A cog in his numbed brain clicked into place. Then it had not been a nightmare.

"God!" he breathed. Might not this, too, be part of a terrible dream? And fighting for an instant to think this, Mark Conrad snapped one hand to his teeth, sunk his molars into its back, clamping his jaws.

As if he were pinching himself to see if he were awake? And he was. God in heaven! He was awake. For his own blood oozed from the hand and its warm salty taste was on his tongue.

Then he was halfway to the bathroom door. The blood trail showed plainly on the deep, bright-colored rug. But it did not lead to the bathroom. Instead, the spattered scarlet swerved toward the dark-paneled wall.

In Mark Conrad's throat now was a persistent sobbing cry. For the bright-haired Linda had been the one and only love of his life. Schoolmates, they had been all to each other for years before their marriage. Gay, always laughing Linda, so sweet. . . .

The pulse pounded at Mark Conrad's temples. The cords of his neck stood out like the drawn thongs of a bow. His hands were knotted into clenched white bone. His eyes strained, following the blood marks that might have been made by Linda's little feet, they were so spaced. . . .

Mark Conrad's progress from that vacant blood-bathed bed to the big clothes-closet in the paneled wall occupied perhaps no more than fifteen or twenty seconds, though he moved with the stiff unnaturalness of a sleepwalker. But in those seconds he was seeing Linda all back down the years.

And in those seconds might have been the beginning of insanity.

Mark Conrad's hand reached at last to the knob of the closet door. So cavernous was the high-vaulted ceiling of the old mansion's guest-room, that the dim night light on the bed only deepened the shadows at its side. The door yielded to Mark Conrad's hand. More than yielded. It swung toward him as if a weight had suddenly been released.

"Linda! Oh God! Linda!"

His big hands caught the slender figure which had pitched abruptly outward. Only vaguely he could see the outlines of the small, pretty face, the curve of the girl's breasts from which the nightgown had been stripped and the torn, gaping redness of the wound which lay just below her throat. It was as if a knife had been driven to its hilt and then ruthlessly twisted to give a final agony to death.

Still soft and warm, the body of the girl lay in Mark Conrad's arms. Blood still oozed slowly from the terrible tear between the breasts. The girl's eyes were closed and now her head was drooping forward, like a bright flower wilted in the sun.

Madness of grief and shock surged through Mark Conrad's big body. His shoulders trembled as he lifted the girl's weight, swinging with her toward the beds. For the moment a dizzying blindness swung across his vision.

The girl was on the bed which Mark Conrad himself had occupied. In an interval encompassing seconds, the man stared down at her. Then with a quick movement he swept the back of his hand across his eyes. Again he stared.

"My God!" he groaned. "I've gone mad! It's Doris!"

HE WHIRLED on his bare feet. This time a new life surged through his veins. With a leap he was beside the bathroom door. He shouted and tore it open.

"Linda! Linda! Where are you? Linda!"

His hand found the wall button, flooded the high room with light. The bathroom was empty. He flung himself toward the door leading to the outside mezzanine landing of the old mansion.

"Norcross! De la Roque! For God's sake! Norcross!"

His big hand clutched at the ancient brass knob of the outside door. It turned and he applied all his strength. The door was locked. Its bolt was of an old-fashioned, ponderous make that defied any man's strength.

Mark Conrad pounded the thick oaken panels with his fists.

"Norcross! De la Roque! Linda!"

No reply came from the outside. In an interval of listening, he could hear only the repeated eerie plaint of the whippoorwill outside the high narrow windows. Mark Conrad crossed the room to these windows, eyes searching for anything that might serve as a weapon to batter through the heavy door.

It came to him then that in all of the big room with its luxurious fittings there was nothing that might serve as such a weapon. He had not noticed this the night before on retiring, but now he saw that the chairs were of only the lightest wicker-work. The twin beds were of a legless box type.

He reached the windows. He had made no note of this the night before, but now he became aware the windows were studded with heavy iron bars. He looked down across the red moon-wash of the lawn toward the Royal Palms that fringed the river shore.

His pulse quickened. Had something moved out there? He couldn't be sure, but it had seemed that the lightless hulk of a launch had moved close to the little landing.

Before he could peer more closely, for the third time that shuddering, sinister sigh breathed in the room.

Mark Conrad's eyes bulged. The girl on the bed had moved. Ever so slightly—but he was sure the sigh, weak as a sob after death, had come from her lips. With a bound he was beside her.

"Doris!"

He bent closely, ear pressed to her throat. Yes, there was the faintest breath remaining in the blood-drained body of the girl who had with such horrifying mystery taken the place of his young wife.

Doris Reynolds, she was. She was the friend of Harvey Norcross, and also a friend of Linda's.

The four of them had come together to the mansion of Professor de la Roque for what was to have been a week-end tarpon-fishing party. The invitation had come through Norcross from the professor, though Mark Conrad had met de la Roque on several occasions down in the town.

Mark Conrad jumped again to the door. He pounded and shouted. No answer came. He caught up a glass and poured some liquor from his pocket flask.

Seeing the hideous wallow of blood on that other bed and the floor, he had no hope for the life of Doris Reynolds. But there might be a slim chance that she could be brought to consciousness.

The liquor bubbled in her death-dried throat. The girl's bloodless bosom rose and fell. Her great dark eyes opened. Her bowed lips moved, whispered. Mark Conrad bent close. Words faint as a far breeze . . . but he heard them with widening eyes. . . .

The faint far breeze whispered out. Mark Conrad drew the golden silk coverlet over the flower-like face. For a full minute he stood listening to the guttural dirge of the frogs in the swamp below.

Thump! Thump! Thump!

The sound that whirled him about was muffled, as if the heel of an unseen hand had pounded the wall.

But in the cavernous room the thumping had no direction. It ceased.

Mark Conrad snapped his brain to patterned thinking. He took a full deep breath, then suddenly he was tearing away the covers of the mattress on which lay the dead Doris Reynolds.

Deathly sweet, the odor struck all the way to his brain. His very proximity to it staggered him for a moment, but his big hands tore at the mattress. He found there a slender rubber tube that ran under the rug. From it streamed the etherizing gas! He tore the tube partly loose, knotting it. Only the open window had aroused him—awakened him too late to become a witness to this bloody crime.

An instant later he had knotted a similar tube in the bed where Linda had kissed him good-night. He turned back to the still form under the coverlet of golden silk. Tangled imaginings seethed in his fevered brain.

Where was Linda?

Had she been spared? Oh had she been stricken by the same diabolical hand that had twisted a knife in the raw, sweet flash of the other girl's bosom?

Except for that brief thumping, silence brooded over the rambling old mansion. Who would be first to open that oaken door?

Doris, with dying whispers, had breathed but little. Extortion, she had said. But what manner of extortion had been plotted?

His being alone in the bedroom with the murdered girl was a circumstance he instantly discarded as having no bearing on the fiendish motive underlying the crime. Those rubber tubes confirmed evidence of long, considered plotting. . . .

ALL this in less than a minute of thinking. Then Mark Conrad was prying at the window bars with his big hands, eyes slanting down upon the dark hulk of the launch now lying motionless as a floating coffin near the river landing. Suddenly he eased his effort.

Under the paling red wash of the half moon two ghoul-like figures were coming up from the river. They carried between them a sheeted burden. A door opened and closed below. Again Mark Conrad hurled himself at the oaken door. It refused to yield.

Thump! Thump! Thump!

Slowly spaced, as if a fisted hand were attempting to signal. Mark Conrad tried to fix the direction. Somewhere behind one of the walls. A surge of hope came to him.

"Linda! Linda!"

Calling the name softly, he started around the walls. The thumping ceased. He was beside the wall near the closet. A prickling sensation crept along the back of his neck. Unseen eyes were upon him. he was being watched. Probably the eyes had been there all the time.

With a quick jump he snapped out the ceiling lights, then the dim light over the murder bed.

As if it had been a sign, demoniac laughter rang from the walls! Somewhere that unseen hand thumped again to the beat of the taunting ribaldry.

Beside the closet in which Doris Reynolds had been placed to die, the wall panels slid apart! And a ghastly blue light flooded the side of the room. . . .

With big hands knotted into fists, Mark Conrad hurled his weight toward the open space. He checked himself only in time to prevent colliding with close iron bars. . . .

He was looking down into another room on the floor below. A gasp of chilled amazement was his only sound for the moment. For he was looking on a scene so gruesomely astounding that his very breath was stopped.

The room below was outfitted as completely as the operating theater of a hospital. A body lay on a table, completely covered by a sheet.

Three gowned figures appeared, wearing gauze masks. Mark Conrad's aching eyes were riveted on one. He was the tallest, with a queer hunch to his right shoulder and a streak of dead-white hair in the blackness of his scalp.

"Professor de la Roque!" he muttered.

The probing fingers of the ghastly blue light must have revealed Mark Conrad's face pressed to the bars. De la Roque looked up and his beady eyes glittered. He spoke with calm incisiveness. His voice still conveyed the impression of culture, but there was something else in it now. A grating, maniacal undertone.

"You are there, Conrad? Yes! Then you are privileged to behold the hands of genius! Study this well, for it is only the beginning, and it is for you to say if it shall go on!"

Mark Conrad's eyes shifted to the bound figure of the man seated in a chair. Norcross! His legs and arms were tied and a gag of black cloth was drawn tightly through his mouth. He was bending forward as if straining to free himself.

Mark Conrad cursed. He tried to find coherent words.

"De la Roque! What is all this madness? For God's sake, man! There has been murder done! Where's my wife, de la Roque? She's all I want! If this is an extortion game, God in heaven, tell me! I'll pay! What is it you want? Anything! Linda! Linda!"

Had the sheeted figure stirred at the sound of his voice?

Again came that demoniacal laughter. It was from the thick and twisted lips of de la Roque. Yet his voice still held a calm, gloating steadiness.

"My good friend Conrad, your wife is alive. Perhaps afterward she may wish she were not. That also we shall see. How much would you pay, friend Conrad, for—well, say one of your wife's beautiful arms?"

"My God, man!" Conrad cried. "Are you crazy? Hasn't enough happened here tonight? Say what you want. How much?"

Was it only the lurid flickering of the light from the blue dome above the operating table, or had the figure under the sheet again moved?

The feet of Harvey Norcross pounded the floor below. His eyes were slanted upward, as if he were trying to tell Mark Conrad something.

"Ah, my friend Conrad! First we must fix the basis on which you will know how to bargain! Watch closely, my friend!"

De la Roque spoke a quick command. His assistants moved to the table. De la Roque's long pointed hands caught up a scalpel. The side of the sheet was flipped suddenly back. One of the others held a white basin.

"God! De la Roque! No, damn you! No! No! No!"

Mark Conrad's cursing speech became a frenzy of appeal.

"Linda! Linda! Oh my God! Linda! . . .

He felt his throat tightening. His words were beginning to bubble as if the blood were being squeezed from his heart to clog his tongue.

The gleaming scalpel flashed downward in the hand of de la Roque. Its razor edge bit through lovely, velvety white skin into the quickly bleeding red flesh beneath. The cries and curses in Mark Conrad's throat were rasping, meaningless sounds. His big hands gripped the iron bars until his knuckles cracked.

Yet de la Roque's hands were steady, swift and sure. . . .

ON THE beautifully tapered hand of the girl under the sheet was the square emerald that had been Mark Conrad's engagement gift, the Conrad family stone. Encircling the finger beneath it was the carved ring of white gold that had welded the love of Linda and Mark Conrad.

De la Roque swung the surgeon's knife in a viciously quick cut. He seized another instrument. A bone grated. Mark Conrad screamed his curses, for the grating had been in his soul.

"Anything, de la Roque! A million! Two million! All I have, de la Roque! I'll pledge you anything! You can take my fortune and go! Spare my wife! Linda! Honey! Damn you! Can't you hear me, de la Roque! Oh, God I'll see you in—"

Mark Conrad's speech died to a gasping moan. The tall figure of Professor de la Roque swung around. Blood dripped, dripped into the white basin. In de la Roque's uplifted hand was the severed arm of the girl! The blood ran unheeded along the fiend's white sleeve. . . .

Before Mark Conrad's hell-tortured eyes the green and white jewels of his love for Linda hung upon the grotesquely quivering fingers of her dying hand. De la Roque shook the amputated arm as a beast might have worried raw meat.

Linda's beautiful hand and arm! Linda maimed for life!

Mark Conrad's curses became shriek upon shriek. And against them the demoniacal laughter of De la Roque rang out. . . .

"You see, my friend! We do not ask your fortune. As she is, you may have her for one million. One million cash! We are not greedy. It is the price—or would you care to see more?"

Mark Conrad screamed out a curse. His fists flailed the iron bars, heedless of the breaking bones in his fingers. Insanity was upon him.

And into the inferno of his brain penetrated again:

Thump! Thump! Thump!

Close beside him in the wall beyond the closet? Or was it in the closet? He heaved his body at the light door, almost tearing it from the hinges. The closet was empty. He whirled back to the bars.

His world stopped, then began again. All the hideousness of this torture became a fantasy no human brain could withstand.

For as he turned, another operating table was wheeled into view. Upon it was another sheeted form. De la Roque's hands pulled the covering downward. Mark Conrad's breath sucked into his lungs with crackling pressure.

His young wife Linda lay upon the table! Stripped down to the waist, she was white and lovely, her face beautiful in the calmness of drugged sleep.

De la Roque's insane laughter filled all the space.

"You see, my good friend Conrad!" he shouted. "That was only a lesson! But it is what will happen if you do not arrange for your friend Norcross here to bring the million to us in cash! Your wife has not been harmed. But unless you accede in silence to our demands, she will be carved bit by bit, as I intend that other one shall be!"

"Linda!" cried Mark Conrad. "Linda!"

Then—"I'll pay it, de la Roque! Before God, I'll pay! Don't touch my wife!"

Linda's lovely arms had been untouched. The tapering fingers of her left hand were ringless.

"Yes. I think you will pay, my friend Conrad," said de la Roque. "We shall send presently to bring you down. You will instruct Norcross what he must do to bring the million. . . ."

Mark Conrad wiped bleeding knuckles across his mouth. With groping slowness his stunned brain strove to free itself from the blood-pounding insanity that had already begun to clog his mind.

Thump! Thump! Thump!

A panel creaked. A step sounded almost beside him.

He whirled. The streaming blue light picked out an imbecilic face, almost at his shoulder. Matted hair fell over burning eyes. Thick beard grew down over the cheeks from the ears. Hands as thin and long as claws were raised.

Mark Conrad's fist already was swinging when the voice hissed: "Wait, Mark! It's Tom! Tom Conley! Do you hear? Don't speak out so they'll know I'm here!"

"Tom Conley?" Mark Conrad breathed.

More than two months before his friend, Tom Conley, and Tom's sister Beth, had disappeared. They had gone upriver from the town on a tarpon-fishing trip. Their car had been found in a swamp. Though a search for the bodies had been fruitless, they were believed to have drowned.

De la Roque and the others were moving down below. The sheet was pulled over Linda's face. Norcross was being unbound. Tom Conley's clawlike hand gripped Mark Conrad's arm. His voice was a hissed whisper.

"Don't believe them, Mark—they'll cut her up anyway. I've been a lunatic, Mark . . . I saw—God! I saw Beth cut to pieces—and I had got them a hundred thousand—They killed her, Mark—you hear? They were keeping me—thought I would regain my reason and get them more money. . . .

"I was crazy, Mark—I think I still am —haven't known anything for weeks. . . Then I saw you and Linda through the wall . . . after awhile I began remembering who I was. I've been hours trying to open that panel. If you get the money they'll cut up Linda—they'll kill all of us. I heard them talking—they're ready to get out when they clean up with you. . .

"They don't mean any of us shall get out alive. . . But there's a way down. Quick, Mark! Come on!"

Dumbly Mark followed him—into the wall—down narrow steps. . . .

INCH by inch the panel in the wall of the lower room slid back. The lurid blue light still gave to faces there the ghastly hue of living ghosts. Mark Conrad pressed close upon the rag-clad figure of Tom Conley.

"When I get the money—"

It was the hoarse, strained voice of Harvey Norcross. The ropes had fallen from his limbs. The gag was off his mouth. His hard-cut jaws worked in the blue light as he stood erect.

De la Roque and the two other men were still in the room. Linda's sheeted figure had been pushed a little to one side. The table on which the other girl lay was close to the panel. The gruesome elbow joint of the severed arm dangled pathetically over the edge of the support.

Mark Conrad saw that it was bloodless! The basin that had been used was setting by. And in it Mark Conrad saw the huge blood-filled sponge that had been employed in De la Roque's trick to make the arm of a corpse appear to be that of a living person—Linda.

Forced to stoop as the panel slid back, Mark Conrad pushed Tom Conley to one side with a straight leap forward. Weaponless, he hurled himself upon the four men. But as his balled fist swung, his feet slipped in the blood on the floor.

A mad oath ripped from de la Roque's thick lips. His hand caught up a gleaming scalpel. Before Mark Conrad could reach him, he had torn the sheet from Linda's body. The scalpel was lifted.

De la Roque's two aides hurled themselves upon Mark Conrad. He went down with their fists hammering at his head. But he slid sideways and one big hand gripped a roller of the table on which Linda's body. The scalpel was lifted.

Linda's unconscious form struck the floor. De la Roque's swinging scalpel had barely touched her smooth throat, leaving a faint red track. A voice cried out, "Hold it! Stop! We'll lose everything!"

De la Roque stood with the scalpel in his hand, lips curled back, eyes glowing with the venom of a disappointed beast of prey.

"To hell with that!" he shouted.

Bending down, he reached out with the flashing knife. Linda's bared bosom was directly beneath.

An animal cry of "Beth! He's cutting you again! Beth!"

The tattered scarecrow bag of bones that was Tom Conley catapulted headlong across Linda's body. The scalpel struck. Its edge went deep in Tom Conley's shoulder.

Mark Conrad struck upward at an evil face. His shattered fist squashed a nose. His knee came up into the shrinking stomach of the other man. As the man rolled over, Conrad got to his feet.

De la Roque, unable to free the knife in Tom Conley's shoulder, had turned to the instrument table. All of the horror, all of the insanity that had come upon him in the room above came back to Mark Conrad as he glimpsed Linda's body lying beside Tom Conley on the bloody floor.

With both broken hands held before him, he dived headlong at the table of gleaming knives. It crashed over and de la Roque went off his balance. But de la Roque had a scalpel in his hand and he struck—and struck again.

Mark Conrad's arms were being slashed to ribbons, but the pain did not touch the madness of what he had endured. He knew not what curved deadly weapons he himself now held. He only pushed his head to one side to avoid the scalpel striking at his throat.

Then with both hands he lashed out—lashed out again and again. . . The face of de la Roque suddenly became a leering bloody mask, crossed like the iron bars in the room above. His screamed curses and the grate and jar of steel on bone shivered through Mark Conrad's maddened senses.

The scalpel fell from de la Roque's hand. He pitched forward, his face shoving a reddened trail across the floor. As he lay still Mark Conrad ceased to strike.

The other two men were crawling through a door. Somewhere a man cursed and screamed in agony. Mark Conrad mopped the blood from his eyes, cleared the haze. Through the dancing mist of his diminishing madness two figures leaped into view.

Tom Conley was on his feet, swaying. He was weaving toward Harvey Norcross and he was pulling, wrenching to free the knife from his shoulder. Norcross smashed his pitiful face with a driving fist, but Tom Conley only laughed—demoniacally.

The knife was in his hand. Norcross cursed and struck again. But Tom Conley surged forward, knife swinging viciously once—only once—in his hand.

The cursing scream of Norcross became a whistling gasp. His huge head rocked back, held on his shoulders by little more than his spine. Blood rushed from the grinning gap of his throat and geysered over Tom Conley.

Norcross sagged forward, glassy-eyed. He crashed as the blood drained out.

"Beth! Dear little Beth! It's all paid now!"

It was Tom Conley mumbling. Mark Conrad pushed him into a chair.

"It's all right, old fellow! All right!"

Some of the madness was leaving Conrad's brain. He went on his knees, gathering Linda into his arms. He kissed her. Her violet eyes were slowly opening. He kissed her again.

THEY were in the launch, drifting slowly down the early morning tide of the Caloosahatchee. Mark Conrad held Linda as if he never would let her go. Tom Conley crouched in the bow of the boat, eyes sick but sane.

"It's all right, Tom," Mark Conrad said. "I knew the whole thing was framed by Harvey Norcross. Doris told me just enough before she died. He killed her when she tried to defend Linda.

"His game was to make it appear he was as much a victim as we were. He didn't intend that either Linda or I was to be killed. De la Roque and the others were to take their share and fade out. Norcross wanted to stay here on the river. He wanted me to keep on believing he had been my friend.

"But you knew, Tom. You weren't insane then. It was best that way. . . ."

A whippoorwill gave forth its early plaint of dawn. Mark Conrad pressed his lips to Linda's warm cheek.

Food For The Devil

Hungry and blood-thirsting, the age-old savage Beast of the Swamp had sucked Janet Randall's sister into the cold maw of the marsh, a warm screaming victim. Yet that did not suffice—still the dark shadow of its lust hung over them, a threat to every living creature in that house of haunted souls . . .

THE driveway from the main road ran along a narrow ridge cutting through the swamp. It turned, climbed a little hill; the lifting beam from the car's headlights pierced the darkness and spread over the house.

It was an immense edifice, just as Janet had written him, dismal and sinister—yet exactly the type of place one would have expected old Cyrus Randall to possess. Obviously it had once been a mansion of some grandeur. Now, however, it had settled; its gables sagged; it seemed to be gradually sinking into the bottomless bog which surrounded it.

Braking slowly, Dick Grant swung his roadster around to a porte-cochère at one side and brought it to a stop. He frowned. This was queer: all the windows in the front had been dark and all those on this side were dark too. But Janet, his fiancée, must be expecting him. He had wired immediately after receiving her letter asking him if he could come.

He twisted, climbed out and started up the steps toward the door. Suddenly, with one foot half raised, he froze.

A wail of anguish floated through the night. . . .

He pivoted on the other foot. He peered into the gloom, listened. For a moment he could hear nothing but the mournful soughing of wind in the trees. Then it sounded again—faint, eerie.

He leaped down the steps to his car, dug a hand in the pocket of one door and

By
George Edson
Novelette
of
Gruesome
Dread

pulled out a flashlight. The weak cry had come from the swamp down the hill. And it was the wail of a woman. He clicked on the flashlight, ran back along the drive.

He stopped as the light caught an opening in the rank growth at one side. It looked like the entrance to a path which might lead down into the bog. For an instant he hesitated in indecision, finally spun and plunged through it.

The path was steep, slippery; it seemed

to be taking him down into the bowels of the earth. The air, as in a subterranean cave, grew cold and clammy. A thin mist swirled up to meet him. A foul odor of stagnant water rose to his nostrils.

But eventually the descent ceased. The single path branched into a maze of ridges twisting into the bog. He paused.

The wail again—nearer, to his right!

He turned, took three or four quick steps along a ridge which seemed to lead in that direction, then halted with a jerk. He heard the patter of running footsteps somewhere behind him. Snapping off his light, he drew out to the side of the ridge and slid back of a clump of brush.

The footsteps approached swiftly. He narrowed his eyes, peered over the top of the brush. A dark figure materialized out of the mist. It ran toward him. And he saw, for one fleeting second, a white face.

"Janet!" He jumped from behind the brush. "Janet! Stop! It's me—Dick!"

JANET RANDALL uttered a startled cry, whirled, stumbled. He caught her in his arms.

"Janet! What is it? What's—"

"Dick!" Her eyes were wide with terror. "That was Elsa—my sister! It's taken her!"

Dick echoed: "It? What—"

"The Thing! The Thing in this swamp! Miss Galt said it would. It took my uncle. He didn't die up there in the house. He died in the mire of this swamp. Now it's got . . . Dick, we've got to find her! Before it's too late!"

"Steady, Jan." He restrained her when she would have broken away from him. "I'll go first."

Switching on his flashlight once more, he turned, pushed through a mass of tangled branches. Then he swung one hand back to grip one of hers.

The ridge grew narrow. Finally it tapered down to a ribbon of firm ground separating two expanses of bog. It ended.

Dick stopped. He tucked his flashlight under one arm, placed cupped hands to his mouth and shouted. The sound of his voice trailed away into the mist.

Then a feeble cry answered, far off.

It came from behind them, still to the right. Dick wheeled, grabbed Janet's hand again and led her back along the ridge of solid ground. He halted, raked the beam from the flashlight out over black mud. It found nothing. He ran on and stopped a second time. And this time the beam found something—white!

A floundering arm! Then a face wrenched around toward the glare cutting the mist! Elsa Randall's face! Her voice pleading weakly:

"Help! Oh, God! Help me! It's pulling me down!"

A choked whimper tore from Janet's throat. Dick gripped her hand tighter. It was well over a hundred feet out to the girl from where they stood. If they could get close, find a log . . .

He dragged Janet behind him as he rushed back vainly in search of another ridge branching off in that direction.

"Dick!" Janet's voice broke into a wild sob. "We've got to get out there to her —save her!"

And from the mire, even more weakly: "Oh, God! Help. . . .!"

Dick stiffened as the cry faded. He wheeled, shot light out on the bog. The arm had disappeared; the face was tilted up to heaven, mud-streaked and terrified.

"Elsa!" Janet strained against Dick's arm. "Elsa!"

A moment of ghastly silence, then: "Janet! Get away! The Thing . . ." And the bog swallowed the white face.

Janet screamed, ripped free, stumbled across the ridge. Dick lunged after her and clutched her by the waist. He pulled her against his chest. "Be brave, dear.

That wouldn't do any good. You've—"

A hideous sound from the darkness interrupted him. A sound like a laugh—a high, insane laugh mocking their grief. It lasted for several seconds; then it trailed off into an ugly snarl and stopped.

Janet whispered, "The Thing!"

DICK swung her behind him, probed the direction from which the laugh had seemed to come with the beam of light. He listened—and sucked a sharp breath between his teeth.

Footsteps were softly tap-tapping. Slow, rhythmic footsteps plodding toward them from beyond the reach of the light. A cold chill stabbed up his spine and pricked the nape of his neck.

"Jan," he spoke softly to her over one shoulder. "someone's coming. I may need both hands. Get ready to take the flash."

He felt her body go tense, heard her breathing quicken.

"Don't be afraid," he continued. "Just do what I say. Run if I tell you to run."

Nearer came the slow footsteps. . . .

"I won't run," Janet said. "I won't leave you here." A glow of warmth almost banished the chill. She had plenty of pluck.

Nearer came the footsteps. . . . Nearer . . . And suddenly a hunched misshapen figure moved into the light.

Dick stared. The man was old; he had an unkempt white beard and long white matted hair. He wore no hat. His shoulders sloped forward as if from some deformity rather than from mere age. His arms, long and powerful in proportion to the rest of his body, dangled limply down below his knees. He blinked like an owl in the bright light of day, asked in a shrill nasal whine: "What's the trouble? I heard someone a-screechin' down here."

Dick didn't answer; he regarded the old man with wary eyes.

"The Thing, eh?" The nasal whine thickened to a croak. "Eh? The Thing?"

Janet said, "It's old Seth Cain. He lives on the edge of the swamp—in one of Uncle Cyrus' huts."

"So it got another one?" The shaggy head cocked itself bird-like over one shoulder. "It'll get ye all, so it will. Like it got Cyrus Randall. If ye don't have the help of old Seth."

"Why your help?" Dick demanded. "What do you know about this Thing?"

Cain started to cackle. Then he sobered, shuffled a few steps. He lifted one long arm, dragged it across his face.

"I know its swamp. I know every nook and cranny of it. I know where the Thing lives"—the arm which he had lowered from his face lifted again and gestured—"out there where no one else can go. Only the Thing—and old Seth."

"He's crazy," Janet whispered. "But he's a harmless old man."

Dick wondered. The hunched body might be aged and deformed; yet there still remained enough strength in those long arms to crush a husky man to death.

"That's why ye'll have to come to Seth," he mumbled again. "Else it'll get ye all—haul ye down into this bog. The swamp's always hungry."

Once more the old man cackled. Then he hitched backward to the edge of the light, turned, slouched into the gloom.

CHAPTER TWO

Spoor in the Shadows

THEY stood there, silent and motionless, for several moments after Seth Cain had left. Finally Dick took Janet's hand in his, drew her away from the spot where they had stood helplessly watching her sister sink into the mire. He found the place where he had met Janet, retraced the route from there.

Reaching the driveway again, they walked sadly up toward the mansion in which Cyrus Randall had lived. It looked more dismal than ever now, squatting there in the darkness like a crumbling tomb—more sinister, with the wind in the trees mourning a monotonous dirge.

They came to the porte-cochère where Dick's car was parked. They started to mount the steps to the door. But suddenly Dick paused, stopped Janet. "Just a minute before we go in, dear. I've got to know what's been happening here. About what you call the Thing. How did it get Elsa? Did you see it?"

"I've never seen it," she answered him in a hushed tone. "I've heard that—that awful laugh twice. Coming from the swamp in the middle of the night. I didn't believe the stories about a monster taking people down to feed the swamp. Oh, Dick" — her face contorted — "it wouldn't have happened if I'd believed! Elsa wanted to leave—wanted to give up all claim to the house! I wouldn't go! I thought it was silly to be afraid!"

Dick slid one arm around her trembling shoulders, murmured: "Easy, Jan. You weren't to blame. Don't let yourself think so for a minute."

"Just a little while ago I went out to the shed behind the house, to get something out of our car. I left Elsa with John and Luther Smith."

Dick knew that John was John Moreau, a cousin to the two sisters and the third heir to old Cyrus Randall's estate; he asked: "Who's Luther Smith?"

"He's a young man who acted as both secretary and nurse to Uncle Cyrus after he became paralyzed. There had to be someone to—"

She stopped, uttered a frightened little gasp and lifted her head as an eerie blue ray of light flickered down over the steps. Dick wheeled. The light came from in-side the house. It was moving toward the door, filtering through stained glass.

And then, as they both stared, the door opened. A lean hand rested on the knob. Janet clutched at Dick's elbow.

Another white hand, holding a kerosene lamp, swung out and up. The light from the lamp played down over a face— the face of a woman.

It was gaunt, sullen—a face which had exchanged a crude beauty for festering hatred. The eyes were two black points of bitterness between narrowed lids.

"Oh!" Janet spoke to Dick rather than to the woman. "It—it's Miss Galt."

Dick had already guessed that. He knew that a woman called Miss Galt had been Cyrus Randall's housekeeper for more than thirty years, ever since Cyrus Randall, soured because of an unhappy love affair, had isolated himself from the world in this forsaken mansion.

The gaunt face twitched, cracked into a leer; the rasping voice jeered: "It got another of you, didn't it? I told you it would. But you wouldn't believe me. No, you thought I was crazy. Maybe you don't think so any longer.

"It got old Cyrus Randall. It'll get all of you if you stay here. All of you!" She uttered a guttural laugh which was like a curse. "It'll feed you to the swamp—to the mud that slowly sucks you under while you squeal like stuck pigs. It'll—"

"That's enough," Dick cut in angrily. "Miss Randall doesn't care to listen."

The black eyes answered his command with a venomonous glare. Then the woman shrugged, turned, stalked down the hall. Presently the light from her kerosene lamp vanished.

DICK snapped on his flashlight, twisted pulled up the cover of the rear compartment in his roadster. He brought out a valise and set it on the running board. From it he produced a revolver which he slipped into a coat pocket. Shutting the valise and stowing it back in the car, he turned to Janet. "We haven't seen your cousin, Moreau. Or this Luther Smith."

"They were with Elsa."

He said grimly: "I know. And that's the reason I'd like to ask them a few questions. If—well, if they're still here. They must've seen this Thing that feeds human bodies to the swamp. Let's go inside and see if we can find them."

Miss Galt had left the door open. They mounted the steps and entered the hall. It was wide and high, but dark panels covering both walls and ceiling made it seem oppressive; the air, despite the open door, remained fetid as air in a crypt. The rays from the flashlight showed a flight of stairs on the right and several doors on the left.

"Down to the end," Janet said. "They were in the library."

There was no carpet on the floor. Their feet, as they walked, made hard sounds which reverberated hollowly through the gloom above them. They reached the corner where Miss Galt had disappeared.

"Here." Janet pointed to a door.

Dick shifted the torch to his left hand, strode up to the door, stretched his right hand out to the knob, stiffened.

From behind that door came a moan.

He glanced at Janet, motioned with his head for her to move back a little. Then he twisted the knob. He swung over the threshold and raked the beam around the room. He centered it on a form sprawled on the floor.

It wasn't John Moreau. It was a young man with blond hair and a stoutish face. Janet, peering through from the hall, confirmed his supposition aloud.

"Luther Smith!"

The young man semed to hear his name spoken. His body quivered, lips twitched; he moaned once more. Dick knelt beside him, slid one arm under his shoulders.

Smith opened his eyes and gazed blankly up into Dick's face. He mumbled: "Where—where am I?"

"You're all right," Dick assured him. "Hold on while I get you up to a chair."

Carefully he hoisted the dead weight of Smith's body and deposited it in the nearest chair. He looked around for Janet. She was gone. He took one lunging stride toward the door, stopped. She had reappeared with a glass of water.

"Don't get out of my sight again, Jan."

They soaked Dick's handkerchief in the cold water and pressed it over Smith's temples. Smith took deep breaths, blinked.

Dick said: "Try to remember what happened to you. Can you?"

"I—I remember some of it." He spoke slowly, laboriously. "We were sitting here—Miss Randall, Mr. Moreau and myself—talking. Suddenly the lights went out—the lights went out and something rushed into the room. It . . ."

Smith's voice clogged in his throat. Abruptly, as if a horrible thought had clicked in his brain, his eyes bulged from their sockets and filled with terror.

"The Thing! That's what came into the room! That's what hit me on the head!" He glanced wildly about him.

"Where's Miss Randall? Mr. Moreau?"

"Miss Randall is dead," Dicked answered in a dull voice. "We haven't found Moreau yet."

SMITH jerked both hands up over his face. Dick turned, crossed to a table, tried the switch on a lamp. Nothing happened. He raised his flashlight and sprayed its rays more carefully around the room.

One window at the end was open. He walked over to it. He leaned out and started to shoot light over the ground—yanked back as Janet cried out to him.

"Dick! Dick!"

He caught her frightened face with the glare from the flash as he spun and leaped toward her. Another face was near hers—a dark, brutish countenance with a low forehead jutting over tiny eyes and yellow teeth between thick, parted lips.

"Who the devil're you?" Dick thrust himself between Janet and the stranger. "What're you doing here?"

The thick lips curled into a leer. "I'm Mose. Miss Galt—she wanted me to come up to the house."

"He works around the place," Janet explained shakily. "He has a room in the barn. I was frightened because I didn't hear him until he was right beside me."

Mose shuffled a couple of steps to one side, his eyes on Janet. Dick saw a lustful gleam creep into them as they wandered down over her body. He clenched his hand into a fist and swung it forward. But Mose jerked his gaze away from the girl, retreated.

"I ain't done nothing," he muttered with a sullen frown. "Miss Galt—she told me to come."

"Get about your business then. She isn't here. Have you seen Mr. Moreau?"

Mose grunted, "I ain't seen no one."

"Where've you been for the last hour?"

"Where?" Mose hunched his huge shoulders, hitched back to the doorway. "Down in the barn, asleep. I'll go find Miss Galt now."

Dick gazed angrily after him as he turned and glided off into the darkness. Then he spun around to Janet, asked: "Has he been bothering you?"

"No." Involuntarily she shuddered. "He hasn't bothered me. Just stared."

Smith, whom Dick had almost forgotten, pushed himself to his feet. He wobbled toward the door. Dick cast a questioning glance at him.

"I guess I'll go up to my room for a minute," he explained wanly. "I feel—a little ill. But if I could help you search for Mr. Moreau . . ."

"Never mind." Dick couldn't keep con-

tempt out of his tone at such cringing fear. "You couldn't help."

Smith gave Janet an apologetic bow, twisted and hurried out of the room. Dick led her over to the window where he had been when Mose had appeared.

"We've got to have a look for Moreau," he told her. "I'll be tough on you, after what just happened to your sister. But I don't dare to let you out of my sight. . . ."

"I want to stay with you," she interrupted. "I'll help you—if I can."

He flashed her a quick glance of admiration, exclaimed gruffly: "You've sure got what it takes!" He swallowed and forced his eyes back to the window. "This Thing—whatever it is—must've taken both your sister and Moreau out of the house through this window. But we haven't heard any cries from Moreau."

Slowly a speculative expression crept over his lean face; tightened the corners of his mouth; his eyes narrowed.

"Jan, you wrote me that your uncle left a queer will. Would John Moreau benefit if your sister and you were dead?"

She hesitated before she answered. And finally breathed: "Yes."

Dick's fingers tightened around the flashlight. The speculative expression became grim as definite suspicion formed in his mind. He straightened—taut.

From the darkness outside came a groan. It quavered through the window to their ears—a groan of pain. . . .

CHAPTER THREE

The Thing Kills Again!

FOR an instant Janet and Dick stood motionless. Then Dick moved. He flung one leg over the sill of the window, ducked his head and shoulders, squeezed through and dropped to the ground. Twisting, he helped Janet follow him.

"It didn't come from far." He flicked his flashlight to the right of them. "There. Just beyond those bushes."

He gripped her elbow as he started to run. With his other hand he continued to spray light over the patch of tangled brush spreading out from the house.

They heard the groan—nearer.

And suddenly, when they circled the end of the brush, they saw a man. He was staggering toward them. His clothes were dishevelled, torn, soiled; his features were distorted with pain and fear.

"John!" Janet cried. "John!"

John Moreau halted, swayed. He was a slender man with black hair. He had black eyes which usually held a mocking gleam; he was something over thirty.

"Janet!" He brought her name out in a whimper. "I—I didn't think I'd ever see any of you again. Oh, God, my head!"

He lifted a trembling hand to his head. Dick caught his shoulder as he reeled, started to crumple.

"Someone knocked me unconscious," he muttered. "I came to in the barn."

Dick lowered his flashlight and gazed at Moreau's shoes. They were covered with mud—black mud.

"Dick," Janet said, "we've got to help him up to the house before he faints."

Dick tightened his lips and nodded. He gave Janet the flash, pulled one of Moreau's arms over his neck and slid a hand around to Moreau's other shoulder.

He dragged Moreau back to the porte-cochère, up to the steps to the library. He let him down into a chair.

"And now, Moreau, you might try explaining how you got so much mud on your shoes. That mud wasn't in the barn."

Moreau twitched forward, stared down at his feet. He stammered: "I don't— yes, I do. I couldn't find a door in the dark and I climbed out a window. I remember I landed in some mud. I had to wallow through it before I could get up toward the house."

Dick grimaced. The story sounded like a feeble attempt to talk his way out of a suspicious spot. Still, wouldn't a man who had guilt to hide plan a better tale in advance? It seemed logical that he would. And Moreau's appearance of great suffering looked genuine. But smart criminals always slipped on simple details; it was easy to simulate pain. And Moreau stood to gain.

"Where's Elsa?" Moreau shifted his eyes from Dick to Janet, and back.

"Elsa is—dead," Janet answered unsteadily.

Moreau jerked stiff, uttered a horrified gasp. He echoed, "Dead? Dead!"

"She died down in the swamp, Moreau." Dick watched Moreau, clipped the words. "In the mire. In the *mud!*"

Moreau started to his feet, sank down to the chair again. His face was ashen. He ran his tongue over his lips and whispered hoarsely: "The Thing! It's true! There *is* a monster in that swamp! And —you believe I'm ..." His voice cracked.

"Oh, Dick!" Janet tugged at Dick's arm. "Don't! He couldn't have done it. He couldn't have murdered Elsa. He's really hurt, Dick. Help him upstairs, to his room. He must lie down a while."

Dick shrugged, murmured: "All right."

He stooped, worked his arm around Moreau's shoulders again. Janet held the light while he lifted Moreau to his feet and almost carried him out to the stairs and up to the second floor. His room was at the end of a long corridor. Janet opened the door. Dick helped him across to the bed and dropped him on it.

For a moment Moreau lay mumbling to himself; then he sighed and became silent.

DOWN in the library once more Dick paced back and forth across the floor. His features were pulled into a frown of deep concentration; his mouth formed a thin, hard line. Suddenly, he stopped, turned and looked at Janet.

"If only there were a telephone here,"

he grumbled. "Somehow we've got to reach the police."

She was sitting in a chair beside the massive table in the center of the room, one hand tightly clenched in her lap and the other holding the flashlight. Her pale face was drawn and weary, her eyes sad. She said: "It wouldn't do any good. Everyone around this district is afraid of the Thing. None of them would go down into that swamp tonight. Besides, only Seth Cain knows the way through it."

"Maybe they wouldn't have to go down into the swamp," Dick mused. Then, as she glanced swiftly up at him: "Jan, do you believe the stories about this Thing?"

"I didn't. But, Dick, I do after—after seeing Elsa. And"—she shuddered— "after hearing that ghastly laugh."

"I don't know," Dick answered slowly. "Tell me how they describe the Thing."

"It's a creature that's half human and half beast. It stands upright—like a man. But it has the head of a huge wolf. Not dark. White, pure white. With gleaming eyes and great fangs. They say it's an obscene hybrid. Really half man and half wolf. And it has roamed that swamp for over two hundred years. It—"

"Two hundred years?"

Janet nodded, explained further: "They claim the devil granted it eternal life and the swamp for a home. That's why it drags living people down to the bogs of quicksand. To pay its debt to the devil. Every so often it has to take one."

"How often?"

"At least every five years. But sometimes it takes more than one in five years."

"Hm." Dick raised one hand and tapped his chin with his fingers. "When did it last take one before your uncle?"

"About three years ago. A young boy from the town. A searching party found the boy's coat near the edge of the swamp. They never found the boy."

Dick dropped his hand, shoved it sav-agely into a pocket. Janet's summary of the stories about the Thing had brought a skeptical light to his eyes. This monster was too fantastical for his practical brain to picture; the entire legend was beyond credence. But what he had seen and heard tonight were things which couldn't be disputed; Elsa Randall had been thrown into a bog of quicksand and some fiend had uttered that insane laugh.

It was reasonable to suppose that the creature who had laughed had committed the murder. But that didn't prove the creature was a monster, half man and half wolf, who paid tribute to the devil with living bodies.

"No," he said. "I don't believe that stuff about the Thing. I believe the Thing's a person. Maybe a maniac—but a person. And I'll think so until I see it myself."

JANET looked doubtful, asked: "But how do you account for the stories, Dick? There must be *something* to them."

"This is how I account for them," he said slowly. "I believe this legend, like all such legends, was built up in the imagination. A couple of hundred years ago, someone wandered into that swamp, slid into a bog of quicksand and was sucked down to death. Someone else knew he'd gone in there and didn't return. It began to work on his imagination. He fancied he heard or saw this monster. And that started the legend. Once started, a legend grows like a weed. Everyone who disappeared was credited to the monster's account. It happened that someone disappeared at least every five years."

"But Elsa—she didn't go down into the swamp by herself! Something carried her there. Uncle Cyrus, too. He was paralyzed and couldn't walk. And what about John and Luther Smith? Who attacked them? Who dragged John down to the barn? What about the laugh?"

Dick nodded. He wheeled, walked slowly across the room and back to the massive table in the center. He pressed one hand to his head.

"I know. There are questions which can't be answered. Who did all those things? And why?"

"You were even suspicious of John."

"I've been suspicious of everyone I've seen so far except you. This old Seth Cain who came shuffling up to us in the swamp right after we heard the laugh. What was he doing there? Miss Galt— why was she so delighted over the tragedy tonight? The degenerate, Mose, asleep in the barn while someone carried your cousin there. Even your cousin, with black mud, like mud from the bog, all over his shoes. And Luther Smith who seems to be an extra around here since your uncle's death. All of them!"

Sighing, Dick heaved himself up on a corner of the table.

"About the laugh we heard, I think someone's making use of the legend. He's committing murders in such a way that people will blame the creature of the swamp. A slick idea—it forestalls too much investigation. But who? A homicidal maniac—a person with a motive?

Janet looked up at him, silently. He knew from her eyes that all his logic had made no impression whatsoever on her; she still believed in the Thing.

He asked her, "Who told you all this about the creature?"

"Miss Galt. And she said she saw the Thing when it came up to the house from the swamp to get my uncle. She told me it had taken everyone who ever owned this house. There were two before Uncle Cyrus. Both disappeared, were never heard of again. She said people believe the Thing resents this house so near the swamp."

Dick thought of the venomous eyes, the bitter face, the jeering manner in which the woman had exulted over Elsa's death. And abruptly he thought of something else. Something which hadn't occurred to him before as being strange. How had Miss Galt known of Elsa's death in the swamp without being told?

HE PUSHED himself off the table. The significance of the detail he had overlooked made his muscles go taut, his breath come faster. He snatched the flashlight from Janet's hand.

"What is it?" Her voice was anxious. "What's the matter, Dick?"

"Something just clicked. Jan, a week ago you received word that your uncle had died and you were to come up here for the reading of his will. You and Elsa. The only other heir was John Moreau, your cousin. You came the day after receiving word. You expected to return the next day. But you wrote me that the will was very queer. It required that you three heirs remain in residence in this house for seven days or forfeit claim to it. What provision was there in the will for your uncle's housekeeper, Miss Galt?"

"She was bequeathed some money. Five thousand dollars. She, with Luther Smith and Mose, was to be allowed to remain here at the same salary as before Uncle's death. And the queerest thing of all—if we showed no desire to possess his property by failing to stay the seven days, it was to go to Miss Galt instead of to us."

"Ah!" Dick breathed. "That's it!"

"What?"

"That's the motive. I'll bet anything that's the motive behind all this. The first idea was to scare you away before you stayed the necessary seven days. That gave birth to the second more desperate idea, if the scaring didn't work. Tonight's the last night of the seven."

"Dick!" Janet leaped to her feet. "You mean you think Miss Galt . . . ?"

"Doesn't the situation point to her— or your cousin? Moreau would have entire possession of this property with Elsa and you out of the way. Miss Galt—with all three of you out of the way."

Janet raised one hand, clutched at her breast at the horrible suspicion.

"You see what that means?" Dick's voice was low, harsh. "It means that you're the next step! In either case!"

Impulsively Janet drew nearer to him; she opened her mouth as if to speak. And suddenly she froze.

From upstairs came a piercing screech.

Dick felt a cold lump rise in his throat. He lurched forward, caught at Janet's shoulder, swung her behind him. He flicked the flash up to shoot light through the doorway into the hall. Frantically he dug his other hand in his pocket and jerked out his revolver.

The screech came again—a banshee cry of stark terror which shrilled through the dismal mansion and faded to an eerie wail. Then footsteps, racing footsteps, sounded in the upper coridor, rushed toward the head of the stair-well.

Dick stood motionless, rigid. The cold lump in his throat stifled his breath. The hammering in his head sent shocks through his whole body. The footsteps reached the stairs, plunged down them.

Dick trained the beam of light past the corner in the hall. It just caught the bottom of the stairs. And a figure streaked into it. The figure stumbled, yanked itself up, whirled. It staggered wildly toward the library. It was John Moreau.

His face was ashen, distorted. His eyes glittered with fear. His lips twitched; saliva drooled over them and slobbered down over his chin. And his neck—a gaping gash stretched up one side from his collar bone to his ear. Blood welled from it in a gushing stream.

"The Thing! The Thing!" Blood oozed from his mouth as he choked out the words. "It's—up there!" He gulped, groaned. He tottered, held himself up to take two more feeble steps—then shivered and sagged to the floor.

And down from the upper corridor of the house shrieked the ghastly laughter of the Thing.

CHAPTER FOUR

Black Terror

DICK swallowed. The throbbing echo of that laughter beat against his ears, beat horror into his brain. Horror, yes, and fear. It had sounded even more evil than it had down in that swamp.

"Dick . . ." Janet cringed against him.

He had to force himself to pull away from her and to spring over to Moreau. He saw that there was no use. Moreau was still gasping but had only a few moments to live. He tightened his lips.

The Thing was upstairs!

He jerked his head toward Janet, said hoarsely, grimly: "Stay here. I'm going up to get that killer."

"Dick!" Her voice shook with fear. "Dick—no! Don't go up there!"

But he had already rushed into the hall and was running toward the stairs. He started up them. At the top he paused, panting just a little; probed light from his flash down the corridor. It was empty.

Moreau's room had been at the end. Its door was open; rays of light shot through to the interior. The other doors along the corridor, Dick noticed, were closed.

Sucking in a lungful of air, he gritted his teeth and strode toward that open door at the end. He held the flash wide of his body, in his left hand. His right hand gripped the hard butt of his revolver. His ears were straining to pick up the slightest sound; his eyes, narrowed and purposeful, were ready to witness anything.

His mind hadn't yet accepted the possibility of an actual monster despite Moreau's choked words, the ugly gash in Moreau's neck, and that last and most inhuman burst of laughter. But he wasn't quite so sure of his reasoning.

He approached the doorway. Now he could see the bed on which he had laid Moreau a little earlier. The spread was twisted away, half on the floor. A dark blotch — Moreau's blood — stood out against the white.

Two more strides to reach the threshold. He took them quickly, grimly, sprayed light around the room.

And then he heard a faint creaking noise from behind him.

He wheeled. His light caught a door part way down the corridor just swinging shut. He raced to it swiftly. It had latched shut, and he had to tuck his flash under his gun-arm to have a free hand for the knob. Ripping the door open, he discovered another corridor. He lifted his left hand to grab the flash. It slipped out of his fingers as he probed for it under his arm, crashed to the floor. It rolled, flickered once.

That single flickering beam struck through another doorway at the side of the corridor. And Dick saw the Thing, or rather, the Thing's head—the head of a great white wolf!

Gleaming yellow eyes stared fixedly at him. Drawn-back lips in a vicious snarl exposed wicked fangs; the head moved. It was exactly as if there were no body beneath it, as if just head were skating along the floor of the next room.

Then the beam of light was gone, leaving him horribly alone. . . .

DICK fired as darkness shut down on him. He fired, leaped across the corridor to fire again. Downward, this time for that doorway gave onto another flight of stairs, not into a room. That was the explanation of the head's queer position.

He heard footsteps below him, muffled as if they had rounded a corner. He groped for a rail to guide him through the utter blackness, found one, and plunged down the stairs into the black abyss. Evidently his shots had gone wild of their mark; the footsteps were pounding through the house. A door slammed, and he could no longer hear them.

Instead he heard a distant frantic cry. It sent a wave of icy terror over him, terror which clutched his heart and turned it into a frozen weight in his breast. That cry had come from Janet! Janet—left alone in the path of the Thing!

Dick shouted, rushed frantically toward the front of the house. He had no idea of the plan of this section; he crashed against chairs, tables, walls. Once he tripped over a low object and pitched to the floor. His revolver flew out of his hand. He heard it carom off something, slide across the floor. But he didn't take the time to hunt for it. He scrambled to his feet, dragged air back into his lungs and stumbled on again.

A second cry, stifled in the middle, quavered to his ears. It sounded more distant than the first. Sounded almost as if it had come from outside the house.

He smashed into a door. Frenziedly he clawed at it, struck the knob and yanked it open. He thought that he must be near the library by now.

"Jan! Jan!"

A breeze fanned his right cheek. He twisted. One hand found the frame of a doorway. He shoved through it; one foot kicked something and again he fell.

His fingers jabbed skin—flesh. Slipped over it, over a spot that was wet and sticky, stubbed against the floor. Moreau's body? He jerked the hand up and fumbled over the clothes. Yes, a man's. He felt momentary relief. Then he heard the third cry.

It *did* come from outside the house. The breeze wafted through the window.

He hurled himself up and across to the window. Squeezed through, rushed around the patch of brush where they had met Moreau, across a stretch of uneven lawn.

Suddenly, out of the darkness ahead of him, loomed a dilapidated building. The barn where Mose slept and to which Moreau had been taken earlier that night.

Peering at it as he ran, Dick thought he saw the outline of a moving figure against one wall. A figure—grotesque in shape, as if it carried a burden over one shoulder—which glided along that wall and vanished through the middle of it.

A chaos of wild thoughts streamed through Dick's head. Moreau had been taken to the barn. . . . There must be a passage through to the swamp behind it. . . . Janet . . .

He reached the wall along which he had seen the figure move, the part of the wall where the figure had disappeared. There was a small door. He yanked it open and plunged through to the inside.

Heavy blackness clamped down on him. He stood motionless, tried to hold his breath and listen. He stiffened. He heard a faint moan. He couldn't spot the direction; it seemed to come from his left. He twisted to the left and groped one foot forward a step.

He heard the moan again—a little louder. And vague sounds of movement. He doubled one fist; the other arm he stretched out before him and swung back and forth in a continual arc. He took two or three slow steps.

His swinging hand struck a body.

He lashed out at it with the doubled fist. He felt the fist land, grind into flesh. Felt that and heard the swish. Instinctively he tried to duck. But he was too late. Something crashed down on his head and hurled him into oblivion.

HIS first consciousness was of splitting pain in his head and churning nausea at the pit of his stomach. He attempted to open his eyes; the agony of the effort made him stop. He lay still for a minute. And gradually the pain in his head and the nausea lessened.

Then memory returned to him. Janet. . . . The Thing. . . . It had carried her down to the barn. He yanked his eyes open and started to push himself to his feet.

Burning agony racked his body when he stirred it. But he tightened his lips, gritted his teeth, and forced himself to rise. He wobbled and swayed, as he came erect. He had to fight off a relapse into unconsciousness.

What was he going to do? He had to lash his mind to think clearly. How would he have any chance to find Janet and save her from the monster? Cold sweat oozed out of his pores. He didn't know how long he had been lying here. By now, perhaps . . .

He cast that thought out of his mind. He couldn't give up hope. Old Seth Cain knew the way through the swamp.

Dick twisted. He had to find Cain's hut on the edge of the bog. Fervently he prayed he could do it soon enough. He dug one hand in a pocket for a match to show him the door.

Match in hand and thumbnail set to scratch the head, he froze. A low murmur, like a chanting voice, struck his ears.

He held his breath and listened. The sound seemed to float up from somewhere beneath him. He dropped to his knees, bent down toward the floor. The murmur was louder. And then—his heart almost ceased beating—he heard a quivering cry. The cry of a girl!

Swiftly he straightened, rose. His thumb twitched; the nail scraped the head of the match and brought flame. He raked his eyes around him.

He was in a small room which had evidently once been used for harness storage. Lines of wooden pegs stretched across the walls; from a few, odd straps and bits of harness hung. An open doorway to his right led out into another part of the barn. He swung through into it, saw a door to his left.

The match flickered out. He crossed to the door in darkness, then lit another. He eased the door back a little and held the match up to the crack.

Stairs, going down into a cellar. The voice was much louder now—a gloating, lustful voice.

Dick extinguished the second match. He pulled the door open a bit wider, slipped through to the stairs. Careful not to make any noise, he let the door close behind him, started to descend. Dank, fetid air assailed his nostrils; clammy dampness oozed over him.

He stopped for just a second. His head had dropped below the level of the ground floor. His searching gaze caught a vertical crack of dim light to his right, across the cellar. He hurried down the rest of the stairs and turned.

The door into a room off the main section of the cellar was ajar. From that room came the voice.

He drew in a jerky breath as he crept toward that crack of light. He reached the door and peered through into the room beyond it. He saw a rickety table against a slimy stone wall; on the table stood a kerosene lamp. He flicked his eyes across the room—and a cold wave of horror swept over him. Then wild fury lashed through the horror, swirled a red mist over his vision.

Stretched on the earthen floor near the wall at that side was a tattered, filthy mattress. Janet lay on it.

Her dresh had been ripped from her shoulders. She was unconscious now; her slender body was quiet except for the faint movement of her white breasts; her face was like a beautiful visage carved from pure white marble.

Crouched over her, slobbering lascivious sounds between gloating phrases which made horrible sense, pawing at her naked torso, was Mose.

HIS tiny piggish eyes glistened with obscene lust as he ran them over the still form; his thick lips, drooling saliva, twitched. His powerful shoulders quivered with passion.

"I ain't gonna let the swamp have ye. . . . I'm gonna keep ye myself. . . . Here where no one'll find ye. . . . I fixed that smart guy upstairs. . . . And I'll toss him in the bog before he ever wakes up. . . ."

Dick clutched at the edge of the door, yanked. He plunged through into the room.

Mose uttered a grunt of surprise as he jerked up his head and saw Dick coming toward him. He lurched to his feet. The grunt thinned into a vicious snarl of rage; the lust in his eyes flamed into a different kind of lust, the lust to kill. He sprang toward the center of the room, set himself, heaved a bludgeoning fist at Dick's face.

Dick slipped under it. Then, straightening, he whipped a hard right up to Mose's jaw. The man's head snapped back. Dick followed with a short left to his stomach.

The degenerate retched out a groan. He staggered, caught himself, lunged forward. He clawed at Dick's shoulders, but Dick ducked and slid out of reach. The thing he had to avoid was the crushing grip of those massive arms.

He seized an opportunity to escape them, to crash another right to the jaw. Bone crunched. He felt Mose totter, ploughed in for a left and right. But the blow on the head a little while ago had slowed his speed. He didn't get out of danger quick enough. The flailing arms clamped around him.

He strained against them, jolted, wrenched. Still they held—held and tightened. It was as if he were locked in a gigantic vise. Air whistled out of his lungs; his head whirled, eyes dimmed. One arm was jammed between his chest and Mose's. He concentrated all his strength on working it up toward Mose's throat.

His fingers touched the skin, dug into the soft flesh and pressed the windpipe. Hissing out a curse, Mose slammed his chin down on Dick's wrist in an effort to break the hold. But Dick gripped the windpipe harder—still harder—and then, with a heave from his shoulder, he pushed.

Mose's arms loosened; he reeled back a step. Dick sucked breath into his burning lungs, shook his head. He dragged himself to one side as Mose pawed at him.

And he stiffened when Mose, half off balance, tried to twist. He struck out with every ounce of power left in his aching body. His fist clipped Mose flush on the mouth. Gurgling, spewing blood, Mose quivered and swayed. His eyes rolled, glazed; his huge arms slowly went limp and dropped. He crumpled to the filthy floor.

Dick turned and stumbled over to Janet. He bent to his knees, raised her head, whispered: "Jan! Jan!"

She stirred and moaned. Then, as if memory had pierced through her unconsciousness, she began to struggle against him.

"Jan! It's me—Dick! You're all right!"

Slowly, fearfully, she opened her eyes. The terror went out of them when she saw him; she trembled and uttered a low cry.

"It's all over, Jan. It's—"

"Where—where is he?" She twisted her head and saw the sprawled form on the floor before Dick could answer. "Oh! —Dick!"

Dick said softly: "Let's get out of here. You've seen enough of that fiend. Put my coat on, dear."

He pulled off his suitcoat and held it for her arms. Rising, he helped her to her feet.

"What are you going to do with him?" she asked in an anxious voice.

"There're some straps upstairs. I'm going to truss him up and leave him here until morning."

She said: "I'll get the straps. I know where they are. He'll recover and escape if you leave him alone for a minute."

"All right, Jan," Dick agreed reluctantly. "But hurry! I hate to let you out of my sight again, even though I'd better stand over this devil until he's strapped." A grim gleam crept into his eyes. "Take the lamp. I've got matches."

Janet took the lamp from the table and hurried out through the doorway. Dick struck a match. Mose hadn't stirred, didn't look as though he were going to soon.

Dick heard Janet climb the stairs and cross the main section of the barn toward the harness room. There was a moment of silence, and then suddenly he heard her scream.

He wheeled, plunged out of the room, across to the stairs. He scrambled up them in a frenzy.

And, from above, he heard the hideous mocking laughter of the Thing.

CHAPTER FIVE

Into the Swamp

HE REACHED the top of the stairs and rushed toward the harness room. Wild thoughts careened through his head.

Mose wasn't the Thing. . . . The Thing was still at large. . . . It had Janet. . . .

The harness room was deserted. The kerosene lamp Janet had carried upstairs with her stood on a shelf on one wall, cast flickering light around it. Dick lunged across to the door. He ripped it open and ran outside.

Another burst of ghastly laughter split the night.

He wheeled, dashed in the direction from which it came. The Thing wasn't far away from him. Down the hill a little, toward the swamp! That discovery sent terror crawling over Dick. He didn't know the route into the swamp from this side; he didn't have a flashlight. Yet the Thing was running toward it, and the Thing had Janet!

Tangled underbrush covered the lower part of the hill. He crashed into it, ploughed through it; he didn't even try to protect his face by holding an arm before his eyes. As yet, he had been able to see nothing, could only hear the chilling laughter.

It rang out again, and it didn't sound so far away this time, from somewhere to the right. He veered, found that the descent became more abrupt. The air, just as before, grew colder. A dank mist swirled over him; the stench of mud and slime struck his nostrils. The ground under his feet got slippery, soggy.

He stopped a second, stifled his breath to listen. Footsteps sounded still further to the right. Then another laugh—almost as if the Thing wanted him to follow. Perhaps it did; perhaps this was a scheme to get rid of him, to draw him into the bog where he was almost sure to make a misstep.

Dick set his jaw at a defiant tilt and pounded on, swiftly desperately, toward the last laugh.

He lost the path of firm land, wallowed into clutching mud, but managed to drag himself back to safety. A few steps more, and he again stumbled into the bog. Quicksand sucked at him hungrily, greedily; he grabbed at some overhanging growth and pulled clear.

Now the laughter which floated out of the mist ahead was mocking and triumphant.

Dick crawled on hands and knees through the brush. One hand touched something cold and slimy, something that hissed, slithered away over his wrist. Involuntarily he shivered. He heaved himself to his feet.

He seemed to be hemmed in by a high fence of thorny growth. The points of the thorns tore his face and hands as he ploughed through. He broke into the open, found that he was running up a little hill.

And then he saw a light.

He jerked to a halt, stared. A light out here in the middle of the swamp! It was faint, unsteady, eerie through the mist. He drew in a slow breath and plunged toward it.

The mist grew thinner as he mounted the little hill; the light became brighter. As he came nearer he saw that it came from a small hut. He crept up to the window. At the sight which struck his eyes, he froze with terror. Janet lying unconscious, half-naked on the floor. Bending over her, jaws parted in a vicious blood-lusting snarl, was the Thing!

HORROR constricted Dick's chest; for one brief instant it made him weak and sick. Then frenzy seized him. He wheeled from the window to rush around the house in search of an entrance. He found the door, smashed against it, crashed it open, lunged through to the inside.

The Thing lifted its great beast's head, jerked erect and rasped out a menacing snarl.

Dick ducked when he saw the knife

flash. He heard it whine over his head, bite into wood; then he rushed.

In the second it took to cross the room, Dick saw that the Thing's body, a human body, was clothed in black. A black scarf bound around the neck separated human shoulders from wolf's head. The head itself was immense, ponderous compared to the size of the body.

Then he was grappling with the Thing.

He realized immediately that he had met his match. The monster had long arms of terrific strength and a crafty brain to control that strength. It avoided telling blows with incredible cunning, concentrated its own efforts on clenching its human hands around Dick's throat.

Finally, it succeeded, but Dick twisted, wrenched until he managed to pull free. He swung a vicious left and right at the snarling maw. The left missed; the right hit it. His knuckles cracked and pain streaked up his forearm from the force of the blow, but it had no effect on the Thing.

The powerful hands clutched Dick's throat as he tried to lash out another left at its body. He choked, jolted back. The hands loosened, almost instantly gripped again. Dick felt his face swell, his tongue loll out of his mouth. He knew his eyes were popping and his face blackening.

His right hand was useless. The knuckles must have broken because he could no longer clench it. He drew back his left, tightened his shoulder and struck cruelly at the Thing's stomach.

The Thing retched out with pain. Dick grasped the opportunity; he forced his chin down and yanked, tore himself free from the throttling fingers.

He jumped to one side as the hands clawed out at him, gulped in great breaths of air. Strength oozed back into his muscles. The blood ran down from his head, but his brain cleared.

The Thing had recovered enough from the blow in the stomach to spin and leap after him. Dick dropped to a crouch, set himself, met the Thing with his left fist swinging into its belly once more. He turned the fist as it struck.

Wind whistled out between those parted jaws. The Thing doubled forward, stumbled. Its long arms flopped; its shoulders shook; it sagged to the floor.

For a moment, it writhed there, choking, groaning. Dick bent down over it. The snarling jaws didn't move. The Thing's eyes were glassy and set.

Then he saw the slits underneath the fixed eyes, saw living eyes glowing out through them. He whipped his left hand under the maw. He jerked at it. Once—twice—and the head held. But the third time he yanked the black scarf ripped. The head came loose, bounced to the floor.

And Dick looked down into the face of Luther Smith.

SUDDENLY Janet's voice screamed: "Dick! Look out!"

Dick whirled. Janet had regained consciousness; she was staring past him, trying to point. He started to twist—and sharp fire dug into his thigh as a roar shook the room.

His body shook from the impact of a searing blow. He tried to keep on his feet. His gaze, centering on the doorway even while he fell, caught Miss Galt. Her gaunt face was distorted, her black eyes glistening with hate. One outstretched hand gripped a snub-nosed revolver.

"Luther!" She took two or three steps into the hut. "Are you hurt?"

"No, Mother." Luther Smith wobbled to his feet. "But you got here just in time. I didn't think this fool"—he gestured toward Dick—"would have the luck to come this far. I drew him into the swamp. I thought he'd slip into quicksand."

"You shouldn't have taken a chance."

"I know." An evil grin curled Luther Smith's lips. "But it doesn't matter now. We'll slip him into it."

Dick struggled to rise. Pain, stabbing pain which streaked from his leg to every part of his body, made him sink back to the floor. He saw Janet pull herself to her knees. Smith strode across the room and smashed her in the mouth. She moaned, slumped.

Dick shouted: "You damned devil! Keep your hands off her!"

"Shut up!" Miss Galt glared at him, then venomously at Janet. "And you! Whine for mercy—like your uncle did! You'll get none! You're going to die! You're the last one between us and the property that's rightfully ours. Mine and Luther's. Luther—Cyrus Randall's own flesh and blood which he wouldn't own.

"Because Luther wasn't by that other woman who ran away from him—his eternal love, he called her—he made me his housekeeper and called Luther an illegitimate brat. But he called him that once too often. We dragged him down and threw him in the bog."

The old crone rasped out a harsh laugh.

"It's easy enough to get away with murder around here where the fools all believe in the Thing. But we didn't want to overdo it. We tried to scare you away before the lapse of seven days specified in that crazy will. You wouldn't go. So you die. Come, Luther."

Luther was standing over Janet and looking down at her. An evil expression distorted his features. Suddenly he stooped, ripped open the coat Dick had given her. She uttered a little cry. He clutched her hair with one hand as she tried to jerk away from him; with the other he smashed her again in the mouth. Slowly he straightened.

"Not this one, Mother. We'll dispose of her sweetheart, but I'm keeping her."

His voice rose, took on a crazy tone. "Illegitimate, am I? Not good enough for the Randalls? Well, I'm going to be plenty good for one of them. You'll crawl in front of me; you'll beg—plead—even pray to me."

Horror twisted Janet's face, glazed her eyes; she tugged Dick's coat over her breasts. In a frenzy of rage Dick tried to raise his body.

"No, Luther," his mother mused. "Better to throw her into the swamp. Seth Cain knows about this hut you built once and he—"

"I'll kill him," Luther growled savagely. "I'll feed her to the swamp, after I'm through with her. But first—"

"SHE'S mine!" The hoarse shout came from outside the hut. "Ye devils! I've found ye! She's mine and I'm takin' her!"

A hulking figure lunged through the doorway—Mose—slathered with mud, his tiny eyes burning with mad passion. He lifted a huge club and went for Miss Galt.

She fired just before the club crashed down on her arm. Dick, pushing up on one foot, saw Mose stagger, saw the revolver fly out of her grasp. He spun, dove for it, grabbed the butt in his left hand. He rolled over as Smith started toward him.

"Get back!"

Smith stopped. Slowly, as he stared at the muzzle of the gun aimed at his stomach, a beaten look crept into his eyes. He wheeled toward the door.

Dick jammed the trigger. Smith's shoulders twitched, but he didn't halt. He disappeared into the night.

"Luther! *Luther!*"

Screaming, the frenzied man's mother rushed after him. Dick levelled the revolver, began to tighten his finger on the trigger again, loosened it. He couldn't shoot down a woman—not even a female devil—when she was running to her son.

His head whirled; he could feel an insidious numbness crawl over him. Vaguely he heard a man's voice utter a terrified shout, a woman's shrill shriek mingle with it. Then he heard nothing. A black heaving void overwhelmed him.

* * *

For a moment he was aware only of the cool soft hands stroking his hot brow, of a soft voice murmuring close to one cheek. But presently he opened his eyes and gazed up into Janet's anxious face.

"Oh—Dick!" Tears quivered on her eyelids. "Are—are you comfortable?"

He gave her a reassuring smile, answered: "Yes, Jan. Where are we? What happened?"

"We're in Seth Cain's cabin. He heard the shots and came out to the hut in the swamp. He carried you back here. Now he's gone to the nearest house to telephone for a doctor. Dick, he isn't crazy at all. I think Miss Galt told me that because she was afraid he might suspect about Uncle Cyrus' death and talk to us. And he did have suspicions too! He knew that Luther Smith could find his way around the swamp, and even that he had built that little hut there years ago. But he didn't dare to say anything until he could prove it."

Dick sighed. His leg hurt like hell, but he didn't seem to mind the pain much while Jan kept a hand on his forehead.

Suddenly he asked: "What happened to Smith and Miss Galt after I wandered into oblivion?"

"The swamp." Involuntarily she shuddered. "He must have slipped in his hurry. She tried to save him but was dragged down, too. Seth saw them."

"Well," Dick murmured, "it's all pretty clear now. Miss Galt turned off the lights when you were out in the shed. Smith knocked out Elsa and Moreau. He dragged Moreau to the barn where he wouldn't be found, probably with the idea of taking him down to the swamp as soon as he had time, using him to shift suspicion away from himself until then. He came back to the house after murdering Elsa and pretended he had been hit on the head.

"Then he ducked off to his room, put on black clothes and that head which he probably got to scare you, and went after Moreau. He'd heard us take Moreau upstairs. There he slipped a little. He had to use a knife on Moreau. Mose grabbed you just as Smith was running away from me. So we got switched to him.

"But Mose furnished the break in the end. When he barged into that hut. What happened to him?"

"He died from the bullet wound. They're all dead. Elsa and John and. . . ."

"All except you murdered for possession of that dismal mansion. It wasn't worth it."

"Dick." Her voice was vibrant. "I never want to see the place again. Never—as long as I live."

Dick gazed into her eyes, replied emphatically: "As long as *we* live you mean, don't you, sweetheart?"

For an answer, she clung a little closer to him.

THE END

Only by Actual WEIGHT RESISTANCE can you obtain muscles like these! My system does not depend on the mere "flexing" of muscles... I use disc dumbbells that can be graduated in weight for the reason that I believe that no other method can give you strong, supple weight lifting muscles!

Send for "MOULDING A MIGHTY CHEST" A Special Course for Only 25c. It will be a revelation to you. I give you my secret methods of development illustrated and explained as you like them. Don't wait... mail your order NOW!

*IF YOU DO NOT ADD AT LEAST 3 INCHES TO YOUR CHEST

...*it won't cost you one cent!"* — Signed: GEORGE F. JOWETT

THREE SOLID INCHES of muscles added to your chest and at least two inches added to each of your biceps, or it won't cost you a penny. I know what I am talking about ... I wouldn't dare make this startling agreement if I wasn't sure I could do it.

All I want is a chance to prove it! Those skinny fellows who are discouraged are the men I want to work with. I'll show them how to build a strong man's body... and do it quickly. And I don't mean cream-puff muscles either. Wouldn't you, too, like to get a he-man's chest like the idealized figure above? I will show you how to get real, genuine invincible muscles that will make your men friends respect you and women admire you!

So many of my pupils have gained

GEORGE F. JOWETT
"Champion of Champions"
Winner of many contests for strength and physical perfection!

tremendous development that I am willing to stake my reputation that you can do the same... remember...if I fail it will cost you nothing!

Nothing Can Take The Place of My Weight—Resistance Method With Progressive Dumbbells!

The Jowett System features the weight resistance method that has been tested and endorsed by many of the world's most famous strong men. By using this proven, scientific system of graduated weights, you can quickly develop your muscles and broaden your chest!

Send for "MOULDING A MIGHTY CHEST" A SPECIAL COURSE FOR ONLY 25c.

I will not limit you to the chest, develop any part or all of your body. Try any one of my test courses listed below at 25c. Or, try all six of them for only $1.00. You can't make a mistake. The assurance of the strongest armed man in the world stands behind these courses!

FREE BOOK WITH PHOTOS OF FAMOUS STRONG MEN!

RUSH THE COUPON TODAY AND I WILL INCLUDE A FREE COPY OF

"Nerves of Steel...Muscles Like Iron"

It is a priceless book to the strength fan and muscle builder. Full of pictures of marvelous bodied men who tell you decisively how you can build symmetry and strength the Jowett way! Reach out—Grasp this Special Offer.

JOWETT INSTITUTE of PHYSICAL CULTURE
Dept. 35Lc, 422 Poplar Street, Scranton, Pa.
Send by return mail, prepaid, the courses checked below, for which I am enclosing $

☐ Moulding a Mighty Arm, 25c ☐ Moulding a Mighty Chest, 25c
☐ Moulding a Mighty Back, 25c ☐ Moulding Mighty Legs, 25c
☐ Moulding a Mighty Grip, 25c ☐ Strong Man Stunts Made Easy, 25c
☐ All 6 Books for $1.00.

Name _____

Address _____

...."I have REDUCED MY WAIST EIGHT INCHES WITH THE WEIL BELT!"

...writes George Bailey

"LOST 50 POUNDS" says W. T. Anderson ..."My waist is 8 inches smaller" writes W. L. McGinnis ..."Felt like a new man" claims Fred Wolf... "Wouldn't sell my belt for $100" writes C. W. Higbee.

■ So many wearers are delighted with the results obained with the Weil Belt that we want you to test it for ten days at our expense!

REDUCE YOUR WAIST 3 INCHES IN 10 DAYS
... or it won't cost you a penny!

■ Because we have done this for thousands of others...because *we know* we can do as much for you...we dare to make this unconditional offer!

■ You will appear much slimmer at once, and in 10 short days your waistline will actually be 3 inches smaller... three inches of fat gone...or it won't cost you one cent.

IT IS THE MASSAGE-LIKE ACTION THAT DOES IT!

■ Now there is an easy way to reduce without exercise, diet or drugs. The Weil Health Belt exerts a massage-like action that removes fat with every move you make.

■ It supports the sagging muscles of the abdomen and quickly gives you an erect, athletic carriage. Many enthusiastic wearers write that it not only reduces fat but it also supports the abdominal walls and keeps the digestive organs in place...that they are no longer fatigued...and that it greatly increases their endurance. You will be more than delighted with the great improvement in your appearance.

NO DRUGS, NO DIETS, NO EXERCISES

■ For 12 years the Weil Belt has been accepted as ideal for reducing by men in all walks of life...from business men and office workers who find that it removes cumbersome fat with every movement...to active outdoor men who like the feeling of protection it gives.

"I suddenly realized that I had become a fat man". The boys kidded me about my big "paunch".

At parties I learned that I had become a "wall flower". Nobody wanted to dance with me.

In a bathing suit...I was immense. The day I heard some children laugh at me I decided to get a Weil Belt.

What a change! I looked 3 inches slimmer at once and soon, I had actually taken EIGHT INCHES off my waist... and 20 pounds off my weight!

It seemed to support the abdominal walls and keep the digestive organs in place . . . and best of all, I became acceptable for insurance!

I have a new feeling of energy and pep . . . work better, eat better, play better...I didn't realize how much I was missing!

DON'T WAIT ... FAT IS DANGEROUS!

Fat is not only unbecoming, but it also endangers your health. Insurance companies know the danger of fat accumulations. The best medical authorities warn against obesity, so don't wait any longer.

■ *Remember this*...either you take off 3 inches of fat in 10 days or it won't cost one penny! Even the postage you pay to return the package will be refunded!

SEND FOR 10 DAY FREE TRIAL OFFER

THE WEIL COMPANY, INC.
4811 HILL ST., NEW HAVEN, CONN.

Gentlemen: Send me FREE, your illustrated folder describing The Weil Belt and giving full details of your 10 day FREE trial offer and Unconditional Guarantee!

Name_____

Address_____

City_____ State_____

Use coupon or send name and address on a penny postcard

125

THE BLACK CHAPEL

HAVE you ever been seized by some such nameless fear as that which held Ralph Dean in its grip that bleak, storm-riven night on Oldun Island? Arthur Leo Zagat tells us that in writing this scene of his masterly tale, *Thirst of the Living Dead, he lived himself this fear.* When the howling of the wind outside was like the wailing of a lost soul, he says, he heard then something that was not the storm fumble at the door. It bristled the hair about his neck, sent whimperings of ancestral fear up from his throat. . . . His blood went cold, and for a moment he dared not leave his desk to learn what waited for him there. Terror, stark gripping terror held him motionless! . . .

If you haven't felt such things yourself, then we know you've wondered. . . . Countless times you've asked yourself, as has every man with a drop of red blood in his veins, how you would react if fear greater than it is most men's lot to bear, came suddenly upon you. Would your eyes distend and your heart leap to your throat? Would the very blood in your veins turn to ice, and the strength drain from your limbs and leave you motionless? Or would something snap within you, and drive you screaming into the night?

Countless times you've asked yourself what your own reaction would actually be. . . . And so, next month, we're offering you the opportunity to learn. . . . If you wonder how, you'll cease to once you've read Laurence Donovan's spine-chilling novelette. *The Crawling Mad-*

ness, in the next issue of Terror Tales. For that yarn will make of fear a living thing within your breast, a breathless reality of stark terror that will stifle you and turn your bones to ice. Read it where you will—alone in the dim lamplight or in a lighted room with your family all about you—it will make no difference. For before you've finished the first page you will be alone—alone in the darkness with horror reaching out its clammy hands to seize you!

Nor need you stop with that. For you'll find other stories, equally terrifying, side by side with *The Crawling Madness* — other hair-raising, spine-tingling yarns by such authors as Arthur Leo Zagat and Frances Bragg Middleton, H. M. Appel, etc. Masters at the art of stimulating you—with the stimulus that terror alone can give!

SALUTE the line-up of first class fighting men you'll meet in the October 1st issue of *Adventure*, on the newsstands now. There's Just Another Jones, who jokes as he rides single handed into Satan's Pit to clean up the West's most dangerous gang of outlaws. Robert E. Pinkerton writes about him in a stirring complete novelette. There's Barry, who proves to a young cavalry officer that he is something more than just a gambler in the draft riots of the Civil War. Donald Barr Chidsey tells his story. The wild night of a Legionnaire— that's told by Kingsley Moses and Curtis Thomas. A young pugilist fights the fight of his life in Eddy Orcutt's story. White men come to grips with dangerous head hunters in a thrilling yarn by Frederick Moore. In Ared White's serial America's ace secret service agent dares a thousand hazards in Germany. Andrew A. Caffrey tells the true story of the first bold balloon flight across the channel. And in Weston Martyr's complete novelette—there are two in this issue—six ship loads of men from as many nations fight for the treasure of a pearl laden lagoon. It's on sale now, the October 1st issue of

Twice a Month **Adventure** 15c

NEW LOW PRICES

GOOD YEAR

Firestone-Goodrich

U.S. AND OTHER TIRES

SAVE ON TIRES NOW

$2.15
29 x 4.40 - 21

Save money on all standard brands, reconstructed by the special Adamite scientific process. Adams tires are fully guaranteed to give best of service under severest road conditions for 12 full months and are backed by the vast financial resources of this well-known company. Now is the time to buy before prices advance.

12 MONTH WRITTEN GUARANTY BOND
WITH EACH TIRE!

BALLOON TIRES		
Size Rim	Tire	Tube
29x4.40-21	$2.15	$0.85
29x4.50-20	2.35	0.85
30x4.50-21	2.40	0.85
28x4.75-19	2.45	0.95
29x4.75-20	2.50	0.95
29x5.00-19	2.85	1.05
30x5.00-20	2.85	1.05
28x5.25-18	2.90	1.15
29x5.25-19	2.95	1.15
30x5.25-20	2.95	1.15
31x5.25-21	3.25	1.15
28x5.50-18	3.35	1.15
29x5.50-19	3.35	1.15
30x6.00-18	3.40	1.15
31x6.00-19	3.40	1.15
32x6.00-20	3.45	1.25
33x6.00-21	3.65	1.25
31x6.50-19	3.60	1.35
32x6.50-20	3.75	1.35
34x7.00-20	4.60	1.65
35x7.00-21	4.60	1.65
ALL OTHER SIZES		

CORD TIRES		
Size	Tire	Tube
30x3	$2.25	$0.65
30x3½	2.35	0.75
31x4	2.95	0.85
32x4	2.95	0.85
33x4	2.95	0.85
34x4	3.25	0.85
32x4½	3.35	1.15
33x4½	3.45	1.15
34x4½	3.45	1.15
30x5	3.65	1.35
33x5	3.75	1.45
35x5	3.95	1.55

HEAVY DUTY TRUCK TIRES		
Size	Tire	Tube
30x5	$4.25	$1.95
32x6 8ply	6.95	2.75
32x6 10 "	7.95	2.75
36x6	8.95	3.95
34x7	9.95	3.25
36x8	11.45	3.95
40x8	13.25	4.15

HEAVY DUTY TRUCK BALLOONS		
Size	Tire	Tube
7.50-20	$6.95	$3.75
8.25-20	8.95	4.95
9.00-20	10.95	5.65
9.75-20	13.95	6.45

FREE

UTILITY LIGHT
With Each Order for One Tire—Also
NEW TUBE FREE
And Utility Light with Each Order For Two Tires

Utility Light—full size complete with bulb—Replaces flashlight, no battery to replace

All Tubes Guaranteed BRAND NEW

Send $1 deposit with each tire ordered. ($4 with each Truck Tire.) Balance C. O. D. If you send cash in full deduct 5%. Remember—12 months' guaranteed service or replacement at half price.

DEALERS WANTED

ADAMS TIRE & RUBBER CO., Dept L-335
2515 South Michigan Ave., Chicago, Illinois

www.ingramcontent.com/pod-product-compliance
Lightning Source LLC
Chambersburg PA
CBHW080913020726
47502CB00008B/2441